Women and Thieves

Of

Two Pan

Book 3
In the Two Pan Series

B. K. Froman

Morning West Publishing

Copyright 2015 Barb Froman

Other Books By B.K. Froman

Book 1: Mornings in Two Pan
Book 2: The Lights of Two Pan
Book 3: Women and Thieves of Two Pan

To those kind souls who help us get through changes in our lives.

1

Not My Rodeo, Not My Livestock.

FOLKS IN TWO PAN have a different outlook about space. We're not talking about the outer limits of the atmosphere, where astronauts duck whizzing meteoroids and the International Space Station zips by every ninety minutes. We're discussing a fizzled-out gold town. Residents here measure their space in earthly terms, such as the distance between a ticked off mama-cow and the safety behind the gate, or the space between a grass fire and the twenty miles a fire truck has to navigate through mountains to get there.

Folks know space is a matter of perspective. The closer they are to the ground, the more they get sucked into the problems around them, like how much money their boss makes or what their neighbors are up to.

They find if they go into the mountains, they'll see space from a different vantage point. At Coyote Bluff, where lovers watch the moon rise, they'll look down on the few lights of town and know they're not the only ones awake with problems—or they'll be reminded that a little lovin' soothes their worries.

If that's not enough perspective, they'll climb to the top of Eagle Cap Mountain and get a good look at the states of Idaho and Washington. They'll notice they're standing on a shelf of granite that was pushed up then smoothed by glaciers that once huddled from there to Canada. In case they need another opinion, they only need to look at the sky and be reminded they're just a speck on a blue marble.

Dealing with space around them is what makes Two Pan folks a little sleepless, a little creative, and sometimes, a little eccentric.

Too much space is what tumbled Belle Chere, seventy-two years old with life figured out, into her knee-jerk plan to murder a very bad man.

~*~

The railroad tie was planted upright in the ground. A fat raccoon stood on the top of it. The tie had a gate and a fence attached with a field spreading wide on the other side. From his lookout, the coon chittered and stared across the bunchgrass to the forest growing on slanted foothills of the mountains. His black paws waved like he was scrubbing windows. A peanut shell bounced off the back of his skull. His black-banded eyes searched the air for more flying food.

"You shoulda shut up and been payin' attention." He dropped to four paws, still balancing on top of the post. Belle Chere, wearing a leather apron around her waist, grabbed a hoof pick. The coon chirped, his eyes riveted on the peanut on the ground. He stretched tiny paws and climbed down the metal bars of the gate, rather than jumping. At the last bar, he slipped, thudded, and rolled end over end, yet coming up with the nut. He sat, splay-legged in the dirt, rubbing his paws over each other, dry-washing his treat.

Belle Chere turned to the mule beside her. Ropes from each side of the halter were tied to the doorway of the barn, keeping the mule from moving her head. Another rope looped over a rafter and kept her left hind hoof off the ground. She'd been standing on three feet all afternoon and showed her front teeth in an agitated warning as Belle approached.

"No!" Belle raised her hand, threatening to smack her. The raccoon scampered back to the top of the post, making *erk, erk* sounds. The mule snapped her lip back over her incisors and looked away as though admiring the scenery. Belle pointed the hoof pick at the blue skies above. "George, if you weren't already dead, I'd strangle you myself." Then she aimed the tool at the mule. "Are you ready to cooperate?" She let the mule's foot out of the rope. As soon as it touched the ground, she tapped its leg. "Up."

The mule lifted its hind foot for her. "That's better, Marly. If you woulda done that in the first place you wouldn't have been a tripod for the last few hours." She rested the hoof on a stand, bent, and began picking at the fibrous heel.

"*Rreeek-rreek-rreek-rreek!*" The coon's loud bark made the mule startle with a sideways step.

"For the love of Pete—shut the hell up, Spanky!" Belle beaned the coon with another peanut. The mule's multi-directional hearing let it point one ear across the field and one ear at the coon, which was on the ground, brushing off his loot and stuffing it in his cheeks.

Belle started on the hoof again. The coon gave three barks and Marly kicked free of her pedicure, both ears directed toward the house. It was a moment before the woman stopped cussing and heard the sound of engines. "Hell's bells. What now?" She rubbed her shoulder as she stood to her full five-foot-two inches She'd fallen off the ladder while pruning her apple tree this morning. It was only a drop of four feet, but the shoulder she'd landed on ached like she'd been pitched out of an airplane. A deep indigo bruise had bloomed. She was getting too old for this crap, but why pay someone to do a lousy job that she could do better?

Two trucks came over the rise on the gravel road that dead-ended into her ranch. They maintained a thirty foot interval between them so the dust blew away before the next vehicle ate it.

She picked up Marly's foot again, sighing, "Push through." Spanky resumed chirping and shaking his paws like he held maracas.

She didn't look up, even after four doors had slammed.

"You got a dead cow?" Sheriff Sol Meyers put on his hat as he walked toward her.

Belle concentrated on flicking dirt, rocks, and manure from the underside of the hoof. "It takes this many people to look at a carcass?"

"Jiggs was at the cafe when I got the call, so I asked him to come along. As part of the Cattleman's Association, he's been helping with stock loss."

A tall forty-five-year-old in a cowboy hat joined the sheriff. He wore the grimace of a man getting his teeth pulled. "I'm only here because I brought someone who wanted to meet you. Truth is, Mabel, I figure you were shooting coyotes and shot one of your own cows."

Belle glanced at him. "I've got a shotgun in the house. Why don't you haul ass across that field. Let's see if I hit a cow or you, Tool."

"And that ... " Jiggs fanned his hand toward the old woman, "is the famous raccoon-tamer, dog-slayer, Mabel Chere, who according to her, can outshoot, out-manage a ranch, and outride anybody in the county. This is Josie Blevins."

A blonde, fortyish woman standing next to Jiggs smiled and nodded. "I've heard so much about you, Miz Belle."

The gray-haired woman picked up the nippers and began trimming the hoof, biting her bottom lip each time she squeezed the snips. "Is your dog tied up?"

"Oh, he's not—"

"That's Rocket," a young man said as he neared the group. "He's mine. He's smart. Blue tick heeler. Won't jump outta the truck."

Jiggs dropped his voice, but it was loud enough to be heard by everyone. "Put a rope on him. Mabel has a bad track record with dogs." He notched his voice louder, "And this is Nap, my son."

Belle dropped the mule's foot, straightening. "Don't you think I know Ox's grandson? He's only been around for twenty-three years. But you—" she pointed the nippers at Josie, "—who are you exactly?"

Josie rubbed her hands, her eyes wide. "I'm ... Buforl Roggs' granddaughter. I used to spend weekends with them as a little girl. I've returned to teach at the school. I've been here almost a year."

"Oh." Belle let go of her scowl. "The Roggs were good people. You come from good stock—mostly."

No one mentioned Josie's gold-digging mother. An awkward space bounced between them as Nap turned to play with the raccoon.

"You've got a beautiful place," Josie filled the silence. "Jiggs says you do it all on your own."

Belle threw a smirk at the rancher. "Talk about me, do you?"

"Only when forced to. Josie has something to ask you." All eyes turned to the blonde.

"Oh ... well it can wait." She looked at the sheriff. "You should do your business first. It's more important."

Sol nodded. "Let's look at the dead animal you called about."

As Belle passed Nap, she pushed the hoof pick and nippers into the young man's hands. "Finish up. Maybe I'll hire you to help out on the odd job." She rubbed her shoulder as she led Josie and the sheriff to the pasture.

"You coming?" Sol said, looking back at Jiggs.

"You're on your own. Good luck."

"Miz Belle ..." Nap yelled, "can I use your bathroom?" She waved her hand as though she were batting down a fly. Nap looked at his dad. "What's that mean?"

"Who knows? Do what you want at your own risk or go 'round to the back of the barn." Jiggs took a peanut from a pail, and handed it to the coon, who seemed content to stay there rather than trek after his keeper.

"Here." Nap slapped the tools flat against his father's chest. "See to the mule while I check out the plumbing."

"Bound to happen," Jiggs mumbled, watching his son get out of work and walk toward the log cabin. He glanced around at the outbuildings. Old, but well maintained for a woman on her own. She didn't socialize much and had been single as long as he'd known her. When her father died, she'd taken over this ranch. As he remembered, there'd been a battle for the land among her lazy siblings, but rumor had it that Belle had intimidated and out-lawyered them. Whatever she'd spent had been well worth it.

Nestled at the base of the mountains, her pasture ran up the valleys and into government acres on the hillsides. It was a postcard setting with a few black calves bounding across the field. Another pasture held round-bellied mothers whose only job was to produce each year and lead the calf back home in the fall. Belle no doubt gathered the cows that she thought would have hard births and brought them in early. She was a good rancher, though he'd never tell her such.

He picked up the mule's rear hoof. The raccoon had returned to his post and his chattering. Jiggs recognized the mule. One of a pair: Winston and Marlboro. He had no idea which one he was working on. They'd been George Jugenmeir's animals, and he was glad Belle had bought them after George had died. If only his handshake on the land deal had gone as smoothly. Some folks had said it was his fault, allowing that urban pirate, Dr. Richard Jarmin, to out-maneuver him and get George's land. He'd proven them wrong, digging a deep financial hole to keep the whole area from being turned into condos and vacation rentals—but for how long? Ranches like this would be gone someday, all divided into parcels that produced nothing.

"You should see the inside of that house!" Nap interrupted his thoughts. "There's pictures down the hallway of this gorgeous gal barrel racing. I think it was Miz Belle. There's at least three custom-made saddles decorated with silver and brass in the living room. Expensive tack. And then there's medals, and military patches along with photos of women in fatigues. Everything's all tidy with big leather chairs and wool blankets."

"Don't snoop."

"I didn't, but I've always heard stories about her like she was some kind of Pecos Bill. I figured she'd be a slob like Gramps was. If those photos were of her, she was quite a looker in her day."

"Ox always said she could make a small dog break a big chain." Jiggs pushed the mule away. "Quit leaning on me. Somebody needs to teach you manners."

After he'd rasped the hoof smooth, he moved around to check the other feet. They'd been done already. The raccoon stood on the post, racketing at the woods again. Nap tickled its tummy. "Why didn't she marry? A woman with a spread like this would be a catch."

"Too mean. Why? You interested?"

"Ha. Funny. Why doesn't she like *you*?"

Jiggs busied himself, running his hands down each of the mule's legs. "Long story." He glanced up at Sol and the women walking toward them.

"Bullet in a pregnant cow," Sol called out. "No footprints. Didn't cut out the loin or backstrap so they weren't grocery shopping. Probably shot from their truck. Found this." He held out the butt of a thin cigar with a filtered end and stamped with the brand name Gaucho. "Cheap smokes. There's no reason to come down this road except to see Miz Belle, so it could be the shooter's." The sheriff's eyes widened and his eyebrows rose as he looked at Jiggs. "She says she hasn't ticked anyone off lately."

"Craphouse crickets, Mabel. There's probably only four people in this county you haven't had a run-in with—and I think two of them died in the '70s." Jiggs threw a crazy look at her. "Did you tell Sol about shooting at a guy?"

"You finish Marly?" The old woman picked up the hoof and looked at it. "You missed a spot." She held out her hand for the rasp.

The sheriff squatted beside her as she worked. "You mentioned to your insurance agent that you shot at some yahoo. He told Jiggs, who told me. What happened?"

"What a bunch of pinhead gossips." Belle burned Jiggs with a hot stare. "That idiot Elmer Scott was trying to sell me theft coverage. I told him I didn't need it. I knew how to scare off the broke-ass bum who'd cut my fence."

"When was this?" Sol asked.

"Oh, crap. How am I supposed to remember? A couple of months ago? No big deal. I was sitting in my recliner. Spanky was rolling somersaults across the floor. It was turning dark. I was tired and hadn't got up to flip on the lights. Across the pasture, some guy was strolling down the fence line. Kinda puny-looking. Beat-up, wearing a hat that was too big and pulled low. He kept walking, never even glanced at the house. I figured he'd been up one of the canyons and got throwed. His horse was probably hoofin' down to the trailhead, and the guy was taking a shortcut back to the road."

"You didn't bother to see if he was hurt or needed help?" Jiggs asked as the sheriff held up his hand to silence him.

"Nope." Belle gave Jiggs a *shove-it* look. "His troubles are his. Not my rodeo; not my livestock. I watched until he walked out of sight. Then in about ten minutes, here he comes again. The same guy walking back *up* the fence line. That was strange. I thought maybe he was looking for something. This time he's going slower, looking at the house, his hands pulling on the top wire. He sidles down the fence that way, real slow."

"What'd you do?" Josie asked, then glanced at Sol with a quiet, "Sorry."

"Grabbed my Remington 870 I keep by the door. It was getting pretty dusky. I went out through the mudroom and walked to the corner of the barn. He could've seen me if he'd looked up. I wasn't gonna sneak around my own place. But he was too busy. He'd clipped the top wire and was leaning in, laying a stem of grass on the electric fence running along the inside."

Josie leaned close to Nap, whispering, "Grass on a fence?"

"So you can tell if the electricity is on," he whispered back. "A little tingle pulses through the green stem."

Belle was saying, "... then he pulled his snips to cut the second wire. So I fired."

Sheriff Meyers looked out to the fence line. "About sixty yards. What was the load?"

The woman shut an eye and cocked her head as she looked at him. "If I say I shot a man, are you going to take my gun and me to the county hoosegow?"

"Depends."

"I'll just say it was dark. I pointed my twelve-gauge in that general direction and pulled the trigger."

"You hit him?"

Jiggs and Nap snorted. Belle Chere stared at him with an are-you-kidding look. "Well, I don't know." She tapped her chin as though she were thinking. "Maybe he yelled because the sound of the gun scared him. It sure panicked the mules."

"What load?"

"Number six birdshot, field load, full choke."

"Shit!" Nap's eyebrows rose. Seeing Josie's confused look, he leaned close. "At that range, she peppered the hell outta the guy. Broke skin." He looked up to see Belle giving him a look usually reserved for dumb cows that couldn't find the gate. "Uh ... that is ... if she hit him. Like she said. It was real dark."

Sheriff Meyers let out a resigned breath. "Okay. Let's go look at it." He pointed at Jiggs. "And you're coming this time."

Belle untied Marly from the doorway. "I'm not traipsin' out there. I've got chores. Go look if you've gotta. I've already seen it. It's where the fence was mended."

"Did you save the cut ends of the wire? We can match it to other cuttings around the county to see if the same snips were used."

"Hell no. You been watching too many of those who's-DNA-done-it TV shows." She rolled her eyes as she led the mule into the barn.

Josie stayed to talk to Belle. The old woman put Nap to work on Winston, her other mule. Jiggs and the sheriff walked to the spot and found the grass mashed down, but no blood. Jiggs pointed to a faint part in the tall grass that separated the fence from the hillside. "Does it look like somebody's been through there?"

Sol nodded. "Follow it. You're the better tracker."

As the wheat grass and weeds gave way to forest, they found what could've been a blood splat the size of a penny in the duff. They found a few other possible spots until, thirty feet into the trees, the trail disappeared. "There's a partial hoof print here." Jiggs leaned close to the ground. "Looks like somebody got on a horse and rode into the mountains. That had to hurt."

The two men spread out, searching a wide swath of the forest. After twenty minutes, Sol called, "Nothing. I got nothing over here." Only a waxwing twittered an answer. "Jiggs?" he called louder, standing at his full seven-foot height, scanning around. The overhead canopy of the firs shadowed him, but the wild current and chokecherry bushes hadn't leafed out for spring, leaving the space of the forest floor visible. "Jiggs?" he called louder.

"This way," came a voice at least thirty yards away. As Sol neared, Jiggs held up his hand in a slow-down signal. "Watch where you step," he said. "I found one bootprint and that."

He pointed to a filtered cigar butt lying beside a tree. A thin thread of smoke rose from the Gaucho. Jiggs' hand lifted, directing Sol's gaze directly across the pasture where they could see—the two women talking. Nap was in the doorway, working on the other mule. On the top of a railroad tie, Spanky chattered and chirred, waving his black paws at them.

2

Sometimes You Get; Sometimes You Get Got

"DO YOU THINK the smoker of that skinny cigar was watching her before we got here?" Jiggs asked, his long-legged stride easily keeping up with his taller friend as they crossed the pasture.

"Whoever it was left quick," Sol said. "And we only found the one butt, so I'd say he—or she—got here after we did."

"You think it might be a woman?"

"No. Most rustling is done by men, but all that gender-diversity training I've had to take reminds me that thievin' is an equal opportunity vocation. Listen, I wanted to thank you for your help here and with the Cattlemen's Association. Ranchers will talk to you before they'll say anything to me. Sounds like we're looking for somebody with a new limp."

"It's calving season. I'm not around town enough to notice anybody. And it's kinda early to start thievin'. Why not wait until cows have dropped their calves, and then grab them before fall round-up?"

"There was a big bust on a meth cook-house in the ION Country."

"The what?"

"Where Idaho, Oregon, and Nevada meet." Sol waved an apology. "That's what law enforcement calls the Jordan Valley."

"You've had too much training. We always called it the 'moonshine capital of eastern Oregon.'"

"Well, they've changed production. Those thousands of acres, few people, and two-hour drives to a paved road make perfect hideouts."

"There are ranchers there, too. Good people. What's that got to do with around here?"

"Someone local has been dealing meth. I haven't been able to find him *or her*. But since the big bust cut their pipeline, livestock loss has picked up. I'm guessing they're looking for other sources of income. What could be easier than loading up a cow with calf and getting a thousand bucks?"

"Crap. I hate to see that problem come here," Jiggs said. "If that's the case, why would someone shoot Mabel's animal and leave it in the field, instead of selling the meat?"

"Maybe her incident was just kids driving by, taking pot shots. Or if a poacher saw deer in her feed troughs, he could've shot, accidentally hit a cow, then high-tailed it. It's possible somebody got interrupted field-butchering, maybe heard a helicopter fly over or a truck coming down the road."

Jiggs gave him a sideways look but didn't reply.

"Yeah. I don't buy any of that either," Sol said. "I think someone's out to teach Belle Chere a lesson. What I don't get is why she'd report someone shooting her stock, but she wouldn't report shooting at a guy."

"I wouldn't report shooting a poacher either. First because you're the law, and second because I'd figure I'd taken care of the problem. End of story. But in her case, I'm guessing maybe she called because she's spooked."

"Belle Chere?" The sheriff squinted. "You ever hear the story about her knocking Aalton Zalman cross-eyed with a branding iron? He's a big man."

"I heard she'd run after him with a red-hot iron, yelling, 'If you put your hands on me, you'd damn well better be wearing my brand.'"

A grin ticked up the corner of Sol's mouth. "Well, that was years ago—I doubt if she could swing an iron now." He motioned toward Belle as they approached the gate. The small woman was shaking her finger at Josie. Nap was running a rasp across the mule's hoof, his smile growing bigger at Belle's colorful cussing.

Jiggs nodded. "Remember how she used to *never* let anyone work on her stock? Doesn't it seem strange she's handing out chores now? This kind of life has to be getting hard for her. Besides, she's not stupid. You can bet she's already been out in that forest, tracking prints and broken branches. She knows someone's after her. I'm guessing she's feeling kind of old and exposed right now."

The mule, tired of his pedicure, U'd his neck and nipped Nap in the back. The young man jumped and swore. Belle whirled, smacking Winston hard in the mouth, shouting, "NO!" Slobber flew sideways as the animal jerked its head back. Twelve inches in front of his muzzle, she held up her hand in a halt-sign. Winston dipped his head as though watching an ant parade on the ground, twisting his radar ears toward the approaching men.

"Okay," Jiggs said quietly as they went through the gate, "maybe she isn't *that* old and fragile."

Sol closed the latch behind them, and the raccoon climbed down, abandoning his post. It scurried between people, sniffing and finally grabbing pawfuls of Josie's jeans, clambering up her leg.

With a disgusted look, Belle focused on Jiggs. "Why would you bring your honey-bunch out here to talk to me about going on a women's hiking trip?"

"Don't you believe in strong women?" Josie's voice wavered as the raccoon noodled its head beneath her vest. "This is your opportunity to mentor other women." She winced as the coon pulled at her dangling earrings.

"Nope. I find it easier to ignore them until they get their shit together, then we'll compare notes."

"Mabel, are you going to help with her Women's Trek, or not?" Jiggs said.

"That's a nuts-and-butts NO! Why would I leave my comfortable home to stump through the woods so a bunch of city gals can *find* themselves? Hell's bells, they'll discover *the meaning of life* if they'll work until they fall over every day, like I do. Rather than wander aimless in the mountains, they can come here. I've got plenty to do. You forget what's bugging you pretty damn quick if you help birth calves at O-dark-thirty."

"Surely you've seen the flyers about the Women's Trek I posted around the county?" Josie winced as Spanky climbed on top of her head, his black-fingered paws pulling her hair. "We're having a Trek meeting at the Latte-Da next Friday; maybe you'd come and greet the ladies? It might change your mind."

Belle leaned back slightly, arms over her chest, an amused smile twisting her mouth as the coon slid around on top of Josie's head. "No. I'm pretty sure I don't want any part of your trip. But let me ask you this ..." She paused, watching Josie steady Spanky's forward drift, his paws grabbing her bangs, his feet scuttling backward. "Why would you let a stupid raccoon climb all over your head?"

"I didn't want to be rude." Josie leaned over and, with Jiggs' help, untangled the animal from her hair. As soon as the coon hit the ground, it grabbed her leg and began climbing again. Josie waved her hand, stopping its ascent at her knee as she blurted, "If you won't come along as a mentor-guide, can Jiggs borrow a mule to pack in our supplies?" She grabbed the coon's front paws and freed her leg. Now she found herself with Spanky upright on his hind legs, clutching her fingers. The coon stepped in each direction that she did.

"Holy moly. Would you look at that." Belle made a pained face as though she were cracking nuts with her teeth. "You *are* desperate if you're dancing with a coon to get a mule. Tell you what ..." She scuffed her furry pet and set him on top of the railroad tie. "Stay!" She held her hand in front of his nose. He tucked into a ball and she gave him a peanut. "I'll let you borrow a mule if you'll muck stalls for a week, and Jiggs and Nap will brand the calves in the pasture."

Nap stopped rasping the bottom of the hoof he held. He gave the old woman a surprised stare. "Now you want us to *brand*?"

"Okay, okay." Belle held up both hands. "I'll brand. You rope and hog-tie them."

"This is typical-Mabel." Jiggs looked at the sky, shaking his head. Behind him, the coon stood and sat, up and down, on its post, making *reerk-reerk-reerk* sounds. "I suppose you want us to start your mules under a saddle, too? Train them till they're bomb-proof."

"Nope. I've worked hours with these animals." Belle cast her voice louder than the coon chirps. "George let them get away with anything. They were rude bastards when I got 'em. Now anyone can handle them, even you, Tool. They're broke to ride and neck rein."

"We'll see." Jiggs bent away from Spanky, who was leaning out from the post, reaching for the brim of his hat. "*What* is the matter with your coon?"

"Probably your stupid dog," Belle said.

"He's not even lookin' at the dog. C'mon, Nap, let's take a walk before Mabel thinks of something else for us to do. We'll check around the house. Get Rocket outta the truck, but keep him on a rope." He gave Belle a hard stare as he left. "I know better than to let you run over another dog."

"Why don't you say what's really botherin' you?" Belle snapped, but Jiggs kept walking.

The flagstone patio at the front of the house wasn't as tidy as the back entrance since no one in the country used the front door. Her big picture window was partially covered by a wrought-iron rack full of firewood. Last fall's leaves clustered around a box of kindling and yellowed newspapers, and were held in place by spiderwebs.

As they searched, Jiggs told his son about the burning cigar in the woods. Nap let Rocket loose, but the only suspects he found were four does passing through the field. The dog, nose skimming the ground, also picked up the scent of a squirrel, which he herded into the dead leaves under Belle's wood rack. He barked a *woof* at the squirrel to stay put and then ran after Nap and Jiggs, who had walked away.

"What's the story on her running over a dog?" Nap scratched Rocket's head when he caught up.

Long strides and even longer moments passed before Jiggs spoke, "Never mind that. Do you wanna help with her calves?" They rounded the corner of the house, heading back to the barn.

"Why not?" Nap said it like a kid who'd been asked if he wanted to splash in mud puddles. "I've heard stories about her all my life. She's the mystery woman. Queen of the backcountry. Look at her." He waved toward the short woman, whose baggy jeans tucked into the top of her boots and oversized, insulated vest made her look even smaller. A salt-and-pepper gray braid trailed from under her olive-drab boonie hat. "I think she's a hoot. Why wouldn't you help her? You'd do it for anyone else."

"Lord, preserve us. You'll see. Put your dog back in the truck."

As the men approached, an argument was in full bloom. Belle had both hands on her hips, feet wide, standing inches from Sol's chest. Her eyes sent a fiery glare into his down-turned face. "I am *not* vacating my ranch because some asshole is shooting my cattle and might be scoping me with his binoculars." She flung an acid look and shook her middle finger toward the forest.

"Miz Belle." Sol used his overly patient voice. "I'm only suggesting you stay with friends for a while. You know this isn't a usual-type of rustling. Most thieves get in, get out, and get a hundred miles away to sell the stock. You hurt this guy who cut your fence. He's in pain with the ounce of lead you blasted into him. It seems he wants to make you pay. Leave, and let him cool down for a while. I'm sure Jiggs and Nap would look after your place while you stay with friends." He glanced at Jiggs, who wore the look of a man sliding down a cliff.

"I don't have anyone I wanna stay with," Belle declared.

"You could stay with me," Josie said. "I'd enjoy having you."

Belle squinted at her then turned, scrutinizing the others. "I see what this is. A conspiracy. You want me to go on this damn women-in-the-woods op. Well, I'm not goin', and I'm not hiding from some jackass cow thief. I'm spending the rest of my days in my home. All I want is to be left alone, happy, comfortable, and safe. And I don't plan on letting anybody," she poked Sol's chest emphasizing her next words, "*take that from me!* Got it?"

"All right. All right." The big man took a step back.

"Mabel, stay here shooting crows or crickets if you want," Jiggs interrupted, "but I'm getting ranchers together to see who's missing stock. If your bad-mannered mules don't nip you to death, come to the meeting at the Bar and Grill on Tuesday. The Cattlemen's Association is hosting the burgers and beer."

"Love to." She grinned. "I enjoy hearing those old windbags grumble about how well I'm doing and how much better I'm doing it."

Josie quickly added, "The Trek meeting is Friday. Maybe you could ... come to ..." Her words faded under the old woman's withering stare.

The sheriff squared his shoulders and put his hands on his hips. "At least promise that you'll call me next time before shooting anybody who's sneaking around."

"Sol Meyers ..." Belle reached up and put a hand on his shoulder. "I've known your daddy since he was a buck-toothed kid in school with me. I remember you crawling bare-butted, around on the Grange floor 'cause your diapers had a full load and had fallen off. If you'd use the horse's breath of smarts God gave you, you'd know I'm not gonna make a sorry-ass promise like that. Even Tool, here, wouldn't do it." She waved toward Jiggs.

Nap cocked his head at his dad. "Why does she keep calling you what Gramps always called you? What's the connection there?"

"Let's go." Jiggs turned and walked toward his Ford F-150, grumbling about one-eared alley cats being more pleasant than Mabel Chere.

3

Never Go Past The Wire

BELLE STARED AT her door, the sheriff's words echoing through her mind. "Be sure and lock up tonight, ma'am."

"Like hell," she'd told him. Now, standing in her pajamas, contemplating the deadbolt, she mumbled, "Like hell," again. It didn't quite carry the same conviction.

She didn't even know if the lock worked. It was a matter of pride that she'd never secured the door—not even when she'd returned to Oregon almost fifty years ago. Back then it had seemed a sad twist that she could barricade herself at home, but when she was far away and had truly needed a locked door, it wasn't allowed.

The nightmares had followed her back to Two Pan, crowding her sleep. Still, she hadn't turned the dead-bolt. The silhouetted man, back lit by fire, appeared nightly, screaming strange words from a doorway. A few times she was face-down on the floor before she remembered that she was in her own house. Still, she resisted the temptation to lock herself away from fear. Instead, she went out to meet it.

She had camped in the Eagle Caps until the open spaces and calm of burbling creeks had healed her. Or maybe it was because there were no doors in the forest. Her nightmares couldn't find her there. Either way, her memories had washed out, eventually becoming submerged under so many years that they had eroded and their sharp edges had smoothed.

Until tonight—now there was the possibility a nightmare would come through the door again.

"Like hell." Her voice carried more grit as she turned and walked to her bedroom. Spanky was already curled on the foot of her bed. "Scat." She prodded him. He ambled to his pillow in the corner as Belle slid under the covers and turned off the lights. He would sneak back onto the bed when he thought she'd fallen asleep, and in the morning he'd be snoozing next to her feet, body stretched out, paws in the air, belly up like he was sunbathing.

She focused on woven rugs hanging on the wall and the dark frames holding photographs of her horses. Pieces of her life took shape as her eyes adjusted to the dark. She waited for sleep to come while listening for the soft thump of a footstep on the porch or the creak of a door.

Minutes ticked into an hour. "This is stupid." She threw back the covers and plodded to the kitchen. Without turning on the lights, she looked out the window, half-expecting to see the tiny red glow of a cigar in the forest.

All was black. Quiet. And yet, the trees on the dark slope had lost their friendliness. A threat was out there beyond her barbwire. *Never go past the perimeter.* That lesson should have faded away, too. It pissed her off. These pieces of survival didn't get to resurrect themselves. She had worked too hard to be free of shadows that went *thump-thump-thump* in the night. She refused to be locked up like a chicken because some coyote was circling the coop.

Her hand massaged the ache in her shoulder. Why had falling off a ladder allowed whispers of getting old and being alone to spread with her bruises?

"Go to hell." She knew how to deal with fear. Her hand passed the lock and grabbed the Remington 870 leaning next to the door. As she walked down the hallway, she shucked the pump on the twelve gauge. The familiar sound of a shell sliding into the chamber was a surprising relief. Carefully, she laid the shotgun on the bed and slid beneath the sheets.

In the morning she'd awaken feeling foolish, scolding herself for becoming an old woman, the kind who let her imagination grow boogey men. She was making a bigger deal out of this than necessary. So what if she'd shot a vandal? Lazy asses avoided trouble. And trouble avoided flinty souls. She'd worked hard to be known as tough. He'd move on to pick on weaker people.

The house was quiet except for the sound of the refrigerator humming. When it cut off, Spanky slowly climbed back on the bed, pausing to see if he'd been discovered. He kneaded the covers a few times then settled at the end. Belle didn't say anything. Tonight ... she'd do what she needed to feel safe. No one would know her uneasiness, except the raccoon. And he wouldn't tell.

4

A Blue Light In Two Pan

ON TWO PAN'S Main Street, in front of an empty store, a single blue light glowed through the night. Spooner Hunter had screwed the specialty bulb into the socket, along with his hopes. He believed the light would draw the curious and they would stare, and then participate in his Two Pan Project: photographs of each local citizen. But so far, folks had been slow to jump in front of the camera.

A late-hatched pine beetle circled the bulb. The blue glow cast an eerie pall over the twenty-five photos posted behind the plate glass: The good ol' boy, Chicken Thief Bob, was frozen in a pose, forever pointing a grin and a wave at the camera. Mayor Bazz Hinton veed his fingers in a Nixon impression. Old Millie Capper wore a puckered smile and untied tennis shoes; for some reason, she was holding up a fork and a bottle of window cleaner. Some people smiled; others simply looked at the camera. Jiggs Woolsey was the last picture in the long row, his cowboy hat pushed back on his head. He squatted next to an old loose-skinned dog; both of them looked like they were waiting for ice cream.

Tonight, below the pictures, the rangy, homeless mutt lay on the blue-lit sidewalk. He had taken to sleeping there. The photographs were his company, especially the picture of his cowboy friend. He raised his head, his wet snout nosing the air. He stared through the darkness at a noise.

Though the fleabag couldn't tell colors, he clearly saw the small light moving down the street. Behind it was a human. The man stopped to shine the red beam into the window of Grubb's Mercantile. After a moment, his footsteps turned and kept coming. The boots toed out and the heels never brushed the concrete, each step remaining on the balls of the feet. Even with such a strange tread, there was a new hitch in the stride as though the hip had to muscle the right leg forward. *Bob. Push. Bob. Push.* The familiar musky smell of unwashed man traveled up the street. The light beam hesitated; it shone down the alley, jumping wall to wall between buildings for several heartbeats, and then it moved onward.

The dog put his head on his paws. His eyes followed the light. The footsteps passed. Stopped. The street was silent.

The steps came back. *Bob-push. Bob-push.* The red beam doodled on the sidewalk beneath the blue light, making a purple circle dance on the concrete.

The hound looked away, staring into the darkness like a kid pretending he doesn't notice a neighborhood bully. He knew this man's smell—one of the kicking rowdies, breathing through his mouth, with a low grunt each time he moved. The dog's rheumy eyes flitted sideways, watching but not staring.

The red light dotted the pictures above him. It stalled on one photograph. For a long moment there was no sound. The sharp scent of anger and alcohol rolled from the man in ever-increasing waves. The dog pushed to his feet, his head low.

Koooouuuggghhhh. The draining sound came from deep within the man's gullet. A loud, wet blast of phlegm flew from his mouth, splatting hard against the window.

The dog took a couple of steps away, his tail hugging his belly, his long claws making *scritch-scritch* noises on the sidewalk. The man looked down and quick-stomped, aiming for a paw. The mutt was old and skinny, but lately he'd been gifted with enough hotdogs that he could skitter backward fast enough to avoid the boot. The misstep made the man stumble, catching himself against the glass, his hand smearing his own spit.

"Dammit to hell!" A few more fiery words shot into the night as the man rubbed his fingers on his pants, careful to avoid his unfaithful leg.

A deep furrow appeared between the hound's shoulder blades. His head lowered, trying to make himself small and invisible. The man palmed his hip and narrowed his stare at a photo. "Just you wait. This is all on you, bitch." He turned and limped away, the red beam jagging back and forth in front of him.

The dog watched until the sound and light disappeared. He gazed up at the photographs. The man had marked the area. In slow *scritch-scritch* steps, the mutt padded to the side of the building, away from the brown drool scented with tobacco, hooch, and hatred. Away from the ooze smeared across the window over two photographs: his cowboy friend and a woman. A woman wearing a coon-tailed cowboy hat and a go-to-hell smile.

5

The Way The Wind Blows

DAWN IN TWO PAN seems to arrive sooner than necessary. The sun pushes the stars away, as though it needs an early start to get over the great expanse of the mountains. Residents may not know the exact hour and minute by the hands of the clock, but they know the progress of day by the movement of the wind. After sunrise, the high mountain air warms and pulls drafts upward from the shadowed valley below. In the evenings, when the slopes cool, a chilled breeze rolls down onto the flats. Folks who live here watch the eagles floating on valley currents and know how much of the day has gone and whether they can finish a job before supper. Visitors don't notice—or if they do, they simply say, "In a place like this, you can't tell which way the wind blows."

A woman in tailored jeans struggled with the buttons on her brown tweed jacket as the valley breeze tousled her hair into her face. She slammed the door of her SUV and walked down the street. Samantha Jarmin would prefer not to be in Two Pan until summer; it took too long for spring to push the refrigerated spaces out of the Eagle Caps. Actually, she would prefer not to be in eastern Oregon at all.

The heel of her knee-high boot snagged on the broken sidewalk. She stumbled, catching herself against a storefront. A banner in the window, above a row of photos, heralded an artistic endeavor with an abundance of exclamation points:

The Two Pan Project!!!

To capture the images of the 165 residents of Two Pan—an invisible America whose roots go down to the bedrock. Come as you are for honest pictures of how living in big mountains, with great distances and few people, has sculpted you!!!!

When the community's photos are completed, they will be archived, and not seen for ten years!!!

In a decade, I will take your pictures again. May change be kind to all of us!!!

Spooner Hunter, Two Pan Artist in Residence.

Come on In!

(Children will be photographed separately from their parents. One pet per person is allowed. No snakes.)!!!

Mrs. Jarmin shook her head, glancing at the motley residents. Having her picture taken should satisfy her husband. "Move," she commanded the old dog lying in front of the door. He kept his head on his paws, rolling his eyes to look at her. "Move," she said again. Wrinkles furrowed on top of his skull as he looked away. She reached over him, trying to push the door open. A tin bell, wired to the handle, clanged into action.

An old woman appeared in the doorway, glass cleaner in one hand and paper towels in another, barring her entrance.

"Here." She shoved the supplies forward. "I just finished cleaning the crapola off that window. Wipe it where you fingered it."

Samantha's eyes flashed wide. "Uh … sorry." She took the spray bottle and paper. Even though she saw no fingerprints, she buffed the glass while the dog kept watch. "Okay … now move, hound." Hints of annoyance flowed between her words.

He looked up at her with eyes too small for the droopy skin on his face and flopped his tail a couple of times. She sprayed him. The tail stopped. He blinked, slowly lowered his head, and stared at her feet. "Oh, all right, I'm sorry." She hop-stepped over the mutt, sideswiping the door as she entered the big room. A wrinkled canvas tarp hung against a wall. A tripod and two unplugged floor lights stood in front of it. The old woman sat at a water-stained wooden desk, pushing her hair under a thick stocking cap.

"Here you go." Samantha set the cleaner down, and held up the spent paper towels, looking for a trash can. "I'd like to get my picture taken for the project."

"Driver's license." The old woman held out a hand like she was asking for alms. When the card was placed in her palm, she held it close to her nose, squinting at the print. She let out a squeaky laugh. "You're only forty-five? You look older. You that doctor guy's mother?"

Samantha's mouth parted, but only for a heartbeat, and then her face hardened. "That's rather rude to say to a stranger."

"Just honest."

"I'm *here* to get my picture taken."

"Nope."

"Why not?"

"Says here you live in Portland. This is an art thingamajig for Two Panties only."

"Did you call them—"

"Well, you're the one who called yourself the stranger here. Now your husband ..." The woman got up and shuffled to the window. "Ever'body in three counties knows who he is. He can't have his picture taken either."

"Why not?" Samantha watched the woman's gnarly fingers wipe the glass around the photos.

"Boy, he sure screwed the pooch when it got out he was buying land so's he could make this place into some big-deal resort. Whatta carpetbagger."

"I beg your pardon? He wasn't trying to ..." She paused, waving away the smell and chemical fog from the old gal's profuse spraying. "When my husband gets a great idea, he pushes to get it done. He doesn't mean to run over anyone. He just gets excited." The old woman kept wiping while making sounds like a horse blowing. Samantha took a breath and let it out silently. Leave it to Richard to bulldoze over these people and squander opportunity. She slid her license off the desk where the woman had left it.

"Why don't he give you some of that nip and tuck he does? Is that the reason he looks younger?"

Samantha's mouth gaped as her eyebrows rose to her hairline. "That's *really* none of your business. There's no reason to be so rude. We've had a ranch north of town for almost a year. We live here part-time. I was on several art foundations in Portland. Now I'm interested in supporting this one. I'd like my picture to be part of this gallery."

"Why?"

"So I can be part of this town."

"Why?"

"So I can get to know my neighbors and they know me."

"Why?" The woman gave her a blank stare as she circled the paper towel over the same glass she'd cleaned before.

"You're going to keep asking 'Why' no matter what I answer, aren't you?"

"All right. Lemme ask you this. Do you have Bikky's chicken casserole recipe?"

"Who?" Samantha topped her frown with a squint.

"No? Ever'body in town cooks Bikky's casserole—the old Bikky. Not the young one; ever'thing the young'un cooks tastes like a cowpie. But Old Bikky ... best one-dish meal ever. Won the state fair."

"There's more than one person in town called *Bikky*?"

"Yep, and what's the number of the Bar and Grill—or anybody's phone here? I'm not talkin' about the area code."

The wrinkles in Samantha's forehead deepened. The questions came faster. "Who walks to the Wash Barn naked 'cause all his clothes are dirty? What instrument does the mayor play at basketball games? Who meets in the Opery House on Thursday nights? Where's the town cathouse? Why's there a canoe at the bakery? Who rides a lawnmower 'round town?" The old woman pointed at the gray-black donkey ambling past the window. "Where's he goin'?"

"Good grief! I don't know!" Samantha threw up her hands, let out a frustrated growl, and stormed to the door.

"See? You don't know squat about livin' here."

When Samantha jumped over the doorway dog, the old gal sprayed her with the cleaner, twice.

Outside, Samantha remembered the paper towels she'd used on the windows were still wadded in her hand. She wiped the side of her neck and jacket for a minute before noticing she was standing in the middle of Main Street. The only movement was the dog, wagging his tail like an intermittent windshield wiper, watching her. A block away, the donkey was wandering back down the sidewalk. Three small children laughed and tugged on his brightly colored harness. He traipsed forward, not seeming to mind or step on little feet.

She let out a long breath and rolled her eyes. This wasn't going to be as easy as she'd thought. No wonder Richard had made her come here after he'd screwed everything up. Ambassador Samantha would gain their trust. She had told him, "You have to do what *they* do. Eat and work alongside them. Relationships first, business later."

"You think your lack of medical training makes you better at dealing with people than me?" he'd said. Sometimes he could be a jerk. She'd help these people understand the economic benefits of having a gated-community down the road. They'd join the twenty-first century with a place to sip wine, gaze at the mountains, and keep donkeys and dogs from crapping in the streets.

She drove the two blocks down Main and parked at a coffee shop that had a canoe sticking out the top and an old Harley frame protruding from the front. Inside, three tiny tables stood in the corner, surrounded by twisted-leg chairs from an old soda shop. Samantha scanned the menu over the cash register as a short, stocky man passed her. "I'm going to the hardware store," he said as he headed for the door.

"Zimm!" a voice thundered, making both of them jump. From the back room, a curly gray-haired woman appeared. "You'd better have this done by tomorrow, or everything you own—" The door closed on the rest of her message. "That man! He tore up the wall in the kitchen and this is his fifth trip to the store ... 'Whups, I need smaller nails,' 'Gosh, I forgot the screws,' 'Oops, I guess I needed wire nuts, too.' He's retired and doesn't have a darn thing to do but get in my way. If I cooked like he remodeled, it'd take me three days to make iced tea. Men!" She shook her head. "I'm Lottie. What can I get you, Mrs. Jarmin?"

Samantha blinked. "How do you know—"

Lottie pointed to the street. "Only Dr. Richard Jarmin drives a Cadillac Escalade. Would you like today's bakery special? Carmel Apple Strudel. I make it myself. Get a piece for the doctor, too."

Samantha's pasted-on smile thinned. "He's not here right now. My husband and I drive matching vehicles."

"Well, that's dandy. I drive a Mercury Marquis that Old Man Tower has hit twice. Twice! Blind old fool drives a lawnmower now. You want coffee with your strudel? I can't fix sandwiches. My kitchen is torn up."

"I ... okay." Samantha shrugged as Lottie walked away. "Who's the lady at the Two Pan project?"

"Nobody's over there right now. Spooner Hunter is teaching at the college in Washington this afternoon."

"Well, I just had a run-in with ..." Samantha paused and shook her head, "an interesting woman."

"We're all interesting. Some more than others," Lottie called from the kitchen. "What was so special about her?"

"Never mind. Why's a donkey wandering around?"

"Hermes?"

"I guess. Where does it go?" She pulled out a chair and sat down.

Lottie leaned through the order window to look at the black kitty-cat clock on the wall. Its eyeballs swiveled side to side as its tail swung back and forth. "Two-thirty. He'll be bringing kids home from kindergarten. If it were summer, he'd be mowing lawns. He delivers baked goods for me in the mornings."

"You're kidding." Samantha leaned back and stared at the air in front of her.

"Why would I?" Lottie carried a mug toward her. "He's a working citizen. He's got his own photo in the Two Pan Project." She set the coffee on the table and pushed a ceramic cat forward, its tummy stuffed with blue and pink sugar packets, and then returned to the kitchen.

Samantha gave an eye roll and a headshake at the news. From the table, she picked up a cat creamer by the tail, examining it before tipping milk through its O-shaped mouth into her cup. "Why's there a canoe on your roof?"

"It came with the building."

"I think you're the perfect person to help me," she called out. "I have lots of questions. Tell me how I can get involved around here. Get to know people. Learn their names."

Peeking from of the kitchen again, Lottie looked over the top of her glasses. "Since your husband finagled that place from ol' George, you've never come into town. It's been almost a year. Now you want to meet everybody?"

"I've been very busy in Portland. I'm finally off the boards of several organizations, and my kids are grown. I'll be here more. It would be nice to get involved, make some friends, you know?" She watched Lottie set a plate of pastry in front of her; butter puddled on top and trailed down the sides. "It's a start, isn't it?" She offered a contrite smile.

"If you say so." Lottie left. In a moment she was back, sliding a purple flyer next to her plate. "A local schoolteacher is leading a Trail Trek. Women hiking. The distances aren't long. There's campfires. It's a chance to get away from the everyday grind. Meet people."

"Are you going?" Samantha asked. Behind her, the door opened.

Lottie gave the newcomer a welcoming nod. "Maybe. But Zimm might not finish this kitchen till Christmas if I don't straw-boss him. Mother Mary and Saint Peter ... if I could send him, that'd be like a vacation for both of us." She beckoned the man waiting at the door. "C'mon in, Jiggs. You wanna coupla specials to go?"

"Yeah," he said slowly, giving Samantha Jarmin a solemn nod as he tapped a handful of papers against his leg.

"Well, close the door," Lottie called as she shoved treats into cardboard boxes. "I just met your neighbor, Mrs. Jarmin. Have you met?"

"Once." He walked to the counter, not looking around. "She tried to hire me to *butler* her property."

"Well, I'm sure you told her how it works." Lottie smiled. "Mrs. Jarmin is going on the Women's Trek. That'll make Josie happy, won't it?"

"Well ... I'm *thinking* about going," Samantha corrected as the door opened again.

"You'll have a wonderful experience. Won't she?" Lottie nudged the boxes against Jiggs' hand resting on the counter.

Jiggs didn't answer; he'd turned to look at the new arrival and continued to stare at the young blonde with pixie-cut hair and a lot of leg, standing in the doorway.

Lottie jammed pastry boxes into his knuckles, calling across the room, "Can I help you?"

"Do you have any of those flyers about the Trek?" the twenty-something asked. "They were out of them at the mercantile. They sent me over here."

"Come in. What a coincidence. We were just talking about it. This fella knows the plans. He helped with the route and is mule-skinning supplies for the trip. Tell her about it, Jiggs." She rapped him hard on the back of his hand.

He could've kicked himself for not going through the drive-up. The wind had quieted outside, and there were chores to get to. He gave a tight-lipped nod, wearing the cornered look of a man caught amid a tornado of women in planning mode. In these situations it was almost impossible to escape without getting sucked into a load of to-do's and errands. Walking over to Samantha Jarmin's table, he pulled the purple sheet next to her plate and handed it to the blonde. "Here's a flyer. Call the number if you have questions."

"Perfect. Thanks!" The young woman flashed a smile as she turned, closed the door, and walked down the street. Both Jiggs and Samantha Jarmin stared.

A wadded dishtowel flew across the room, knocking his hat lop-sided. "Men!" Lottie huffed. "You could've helped Josie get another Trek client."

Jiggs re-settled his hat as he went to the window and scanned the sidewalk. "She seemed familiar—like I'd met her somewhere."

"Yes, she did ..." Samantha nodded slowly, "and I don't even live here." She quickly added, "Full-time." They stared at each other, sharing a moment of befuddlement. "And why'd you give her *my* flyer?"

"You should've kept her here and asked a few questions," Lottie said. "Obviously she's from California—she has a tan. You could've at least gotten her name. Found out why she's interested in the Women's Trek. Now I'll have to go over to the mercantile to get the full story."

"From now on, I'm only using the drive through," Jiggs said, pulling out his wallet as he walked back to the counter. "It's too dangerous in here with all these nosy *cats*." He gave Lottie a pointed look, slapped a five on the counter, and headed for the door with his boxes.

"Is this something you want me to hand out?" Lottie held up the papers Jiggs had left on the counter.

"Oh!" He grimaced and stopped. "We're having a meeting at the Bar and Grill. Could you give a flyer to everybody who's got stock? We may have a problem with thieves. Somebody road-shot one of Belle Chere's cows."

"Wow." Samantha frowned. "This is like being in a TV western. Rustlers. Donkeys in the street. Shots fired ..."

"This is real life for us." Jiggs narrowed his gaze. "For you, it'd be like having a twelve-hundred dollar sculpture sitting in your front yard. Somebody drives by and takes it. That's exactly what thieves think when they cruise around and see cows in a pasture."

"In the city, we lock and bolt everything. I didn't think you had problems like that here."

"Used to be, you could count on neighbors to watch out for you. Sadly that's changing as amenity ranchers who aren't here most of the time move in." He and Samantha exchanged a look. "Your man is welcome at this meeting."

"My man?" Her voice rose. "Do you mean a husband or a hired hand or anyone I know with a Y chromosome? Why not me?"

"Okay. Sorry." He headed for the door. "You've got expensive horses. You should come. Another ranch woman may be there. You two should get along swell. Just swell." He hurried onto the street calling, "Thanks for handing those out, Lottie. See ya in the drive through."

Samantha pushed her dishes aside. "So help me, I don't see how you put up with these guys. It's harder being a woman in the country than in the city."

"For the love of Saint Pete!" Lottie huffed. "You tell me where life isn't hard. Here ..." She shoved another purple Women's Trek flyer onto the table and took away the dishes.

Samantha paid and left. Outside, the sun hadn't moved. She didn't know why the locals complained about being busy. Time dragged so slowly here, it seemed everything could get done by nightfall. She drove two blocks to the other end of town and ordered feed.

"Thanks for your order, Mrs. Jarmin," Tracy, the owner, said.

"Have we met?" Samantha arched an eyebrow as she looked at her.

"It's a small town. By now, everyone knows you're here." She turned to her hired hand. "Gil, after you load Mrs. Jarmin's order, you can leave. That's all I've got for you today." The seventeen-year-old pulled at his sparse goatee, mumbled a few words, and disappeared. "He'll meet you around by the dock."

Tracy pointed. "And that was Millie Capper you met by the photos. Pay her no mind. She likes to clean windows."

"Uuuuuh ... how did you know ..." Samantha squinted at her.

"As I said, it's a small town." Tracy shrugged.

"Do you think if I go back, I can get my picture taken?"

Tracy's mouth twisted into a regretful smile. "Spooner is the head of the project. He has the final say, but I'm guessing your photo wouldn't go with the residents because you don't really live here full time. But there's a corner for *Others*. Jim the propane guy is there."

Samantha thanked her and got into the Escalade, cursing through clenched teeth as she backed to the dock and popped her rear door. Great. A jackass was a member of a two-bit club she couldn't buy her way into. The vehicle bounced slightly each time the young man tossed a fifty-pound bag in the back. When he'd finished, she waved out the window. "Here."

"What?" He watched her waggling hand.

"A tip."

"What for?" He took the bill, staring at Abe Lincoln.

"For doing a good job. Are you interested in more work?"

"Not really." He shrugged. "Well, maybe. What is it?"

"My husband and I have a ranch north of town. We have a man, but I'm sure he could use help a few hours a week. Would you have any time to spare, doing regular ranch things?"

"Uh ... I guess I can help out a few hours here and there."

"It's the Jarmin ranch." When he shrugged and shook his head, she added, "People still call it George Jugenmeir's place."

"Oh, sure. Are you ... never mind." He gave a single cock of his hand as he left.

She recognized it as the wave young men gave when they didn't know how to close a conversation.

She'd done well, today, spreading Richard's money around. She'd created a job, made several contacts, had been invited to a cattlemen's meeting, and that tour thing ... she read the flyer's header, *"Women's Trek: Discover what you really want."*

She already knew what she wanted. She'd given up selling real estate twenty years ago. This was the life she'd married for. Richard could be a jackass sometimes, but he wasn't stingy. At times his creativity and restlessness to create wealth was even inspiring. It allowed her to be a distributor and connector. She'd joined the right organizations, volunteered, and donated to the most prestigious charities. Her kids were finished with college. She'd paid her dues.

Richard didn't agree. He'd gone underwater on his last land deal, endangering his practice—and Jiggs Woolsey was partly to blame. "We have to sell your horses," he'd told her.

It was the one luxury that was solely for her pleasure. She didn't use them to compete or impress or make connections. She simply rode. She escaped.

"Too much money," he'd explained. "Stables, feed, vet, farrier, insurance."

She'd sold the thoroughbreds, but begged to keep her two Tennessee Walkers. She'd give up her board positions and sponsorship for several organizations.

"It's up to you, but that'll only save your horses for a little while."

He'd never liked her animals. He only liked the dog because she'd let him pick it and name it.

"I'm truly sorry, honey, but we can't afford your hobby right now. They've got to go ... unless ..."

Unless she convinced residents that the Jarmins were just folks. And the idea of selling land to them wasn't the end of life as the locals knew it. It was economic development. Jobs for these folks' children. It could actually be money in their pockets. He could be very persuasive. Now the horses were stabled at Two Pan—and so was she.

She read the flyer again. This could be the chance to check a bunch of items off her list. It would support a local teacher's business—that had to go a long way in promoting goodwill. She'd meet people in the community; she'd have a chance to ride her horses; and best of all, Richard would be pleased. When Richard was pleased, life went better for everyone, especially her.

A week in the woods? That might even earn her enough points to keep her horses, or at least get back to Portland. She could do this.

Far away, from a space deep, deep inside of her, she heard a small mocking laugh. Or maybe it was just the wind.

6

Trust Your Neighbors, But Brand Your Cattle

SAMANTHA JARMIN HADN'T planned on going to the Tuesday night meeting full of men in boots and cow talk. Instead, she'd asked both her ranch manager and her new hire, Gil, to attend.

Unfortunately, there was nothing else for her to do, and an event like this might be a good place to make connections. So she'd arrived early, sitting spine-straight on the bench in front of the Two Pan Bar and Grill, analyzing the characters she hoped would sell their land.

Activity had picked up in town. Trucks with dogs peering over the tailgates drove past. Lights began to flick on in the few houses along Main. People passed in front of her on the covered boardwalk. Most nodded, though a few strolled by as though she were a cigar store totem.

A faded '53 Ford motored up the street. The old woman driving it parked parallel to the walkway, taking up more space than she needed. She got out and clomped along the boardwalk, stopping beside the bench.

Samantha extended a hand to the mature, brown-eyed woman wearing a suede jacket and cowboy hat with a raccoon tail trailing off the back. "Hello—"

"Scooch over, Tinkerdink." The woman rapped Samantha's leg with the back of her hand. Blinking a couple of times, Samantha complied. The woman leaned down, studying a small brass plate on the backrest. "Will miracles never cease?" She stepped back, inspecting the bench as though it were empty, then turned and clomped inside.

"I hate this place," Samantha mumbled, her eyes closed. After a long sigh, she turned to read the plaque: *Built by Ox Woolsey.* So what? This was like visiting another country. There was a lot of history, but none of it made sense, and everything reminded her she didn't belong. Taking a deep breath, she stood and entered the Bar and Grill.

The lights were dim and most of the tables were full. She'd hoped to see the coon-tailed lady, guessing that she was the other woman Jiggs had said would be at this meeting. It would be helpful to have someone to watch like a guest watches their host to know when to sit, stand, and which fork to use. The old gal was nowhere around.

"The backroom is thataway," a waitress called out, balancing a tray of empty mugs as she paused.

Samantha opened her mouth to ask how the gal presumed to give directions, but then she nodded and put on a smile. In a town where everyone knew who she was, where she lived, what she drove, and who she talked to—of course they knew where she was going.

"You look like a 'well-done' on your burger." The server snagged another empty mug from a table. "Beer or soda?"

Samantha blinked at her. "You tell me."

The waitress rolled her eyes and headed for the long oak bar.

Samantha followed a group of men in cowboy hats stepping behind a black velvet curtain. As soon as she passed through the doorway, her eyes were stunned by the fluorescent-lit room.

"I'm Bazz Hinton, the mayor," a friendly male voice greeted her.

She squinted, shading her eyes, "I'm sorry. I'm temporarily blinded. How do you do? I'm—"

"I know," Bazz said. "Sit down till your eyes adjust, Mrs. Jarmin. Have a burger and cheesy tater tots." He set a red plastic basket loaded with cholesterol in front of her and was gone.

It was a minute before she could take in her surroundings. She'd intended to sit near the front. Richard had taught her it was the best power position, but those seats were already taken. Her ranch manager sat in the middle of the room. He barely gave her a chin nod. He was angry she'd hired Gil Gedding. "White trash kid," he'd called him. "His brother O.D.'d. No family to speak of."

"Then we should help him," Samantha had replied. "I want you to give him something to do for several hours a week. Is there a problem with that?" He'd mumbled an incoherent reply.

She'd offered to pay both of her employees for attending this meeting. They'd understand more of the discussion than she would. The kid sat on the other side of the room, eating a burger. With some satisfaction, she noted that they had come. Her money earned that much respect, even if grudgingly.

The server handed out drinks, seeming to know what folks wanted without asking. "Thanks, Misty," a fellow called out. She placed a Seven-Up in front of Samantha as she passed. "Wait!" Samantha called after her. "I'd like a beer, instead."

Misty swirled a U-turn, her head in place and her body and tray pivoting beneath it. "What kinda beer?"

Samantha hadn't thought about that. Actually the 7-Up was fine, but she'd noticed most of the men were drinking beer, and she wanted to blend in. Everybody was probably watching her and would talk about it at the feed store or water tank or wherever these people talked about things tomorrow. "I'll have what he's having." She pointed at Jiggs Woolsey. Misty smirked as she walked away.

"Move over, Tinkerdink. I like to sit on the end." The coon-tailed woman rapped Samantha's chair with her boot. Samantha shrugged and slid to the next seat. The old gal plopped her burger on the table and her bottom in the chair. "Belle Chere," she announced.

"I'm ... well ... you probably already know."

"Why in hell would I know you?" Belle said around a cheek full of burger. "I've never seen you before tonight, and don't really give a damn who you are."

"Oh. I'm Samantha Jarmin. Thanks for sitting with me." She looked in any direction except at the old woman. "I thought I might have to eat alone."

"Hate small talk."

"Oh." They both ate in silence.

Men passed the table, giving Belle a nod. A few of them asked where her Range Rover was or if she'd shot her buck yet?

Samantha lowered her head, venturing a question. "What does that mean?"

Belle raised her voice, "Just the hot air from jealous windbags. On the first day of hunting season, I *always* get at least a six-point buck. I tie him across the hood of my Range Rover and drive around town to remind these knuckleheads they're not the only ones who can shoot."

"Is hunting season soon?" Samantha nodded *thanks* to Misty who'd delivered an Oly in a frosty mug.

"In seven months. They think I hunt early. They also think they're funny."

At the front of the room, Jiggs stood and rapped on a podium. "Mabel, if you're finished bragging, we can get started." He didn't give her a chance to spike back a remark. "Tonight, we have a brand inspector here to talk about our livelihood and theft. Ollie Starkson."

People continued eating as the man limped to the podium, favoring his right leg. "Excuse my sitting down." He pulled a bar stool beneath him, resting his left cheek on it. "I pushed a bull into a chute. He didn't want to go in." Commiserating murmurs floated through the crowd, and the presenter launched into a PowerPoint presentation.

"There are five cows for every person in the area. You all know the space is huge and the humans are few. So far, two hundred cows are missing from Umatilla to Harney Counties."

Fifteen minutes into his presentation, Samantha raised her hand. "My husband and I would gladly contribute to any rewards to catch these thieves."

Belle's chin rested in her palm, her elbow propped on the table. "Wait until something of yours is stolen first, Tinkerdink. Being too eager makes you look like you're after something. Are you?"

A ghost-shadow of Richard Jarmin's slick development presentation passed through the room, touching off frowns. No one spoke of how Samantha's husband and his realtor had told folks he was building a small executive conference center to help the town. But it was actually a front for the gated vacation rentals and new businesses he wanted to develop a few miles away.

"Rewards are good," said Ollie Starkson, trying to reclaim the topic. "Thank you. It all helps. We also encourage you take blood samples if you've got a carcass butchered in the field. Dip a piece of paper in the blood and let it dry. We can match bovine DNA to thieves' gloves and instruments. Most important, take videos of your stock. Capture their tags and brands, and be sure to show your house or barn in the background. This has been great evidence in court.

"Of course, nothing beats a good eyewitness. You see any-thing fishy, write down descriptions and license plates. Whoev-er is doing this knows the area and the people. They hit during a rainstorm or when everybody is at the local basketball game. A couple of months ago, a private helicopter reported a couple of men herding cattle on horseback. The riders never looked up. Just disappeared over the rimrock. Abandoned the herd. Because of the brands, we were able to get the stock back to the right owners."

Samantha waved her hand again. "Are you saying I'm sup-posed to brand my horses even though their lips are tattooed?"

"Ma'am, a brand is like a return address label. It's the best chance of getting your animals back. Tattoos are recommended for race horses if that's what you've got. Even so, some thieves haul stock to Nevada. No brand is required to sell or slaughter the animal there. Your sheriff … " he waved toward Sol Meyers sitting in the back of the room, "is always vigilant about stock trucks in the area."

Samantha whispered to Belle, "I'm not branding my horses. It's ugly, and they are expensive and beautiful."

"That's good to know." Belle nodded.

A skinny man in overalls called out, "Aw … c'mon. We all know a neighbor's cow can get into our herd. We might not notice it. They get returned later. I don't think there's a rustling problem around here."

"What about the shooting at Belle Chere's?" Jiggs said.

"Well …" the man glanced at the ranch woman. "That was a single occasion. No reason to hawk-eye your neighbor." The low hum of grumbles rose through the room.

"Okay. Okay." Jiggs held up his palms as he stood. "There are more incidents. How many of you have missing stock?"

Everyone looked around. Not a hand was raised.

"C'mon. Sheriff Meyers and I have talked to some of you. We've been to your ranches. Don't make me call you out."

"Oh hell," Belle yelled. "You know nobody in this room has the cajones to admit they have missing cows. They're afraid it'll make 'em look like bad ranchers who can't keep track of what they've got."

"Somebody stole my truck a month ago," Guntis Kral's heavy German accent called across the room. "I had a '57 Chevy rusting in the field for twenty years. While I was over at the bank in Minam, somebody drug it outta my pasture and sold it for steel—cash. Sheriff found it at one of those crusher places."

The hum of discussions rose. The brand inspector was trying to tell people to lock their tack rooms, but the noise overshadowed him.

"HEY! HEY!" Bazz Hinton yelled as he hurried into the room. He didn't wait for the din to quiet down. "We just got a call. The phone tree's been activated!"

Voices went silent.

He turned and looked at the back of the room. "Lights at the Flying Bell."

Belle Chere stood and darted from the room much faster than Samantha thought possible for an old woman. Noise and shouted directions filled the air. Samantha sat, staring at the chair Belle had knocked over.

Within a minute, she was the only one left in the room.

7

Where Your Treasures Are...There Your Heart Will Be Also

~Matthew 6:21

BELLE JAMMED HER foot against the gas pedal, mashing it as far as it would go. The old Ford sputtered, considering whether to die or catch up with the pounding pistons. When its pulse finally found a normal rhythm, she peeled out, bouncing over washboard roads, the chassis chattering and dancing sideways. She whipped the steering wheel back and forth, keeping the tires going down the lane. On a hill, she caught a couple inches of air and imagined bolts and rivets popping in all directions when the Ford slammed back onto the gravel.

The corner for Chere Road appeared too soon. She stomped the old brakes, willing the front wheels to slow as she began the turn. The truck leaned and skittered sideways. She cut the wheel back, straightening, but still sliding for the ditch. If swear words would have helped the brakes, the truck would've stopped dead, but just as she hit the soft dirt at the edge of the road, the tires grabbed a patch of ground and the rear of the Ford spun around.

When she came to a stop, she was facing the way she'd come, with her front tire in the ditch. Gears ground complaints as she jammed the shifter into different positions and stomped the gas pedal, trying to break loose.

The headlights following her cut through the dust cloud. In minutes she was surrounded by people pushing her free. The other trucks could've gone past, but no one did. People yelled and gave orders, making space for her to turn around.

"Steady ..." she told herself as she peeled away again. "Nobody ever won a war by sinking the ship before it got to its target." Behind her, headlights followed at a safe distance. No doubt they thought she was going to do something crazy again.

She drove fast but sanely—until she reached the top of the rise. An orange glow wavered at the end of her road. She stomped the accelerator again.

In a half mile, her truck skidded to a stop, narrowly missing the Kleggs' Chevy parked in her driveway. Carl Klegg was using a garden hose to spray flames snaking up the sides of the barn. His wife, Cleova, aimed a second hose at the ground around the building.

Jumping out of the truck, Belle focused on the dark gap of the doorway between the flames; she ran for it. Within a few feet she pulled up, her arms in front of her, bracing against the heat claiming an ever-growing space around the building. Someone grabbed her by the waist, hauling her backward, yelling over the snap of the blaze, "Animals?"

When Jiggs set her down, he kept a tight grip on her arm, as she tried to run back to the burning barn like a horse. He gave her a shake, pointing and shouting, "Are there animals in there?" She stared at the clouds of rolling smoke, mumbling as she shook her head.

"What're you saying?" he yelled.

"My tack." She was glued to the spot, staring through the door as cobwebs in the rafters turned into orange, starred patterns, burning like fuses and dropping into stalls and hay. In a minute, the loft was also aflame.

Jiggs stepped in front of her, blocking her view. "Mabel! Where are the mules?"

"The vet ... in Minam." She was dimly aware of Nap yelling that he would check the pasture for other mishaps. Trucks passed through her gate, their headlights spreading into the field. People were on her tractor, pulling equipment farther from the burning building. Others stood in a line behind the barn stomping on sparks that settled in the pasture grass. Some people simply watched, mesmerized by the yellow ripples of fire traveling up the studs.

Jiggs was saying something. She looked at him. His mouth was moving, but she only noticed the orange embers behind him, swirling and floating in a fiery dance in the night sky.

At the front of the house, the squirrel listened to the noise coming from the back. He hid in his favorite spot, under the wood rack, watching bright dots float through the sky. One of them gently see-sawed through the air, landing in the leaves in front of him. He watched it pulse bright and dark as though struggling to breathe.

A thread of smoke rose beside it. Edges of an old oak leaf turned orange, spreading color to leaves around it until a bright yellow flame popped upright. The squirrel scampered from the wood rack, scattering the burning debris. The cord of wood had been half depleted from the winter, but it was enough. Tiny flames explored and licked the pieces of bark and tinder, nursing a blaze to life.

Nap drove into the pasture to check on the cattle. The glowing eyes of Angus stared when caught in his headlights. The cows took off running from the shiny monster moving through their field. He drove along the fence line, looking for cut wires, but didn't find any, so he turned back to help with the fire line.

Unsure if what he was seeing was right, he squinted and drove faster, bouncing over the field. "Shit!" he yelled and began beating on his horn.

Cows and calves huddled in a corner, watching the monster race by.

"The house is on fire!" Nap yelled as he jumped out to open the gate. "The house!" People turned to look, but saw nothing, except night sky and a possible smudge of gray above the log home.

Laying on the horn, Nap waved people out of the way as he drove down the driveway and circled to the front.

In a few minutes, frenzied people were running, unscrewing hoses and dragging them to the new blaze. A bucket brigade formed, dousing the back of the house. Folks at the front of the line reported flames in the window, crawling up the walls.

"Spanky!" Belle yanked free of Jiggs' grip, but Bazz Hinton grabbed her arm.

"We've gotta shut off your propane, or it'll blow," he yelled.

"Over there." She pointed. "Tools are in the—" She waved a hand toward the barn. "Shit!"

"I've got wrenches in my truck!" Bazz yelled. "Stay with her, Jiggs." He took off, hollering for folks to push a vehicle out of the way so he could get to the propane tank.

"The raccoon and everything I own is in there." She tried pulling her aching arm free of Jiggs' grip, but ended up wincing and holding her shoulder. Far away the siren of the Rural Fire Department drifted across the rolling acres. "If it started in front, maybe it hasn't reached the kitchen yet. He likes to hide under the sink," she said, pushing Jiggs in front of her toward the side door. "It's just beyond the mudroom."

"Crap!" Jiggs glanced at the dark spots starting to spread on her metal roof. With two fingers, he tweezed the outer doorknob to the mudroom. It was cool. "Okay. But you stay back. Got it?" He didn't wait for an answer.

A hazy blanket of smoke filtered through the tiny room. Jiggs immediately, dropped to his knees, his nose against Belle's linoleum. Already, this was a bad idea. "Here kitty, kitty," he sing-songed, trying to remember the stupid coon's name. Scuffling to the closed kitchen door, he coughed into the floor as he reached, searching for the knob. His hand jerked away from what felt like a branding iron instead of wood. He scuddled backward, running into something.

"Ow, dammit!" Belle yelled.

"What are you doin'? Get out!" Jiggs yelled, but Belle didn't answer. She also didn't move fast enough for him. On hands and knees he squiggled around, feeling like a chick maneuvering out of its shell. With his head and one hand, he scooted and butted an unwilling Belle across her floor, back toward the way they'd come in. She clutched at the side of the doorframe as hands grabbed her from the outside, pulling her away. Jiggs followed, coughing and crawling forward. Behind him, spikes of fire drilled holes through the door. Smoke and heat poured out. Someone in a yellow fire-retardant suit dragged Jiggs away, putting him beside Belle. "Didn't find your stupid coon," he coughed just before they snapped an oxygen mask on his face.

Belle sat on the tailgate of Nap's truck, watching her cabin burn. It made a roaring noise with small pops and explosions coming from inside the house. Ashes drifted around them, settling on Belle's hair, dusting it as though it had snowed.

A pile of her belongings sat in the back of the truck. Several people had smashed windows and crawled inside. Their choice of rescued items was strange, but well-meant. One had grabbed a saddle, for which she was thankful. Another had snatched pillows and bedspread. The top drawer of her desk sat next to her, its rescuer explaining that was where he kept his important papers. She had salvaged her father's 12 gauge by the door as Jiggs had pushed her out.

People patted her shoulder. Others wanted to know where she was staying, so they could bring food and clothes. "Right here." She stared at the window frames melting and twisting. The panes bowed and broke with the heat.

A group of men had gathered around the sheriff. Hands on hips, grim mouths, they shook their heads, darting glances at Belle or staring at the blaze.

Nap came and sat beside the old woman. He wanted to tell her he was sorry he hadn't seen the flames sooner. He'd kicked in a window to spray water inside, but he was pretty sure he had made the fire worse, allowing more air to feed the flames.

And he had seen Spanky. The coon jumped through the window a few seconds after he kicked it out. Flames danced along its back end as it ran. He'd tried to follow, but couldn't catch him.

He wanted to let her know, so she wouldn't picture the little fella cooking in the house. But she was smart. She'd know how a creature screeches its injuries as it runs; she'd understand that a hurt animal was coyote chow. She didn't need to know or even imagine any of it.

He wasn't sure what to do, so he held her hand. They sat, watching the ashes of her life drift down.

8

Ladies Love Outlaws

"MIZ BELLE?" JOSIE joined the old woman and Nap as the Rural Fire Department coiled hoses. Beyond them, the metal roof of her cabin lay in warped pieces. The north and west corners of the house had collapsed. Threads of smoke floated from the remaining two walls while men poked logs, looking for glowing spots.

"You're coming home with me." Josie took the old woman's hand from Nap.

Belle jerked free, crossing her arms and pressing her fingers to her sides.

"Ma'am, there's no place here for you to sleep." Josie gave Nap a look, encouraging him to chime in. He stared at her, keeping silent.

"Move." Belle nudged Josie with her foot. "I'm watching my belongings turn to charcoal. Seventy-two years—gone. So stop badgering. Tell me what justice will ever put this right."

"Mabel," Jiggs said as he neared, "she's just trying to help."

"Dammit to hell. You can't fix this, so stop acting like it's gonna be okay." Pushing Josie aside, Belle eased herself off the tailgate. She cupped her hand around her mouth, calling, "Thank you. All of you. I appreciate what you tried to do." Shouldering past Jiggs, she mumbled, "Now leave me the hell alone."

She made it ten feet before Jiggs grabbed her shoulder. "Mabel!" She winced and let out a gasp. He leaned back, as though expecting her to turn and punch him. "I'm sorry. You okay? Are you hurt?"

Her body sagged as she let out a long breath, rubbing the top of her arm. "I pulled a muscle a few days ago. It's still giving me fits."

"I'm sorry. And far be it from me to tell you to where to sleep tonight. I only came over to see what you needed. You got a blanket? Any food?"

"I've coyote camped many a night."

"Yeah, yeah. You're a lone wolf. But neighbors will keep pestering you if they think you're curled up under a tree. They're going to bring supplies whether you want them or not. It might as well be what you need."

"Do whatcha want. I'm sleepin' in my pickup. And the only thing I need is to kill the S.O.B. who did this."

"Don't jump on *that* wagon. This could've been an accident. Wiring. Space heater in the stalls. They'll investigate when it cools down."

She gave him a look that made it clear he was an idiot. "I'm goin' to the outhouse behind the barn—if that hasn't burned down, too. You gonna follow me out there and pester the shit outta me?"

"Geez!" Jiggs turned and walked away, shaking his head.

Josie, Sol, and Nap were waiting for him next to his truck. Most of the neighbors had gone. The firemen were shucking out of their gear. "She's staying here," Jiggs announced. "Protecting her ashes."

The sheriff gave a single headshake. "If this wasn't an accident, her situation has escalated to a whole new level. I don't know that she should stay alone."

"Why don't *you* go tell her that? She's in the privy," Jiggs said. "Maybe you can nail it shut from the outside and contain her for the night. Go for it. But when she busts outta there, you'd better duck, 'cause she'll clock you with a board, then do as she pleases."

"Oh good grief!" Josie gave them a scowl. "She's in shock. She just lost her world. You two are acting like twelve-year-olds, afraid to get their baseball from a crotchety neighbor's yard. I'm surprised you don't push over her outhouse and run."

"Been there. Done that. We were about what … seventeen?" Jiggs looked at Sol, who wore a grim countenance. "Then we had to spend a month filling in her cesspit and building a new john for her. Why do you think she's in there now? She knows we won't touch it." He gave her a warning look. "But you can go talk to her if you want. It's a two-seater."

Nap said, "I'll stay." All eyes turned toward him. "I'll stay the night. I can sleep in my truck. I've done it plenty of times."

"No." Jiggs stood, hands on his hips, surveying the dark field and their surroundings.

"Why not?"

"We'll need you later." Jiggs waved a *thanks* to a fireman climbing onto the tanker truck.

Nap frowned at his dad. "Well, as Gramps often said, 'Nothin' speaks louder than a good deed, so stop yakking and get doin'.' If she's staying here, I'm at least gathering dry wood and making a small fire so she's not sitting in the dark."

"Here's what we'll do," Sol said. "We'll let Belle stay the night and say goodbye to her home. But tomorrow she's staying with somebody."

Jiggs elbowed Sol. "You go tell her that. I wanna see what happens."

The sheriff pulled a quarter from his pocket. "How about we flip for the job?"

*

Jiggs stood ten feet from the outhouse, feeling like a fool. "Mabel?" he called. "We're leaving now. Nap made a little campfire so you'd have some light. He didn't use any of your house. Sol and I will be back in the morning. Whaddya want for breakfast?"

Only the peepers, croaking in the weeds, answered him. "Mabel? You hear me?" With a sigh, he stepped forward and knocked. The door moved with each rap. Grimacing, he slowly tested the latch. It pulled open, dimly revealing a roll of toilet paper between two white Sears and Roebuck toilet seats covering the holes.

"Son of a monkey." Jiggs closed his eyes and shook his head.

As he walked back toward the group, he called, "Your turn to deal with her, Sol. She's gone."

"Where?"

Jiggs waved toward the forest. "I'm guessing someplace safe. She knows these mountains. Let her have her space."

"We're really gonna leave her out here?" Nap said.

Speaking quietly, Sol opened the door of Nap's pickup, "Just go along with what we're saying." The young man gave him a doubtful look as he got in. "Your dad ever tell you about the time we showed off our hunting skills?" Nap shook his head. Sol leaned against the door frame. "One year, your dad decided we'd be the first ones to fill our deer tags. Usually, Belle Chere took that honor. When she'd bring her deer to town to brag about it, we planned to be leaning against my truck with a big buck tied to my hood, and possum grins on our faces.

"She always shot a giant deer, so we figured she'd scoped out herds in the valleys behind her house. It was hours before dawn when we parked way the heck down the road, crossed her fences, and headed into the canyon back there. We set up, fingers numb, frost covering everything, and we waited.

"The sun was just peeking over the rim when four does came through, grazing in the open. The biggest buck I'd ever seen was with them, but he stayed in the trees. Jiggs and I were covered in dirt and deer urine and upwind. Perfect. Each time we moved, deer heads periscoped up, and we'd hold still like rocks till they went back to browsing. It must've taken Jiggs ten minutes to move his .270 to his shoulder. The buck finally decided it was safe and stepped into the clearing. Jiggs slowly sighted him in, freezing whenever the deer looked spookish— and you know your dad —he is not a patient man. He did good; didn't rush the shot. The buck took a step, lowered his head to graze and—"

"The ground exploded ten feet in front of me." Jiggs grimaced as he walked up. "All I saw were tails bouncing into the forest. Guess who'd ruined the shot?"

"Miz Belle?" Nap said. "She missed?"

"She doesn't miss." Sol shook his head, his cheek muscles bunching in disgusted wonder. "Go look at one of her kills. One shot. Through the heart. She doesn't take a shot unless it's clean."

Jiggs shined the flashlight back and forth across the dark fields "You know what she told us?" He snapped it off. "That she didn't want that buck killed. She'd been watching him for five years and needed a big, healthy stud like that to populate the gene pool around there. You'd think she was raising them like cattle."

"In the long run, she was right." Sol shrugged.

"That wasn't the point. Here we were, two young warriors, and that ancient, fifty-year-old *woman* blew my shot. I could've strangled her."

Sol slapped Jiggs' back. "Tell him the real insult."

"She told everybody about it when she brought *her* deer in. Said she'd schooled us and *still* brought in the first buck of the season. We were twenty-two. It was more than a little hard to swallow." Jiggs leaned close to his son and quietly said a few words. Nap nodded and shut the door. Raising his voice, Jiggs told him, "So now you know. Belle Chere can take care of herself." He gave the hood two pats as he walked away.

Nap started his engine and drove off. The men stood without speaking, watching the taillights of the Dodge Ram get smaller and the road noise grow fainter. When the lights disappeared over the hill, Jiggs went to tend the fire.

"She can sure be uncooperative," Sol mumbled.

"Yep. And she's intent on evening the score," Jiggs said quietly, picking out a branch to use as a pokey stick to stir the embers. "Her shotgun is missing from the pile of salvage. I checked while you and Nap were talking. But she probably only has four shells."

Sol let out a long breath, his head down, but his eyes scanning around them. "Maybe we oughta go looking for her?"

"Nope. We wouldn't find her." Jiggs walked to his truck calling, "As they say ... we left a light on for her. She'll find her way home." With a last glance around, the men got into their vehicles.

The fire glowed, casting warm shadows around it. From the field, the small orange flames could be seen, as well as the red taillights driving away.

As soon as the sound of the engines faded from the countryside, Belle walked out of the field. She studied the ruins of her barn. The firefighters had done a good job. Formless mounds and a watery black mess stood where walls and stalls had been. She'd wait for daylight to scratch through the ashes. Maybe she could find pitchforks and shovels. Their handles would be burned off, but the metal could be refitted.

The house though … she turned to the debris and charred studs. Her throat closed, choking off half of her breath. "I'm sorry, Spanky."

Nothing remained of her life. No pictures of her sexy legs in boots or photos that showed she'd once been good-looking and didn't need anyone—except the camera to show it. Foolish young men had hung over rodeo fences, cheering for her. She'd kept four guys fighting to see who would carry her gear from the barrel racing event to bareback riding to roping. She'd had the medals and pictures and ribbons to remind her whenever she began to doubt that she had once been lovely and a somebody.

The displays in her picture gallery lay in ash and broken glass. She had nothing. The trophies had melted. News clippings baked into puffs of fibers. Photos had curled as they burned, their chemicals flaring blues and greens into a fire too big to be anything but the color of hell.

The only heirloom her family had, her father's Winchester bolt action .30-06, manufactured in the '50s—gone.

Her mind numbed into white fuzz. She plunked down hard on the ground. Carefully and slowly, as though it were a precious treasure, she laid her shotgun across her lap. All this happened because she'd shot one lazy sonuvabitch. How could that be?

A folded plastic tarp lay nearby. On top lay a foil packet and a blanket. Peeling back the aluminum revealed a burrito. She tossed it in the fire.

She sat long enough that the flames died—several times. Each occasion, she stirred them back to life, turning the same question over and over: how had she read the situation so wrong?

She was so damn sure she knew what to expect of the worthless shithead who cut her fence. She'd shot him, so he'd shot one of her cows. They were even. Done and done. She had him pegged as a doddling bastard. Too lazy to take this much offense.

Letting out a long breath, she looked overhead into the night sky. Obviously she'd been wrong. She hadn't made such a bad mistake since ...

She turned around to stare at the mountains behind her, checking if they were still there ... so many things had disappeared. Her trust for one. That had started with Del. She'd been wrong about him, too.

Of all the young men she could've picked, she'd chosen the most beautiful. Dark eyes. Dark hair. And unfortunately, a dark heart—though love wears a blindfold and gladly broad jumps over the truth when it gets in the way. It was true. There was something about a bad boy.

But those long lazy weeks in the mountains had seemed worth it. Together, they'd planned the ranch of their dreams. They'd grown to know each other, heart and soul.

Sure, they'd taken cows, but only for a starter herd. They planned to send them back after birthing several calves. Sure, she'd helped steal them. She was the best rider and roper in the county. She had the ribbons and pictures to prove it. How could she not help her beloved?

And later, when he'd been caught and stood alone in front of the county judge, she'd tried to catch his eye, letting him know she'd wait for him.

When he saw her sitting in the gallery, he'd given her one of those looks that made her heart hop and her breath catch. Then he'd pointed and told the judge that she was the talent of the outfit; he was only the hired hand. And dammit to hell if he hadn't given her that smile again when the judge thanked him for his cooperation.

The fire in front of her popped, arcing embers into the air. A branch rolled off the top of the pile into the dirt. With the pokey stick, she boosted the smoking wood back against the flames.

A sick, stunned feeling pierced her stomach, its talons gripping her guts and holding on. It was the same sick feeling she'd had at twenty-six when they'd snapped handcuffs on her at the courthouse, in front of God and everyone. And Del had smiled—that gorgeous grin.

She shook her head. You couldn't trust men—not any man. She'd been so damn sure of herself. And now she was in one more shit storm. Another man was sucking her into another crime—because if she didn't wring justice out of this, then it felt like God had walked off and left the whole experiment to spin itself to pieces. Fortunately, in the space of life between her past and now, she'd learned how to handle a FUBAR. And sitting in the dirt wasn't on the agenda.

A fine mist had begun to drizzle. Gentle spring moisture pushed from canyon heights by the mountains making their own weather. She stood, whacking the dust from her pants, holding onto her shotgun. "Suck it up. Push through!" she told herself, walking to her '53 Ford.

She was climbing into the cab when she saw, at the end of her long gravel driveway, a pickup, parked with its lights off.

9

No Matter How Fast You Run ...

THE WINDSHIELD WAS beaded with water. Belle could make out a dark form in the driver's seat, the head leaning back, a hat angled over the face.

She tapped the driver-side glass with the muzzle of her shotgun.

A hand dragged the hat away, revealing a man, yawning and squinting through the darkness. He jumped, banging his knuckles on the steering wheel as he threw his hands up. "Crap! Don't shoot."

"Whaddya doin', jackass?"

Jiggs rolled down the window. "First shift. You didn't really think we'd leave you here? We just said that in case you were listening in the shadows."

"Well, aren't you sneaky snakes? I figure the bastard who did this has done all the damage he's gonna do and is gone. But whadda I know? Men are unpredictable peckerheads."

"Maybe this was an accident. Faulty wiring?"

"Yeah, I bet that's why you're here instead of at home. You stayin' all night?"

"Nap will be here at two." He talked louder, watching Belle circle the truck. He paused as she opened the door and climbed in the cab. "Chicken Thief Bob relieves him at six. When he goes to work, Sol will come back, unless you kill one us of early."

"I feel so safe with you sittin' in my drive, sleeping like a hibernating bear."

"I figure I'm here to protect everybody else from you. Not the other way around."

The silence unspooled, both staring straight ahead. Jiggs' hands rested on the steering wheel. He tapped out a short rhythm with his thumb before finally speaking. "I'm sorry about your house and barn."

"Why are *you* sorry?"

"Mabel, I'm trying to express some sympathy here. I can't imagine watching all my stuff go up in flames."

"I've seen bigger burns." She stared into the dark, watching the movie screen in her mind. "I'm sure Ox told you how I cooked myself with stupid choices when I was younger."

"Nope." Jiggs kept his focus in front of him. "We made it a point not to talk about you."

Belle slid the butt of her Winchester onto the floorboard and rested the barrel against the dash as she leaned back. "Your dad was good at keeping secrets."

"That he was." Jiggs tapped more mindless rhythms on the steering wheel. The thumping seemed to fill the cab with too much sound. He stopped. The silence was even louder. "Well, since you brought it up, what bad decisions did you make?"

It took several heartbeats before Belle answered, "Broke my dad's heart. Now there's something you get to lug around the rest of your life. Your father's face when … a judge sentences you to the penitentiary. Too bad images like that don't burn up."

"I wouldn't know. Every time Ox spoke to me he looked disappointed. I got over it." Several moments passed in silence. Jiggs cleared his throat. "How'd you keep jail-time hushed up in a town like this? There's lots of stories about you, but not that one."

" 'Cause I didn't go. Judge Jackson, being an old country peacemaker and a patriotic gavel-pounder, full of himself, gave me a choice. Two years in jail or three years in the Army. That was a no-brainer. Two years and I'd be done with the mess. Then I saw Dad's face. He sat in the courtroom through the whole trial, never looking at me, just staring at his lap, fussing with his hat. I'd ruined our name. Mortified him. My mother wouldn't show her face around the county, but Dad was there for me, always fiddling with that hat. I can still see him through the window of the bus as I left for basic training. Waving. Wearing a big smile and that damn hat. By then it was nothing more than the crown and two rolls of felt along each side."

"Fathers are like that—well, some of them." Jiggs nodded at the 12 gauge. "That his gun?"

"All I have left of him. My former life is gone now, except for bad memories."

Silence, heavy with questions, spread throughout the cab. Jiggs waited, hoping it would settle on the floorboards and leak under the doors. When it didn't, he ventured, "What'd you get arrested for?"

"Ox never told you any of this?"

"We had plenty of other things to shout about."

"Oh."

A second layer of weight blanketed the air. Jiggs leaned his head back and rested his hat over his face. "Where'd the army send you?" The question hung for several seconds. Then he heard the door open.

Belle was sliding off the seat with her gun. The door slammed, leaving him looking through a water-streaked window into the darkness.

*

The Whitman County Sheriff's seal reflected from the door of the truck pulling into the driveway. At 7:30 am, Sol Meyers unfolded his seven-foot frame from the cab, carrying a brown bag and white boxes. Trails of fog and mist were retreating back up the canyon. The air was damp enough to chill fingers, the ground wet enough to cake the edges of boots without being called mud.

Chicken Thief Bob had parked his Toyota next to the pile of house. His long angular body was bent like an A-frame as he blew on a teepee of sticks, shavings, and pine branches.

Sol held up the boxes. "The Bar and Grill provided breakfast. Junior sent your usual." He set the supplies on the tarp, took one of the boxes, and dug a plastic fork out of the bag. "Where's Miz Belle?"

"Asleep in her truck." Without looking up, Chicken Thief blew again. "She's tuckered." Threads of smoke filtered through tree moss and the sticks he'd feathered with cuts. The sheriff squatted on his hocks, opened the box, and began eating. With a few more breaths, the glowing pieces of bark and pine needles grew into a flame. White smoke dissolved into invisible heat. Chicken Thief opened a box marked C.T. and dug into banana pancakes and eggs. "I couldn't find Miz Belle when I first got here. Next thing I know, she's asleep in her pickup. Probably checked her cows. You think somebody did this on purpose?"

"The fire investigator is coming this morning. No use spreading rumors till then."

"He'll only confirm what everybody's saying: we've got a cow-killing arsonist around here. Maybe he'll move on now that everybody's hackles are up."

The sheriff tossed his empty box into the fire and slipped the fork into his shirt pocket, twisting to stare at the mountains. "I think he *or she* is local. They know the Eagle Caps, the ranchers, what time they feed, and what's in their pastures."

"Good grief." Chicken Thief shook his head. "That description fits any of us."

By nine o'clock the driveway of the Flying Bell was full of trucks and people. Lottie had baked a big batch of Wednesday specials and sent Zimm out with the *sopapilla* cheesecakes and a couple thermoses of coffee. Even though she had warned him to "Get back here and get this kitchen finished," he hung around, doing whatever odd jobs he could see needed doing.

After the fire inspector gave the okay, people raked through some sections of the burn, knocking off the damp top layer of the ash. With every step, feathery powder churned into air until the molecules of Belle's home were floating across her fields.

For the fifth time that morning someone asked, "Any cattle missing?"

"You know what?" she boomed across the work area. "Why don't all of you circle up. Have a campfire meeting. Make a list of what to ask. Then pick a representative because I'm only answering a question once from now on. I'll be in my truck."

"Eat something." The sheriff nodded toward the last treat in the box. "You'll feel better."

"Ya think?" She snagged the *sopapilla* out of his hand, taking a bite as she walked away. "You're all like a buncha squirrels. No matter how fast you run around, your tails and your stupidness keep following you."

A half hour later, a short man in khaki slacks, white polo shirt, and windbreaker knocked on the truck window. Belle rolled her head to the side, checking him out. "Oh Lord, take me now," she moaned. "Don't tell me they picked you as their representative." She could only push the door open an inch at a time because Elmer Scott, her insurance agent, shuffled backward instead of stepping to the side.

"Oh Belle, this is a catastrophe," he moaned. "A total loss. Are you missing any cows?"

Jiggs shook his head, eyeballing Sol. "*You* were elected to tell people things like this, not me."

The sheriff glanced at Belle, sitting in her truck, door open, her feet perched on the running board. Elmer stood in front of her, his pen pointing out sentences on a piece of paper. "Naw, you know her better."

"How do you figure?"

"She ran over your dog. You've got a connection."

"Yeah, that was a Christmas card moment."

"You gotta admit that mutt was half-blind and mean enough to bite rocks." Sol stared at Belle, who was smiling and nodding at Elmer.

"Still ..." Jiggs shrugged, following his gaze.

"Yeah ... still ..." A gust circled through the site, shimmying the yellow caution tape the fire investigator had put around sections of the burn. Zimm had made tidy lines of items he'd found in the ashes: cast-iron skillets and pots, chains, tools, and the barrel of a Winchester .270, the bluing burned off.

"Why's she being nice to Elmer?" Jiggs lifted his hat slightly as he scratched next to his ear. "Why isn't she ripping his head off? He's the only man I know who can make a three-word sentence so confusing your blood pressure will spew out your ears."

"Because her insurance agent is giving her something." Sol waved toward the ruins. "To Belle we're a couple of kids who don't know shinola, and we're going to keep her from doing what she wants—to get even."

"Then give her something. Here, tell her you found this." Jiggs grabbed Belle's cowboy hat from the blue tarp. The brim was streaked with ash. The coon tail hanging on the back looked like a dirty, matted rope.

"No." Sol leaned away, giving him a crazy look. "That'll make her think of Stinky or Stanley or whatever that baked coon's name was."

"Kitty. It was Kitty," Jiggs pushed Belle's hat into the sheriff's hands as they walked toward her. "And she's had a pet coon die before. Why do you think she wears that tail on her hat?"

Belle was speaking as they neared. "... supposed to be good news, but ..."

"I know. I know." Elmer shook his head as though comforting a widow. "Nothing will replace your memories." He looked at Sol and Jiggs as they approached. "Aaaah, Sheriff Meyers. Do you have news?"

"I've got good news and bad, which do you—"

"I hate that game." Jiggs grabbed the hat. "Here." He shoved it at the old woman. "The good news is I found this under a truck. The bad news is ... tell her the bad news, Sol."

Sol threw a stink-eyed look at Jiggs. "Miz Belle, the fire investigator has a bit more work to do to make it official, but it looks like arson. Started by a flare."

Belle didn't speak, her mouth tightening, her eyes boring into Sol.

"Don't go outlaw on me, Miz Belle. I'm starting a full investigation. I'll catch the perpetrator." His face hardened and voice deepened as he stared back. "If I hear you're on those mules, looking for whoever burned you out, I'll come after you. Let law enforcement handle this. I believe this person might've been pushing drugs around here. No telling what he or she is strung out on. As a matter of fact, I think you should stay with Jiggs. He'll help with your animals and whatever you need." He glared at the rancher. "Won't you? Your dad's house is empty, right?"

"No, because she's staying with Josie." Jiggs gave him one of the looks they'd commonly exchanged in high school that said *Anytime, anywhere, we'll sort this the hard way.* "It's already been worked out. Catch up."

"Who in the hell are either of you snot-nosed boys to tell me what I *can* and *can't* do?" Belle gave them a disgusted head-shake. "Do you think it's right that I sweated harder than most men to build the Flying Bell, and some crazy-ass takes it away with a flare? That's not justice, and I don't wanna live in a world like that."

"We'll catch him or her, Miz Belle," Sol said. "I guarantee it."

The old woman leaned close, poking Sol in the chest. "It's a man, stupid. And either he has to go or me. I'm telling you ... I have nothing to lose anymore."

"Oh ... " Elmer held up his folder of insurance claims. "Yes, you do, Belle. You have plenty—"

She lashed him with a hard stare.

"Oh. Okay. I'm going to go before I hear anything I don't want to hear." Elmer hurried away, calling, "Where can I get in touch with you, Belle?"

"I'll be at Josie's." She gave Jiggs a pasted-on smile. "I wouldn't stay with you even if my only other choice was a cave full of bears."

"Why do you have to mouthwhip people around, Mabel?" Jiggs asked.

"Because ..." She clamped her dirty hat on her head, her eyes narrowing at him. "It's anger that pushes me on. The truth is, there are some men who need to be killed. And I'm gonna take care of this. Ox Woolsey or any of the old-timers, would've helped me. All the *real* men in this county have died." She hopped out of the truck, walked away, and began hefting her dutch ovens into the back of her old Ford.

Jiggs and Sol gave each other the hopeless glances usually exchanged in front of avalanches or oncoming freight trains. Without speaking, they helped her load her truck. When they'd finished, they cut a wide space around her, giving her time to wander through her ruins once more.

She'd selected this spot to build on. To the west, glorious sunsets. To the north, rolling hills. At her back, her refuge, the mountains. Now ... they'd been tainted. Something poisonous had come out of them to get her—fear. She picked up a fistful of the remains of her house, letting clumps and soot fall through her fingers. "Ashes to ashes," she whispered. Wiping her hands on her filthy jeans, she walked to her Ford, got in, and drove away. She didn't look back. Her eyes kept glancing toward the seat beside her.

Last night, she'd slipped into the forest, hoping to find someone watching her home burn. No one was there—or if he was, he knew as much about hiding there as she did. Before morning broke, she was back, searching around trees and scanning crushed leaves. A hundred yards up the hillside she'd found an empty Gaucho package with five smashed butts inside. He had been there. He'd watched.

No need to tell anyone; she'd take care of him.

"Looks like another front moving in." Jiggs watched Belle drive away. They covered the tools Zimm had salvaged, the wind flapping the tarp in their hands, threatening to tumble it across the pasture before they got it anchored. Ashes blew in their faces, making them turn their heads and squint.

"You think she'll do something stupid?" Sol rubbed the corners of his eyes as they walked to their trucks.

"Like kill the guy who burned away her home and safety in her old age? Why, no. Why would a hard-core old rancher, who doesn't like people, do something mean? She'll simply sashay into an assisted living center and be happy."

"Her mules are at the vet. I checked. They'll keep them as long as she needs."

"Poor Josie. She volunteered for a bad job."

"I checked the woods last night," Sol said. "Didn't find anything. I saw you checking this morning. You come up with something?"

"A hoof print, The shoe is worn on the hind right heel. Maybe it's important." Jiggs shrugged. "What's worse is I found Mabel's boot prints. She'd already been out there. I'm guessing she's figured out more than you or I put together."

"I need to come up with a plan before she does." Sol watched the gusts bend the tops of the grass.

"Well, we're sure not having a town meeting to discuss it, so our thief knows we're not at home."

The wind blew his last words away, skittering ashes across the open pasture. Particles rose and tumbled on the air. They floated miles into the mountains and drifted into canyons that could easily hide a man or a herd of stolen cattle—or the past.

10

Valley Of The Thieves

SPACE IS DECEPTIVE in the mountains. A peak may appear only a day's hike away, but once you start toward it, the mountain mysteriously moves farther than you'd imagined. The place you're searching for is a mile off as the crow flies, but to get there, you'll have to climb up crags, down canyons, cross creeks, and get off your horse to lead it through narrow gaps between ridges for five miles. That's the easy part. The hard part is knowing that the gaps exist.

~*~

The flat area at the base of the cliff was half the size of a basketball court. A few cattle milled near a two-wood-chunk campfire. An open can of chili sat inside the fire ring, its lid squeezed down to keep ash out. A man sat lop-sided in a yellow plastic folding chair, favoring a butt cheek. He took a final drag on his small cigar and threw it into the flames. White hair at his temples was starting to migrate to his short beard, but the whiskers on his chin were still brown. An involuntary groan escaped as he leaned to check the chili.

Close by, a young man hopped off one of the six-foot boulders surrounding the area's perimeter. "You do that?"

"You're supposed to be in town." The man grunted and clamped pliers on the can, turning it to warm the other side.

"Belle Chere's house burned down last night. That's all everyone is talking about."

"The hell, you say. How about that?"

"You do it?"

"Nope."

The young man eyed his father as he plopped into a chair. "Bullshit."

"No ... I only put a torch to the hay in the barn." He scratched grubby fingers around his mouth, ending with smoothing his whiskers. "I don't know how the house got to smokin'."

"The meth has screwed you up. Not that you were firing on all pistons anyway, but your head's like shit soup now days."

"You didn't care what I did when the money was coming in." He gave his son a disgusted look. "Besides ... any bitch puts birdshot in me deserves what she gets. All those high and mighty cowhacks will think twice before taking a shot in the dark now. That the peroxide?"

The young man tossed the paper sack. It bounced off his dad's knee, plopping in the dirt. Two cows startled and dashed to the other side of the boulder-lined area.

The man hefted himself off the chair and pulled down his pants. "Pick it up, dammit. I swear there's more shot in my butt. I can barely stand my pants touching the skin. Pour that on while you tell me what those sonsabitches in town are flapping about."

The young man stared for a long moment before grumbling curses and uncapping the bottle. The peroxide foamed over scabs and bumps in the white, saggy flesh. "Looks like the shot is working its way out. Some of these are right on top."

"Scratch 'em loose."

"Oh ... hell no." The young man backed away, shaking his head. "Screw that shit."

"You're a worthless piece of trash, like your mother." The older fellow picked at an angry red wound, his face pinched as he made painful grunts. After a moment, he held up a small steel ball, rolling it between the blood and pus on his fingers, inspecting it before flicking it into the fire. "Stupid bitch."

The young man turned away. "I'm outta here. I just came to tell you to stay outta sight. And don't pull any more dumb-ass stunts."

"If this had happened to you, you'd be singin' a different tune. What went on at the cow meeting last night?"

"There's talk of a reward, but I don't think most folks have noticed cattle missing yet."

"And they won't till we're long gone."

"Well, because of your shit-for-brain fire antics, everybody's on high alert. They're calling in the highway patrol to help watch the roads. They've handed out cards to write down descriptions and license plates of suspicious vehicles. How long you think before they're searching through these mountains?"

The old man clenched his teeth as he dug at another scab. "Nobody climbs to this canyon." He sucked in air with his words, "Too ... damn ... hard." He held up the ball, inspecting it. With a disgusted grunt, he threw it in the fire. "Nothin' but damn rocks when you get here. Hikers and hunters stay over on Hurricane Trail. Pour some peroxide on this."

The young man held the bottle out, staying at arm's length from his father. "Do it yourself."

"If I wasn't hurt, I'd kick the livin' shit outta you." He grabbed the bottle.

"You've already done that." Picking up a shovel, the young man scooped up a green cow patty, carrying it fifty feet. He dumped it on the pile beside one of the slabs broken from the canyon cliffs centuries ago. A few boulders sat next to the cliff face, but most had rolled, creating the lopsided ring.

An inch at a time, the father tugged his pants up, easing them over his sores. "Anybody order extra feed or say they're goin' outta town?"

The young man flung a cow patty at the manure pile, his face dark as a thundercloud. He turned and scooped up another.

"Listen," the man eased himself into a chair, "don't feel sorry for those damn snobs. You have to hang around them, but don't forget, they killed your brother."

"Drugs killed him. Drugs you supplied. You didn't even pay to bury him, just lit out like usual. Those people in town were the ones who took care of it."

"Whose fault was that? I told him not to use that shit. He had about as much smarts as a flea. Hell, the Archer family has been planting folks long before the gold fizzled out. They can afford to give away a casket or two. They'll probably bury you and me."

"That's something to look forward to. Penitentiary or a free funeral."

"Quit'cher bitchin'. Get on down the road if you don't like it."

"As soon as I get my share, I will. I'm starting over in Montana. Maybe Vegas."

The father gave a laugh. "Well, shithead, to get money we gotta get these beeves to Nebraska."

"Take what we've got. Herd them through the gap and truck 'em to Utah."

"Utah has brand laws. We can't sell unless they're registered to us. And you're worse than me at changin' a brand. So unless you want a sure ride to the Oregon State Pen, we'll finish gettin' a full load." He cussed the pain as he bent over, using the pliers to lift his chili from the fire ring. "I know an ol' boy who's got trucks; he'll haul 'em to Nebraska. We'll have to split with him, but if anyone's gonna get caught it'll be him. Quit your pissin'. You'll have plenty of money soon." He groaned as he leaned back into the folding chair.

"Not soon enough." The son heaved more manure at the pile.

11

You Had The Cat Wearing Pants

TWO DAYS LATER, at the Latte Da coffee shop, the ceramic kitty-cat bell on the door sounded a delicate *tink-tink* as Samantha Jarmin entered. She waited at the counter, inspecting the Friday Special arranged under a glass dome: carrot-cake-muffins with cream cheese centers. Lottie Lubach had her back to the counter, gabbing at the drive-up window. It sounded like a doorbuster sale was happening a couple of towns away at the Clothes Horse.

From the corner of the small dining area, a voice whispered, "You'll have to wait until she's finished at the drive-through. I had to. This is the second time I'm hearing about the sale." The tanned, long-legged young woman who'd taken the Trek flyer smiled.

"Oh. I see." Samantha made a can-you-believe-this face. The young woman returned it with an equally this-is-weird smile.

After a minute, the sale conversation had moved to another town and its Saturday's specials. Samantha shrugged and introduced herself, adding, "May I sit?"

"Sure. I'm Melane McCurry."

"Are you here for the Trail Trek meeting?"

"I thought I'd check it out. I'm new to the area."

"Me too." Samantha looked around at the inspirational cat posters on the pastel yellow walls. "Can you believe this place? It's like a step-back into the '50s. I miss my gourmet coffee."

"This is really good." Melane held up her mug.

"If only I could get a cup ..." Samantha looked at Lottie, whose conversation had changed to the weekend leftover remnants at the Stich'n'So'n'So.

The kitty-cat on the door tink-tinked again, announcing two women. "Sorry, I'm late." Josie leaned over, letting the notebooks in her arms plop onto the table. "I put the last kids on the bus and ran out of school. This is Kathleen Carter." She nodded toward the twenty-year-old, who had maps and colored folders clutched to her chest.

"Kick Carter," the young lady corrected.

Josie yelled across the room, "Lottie, can I get two Dr. Peppers and ..." she pointed at Samantha.

"A coffee?"

"And a refill?" Melane held up her mug.

"I'll do it." Kick grabbed Melane's mug out of her hand and the ten-dollar bill Josie held up at the same time.

"I guess that's the way it's done." Samantha looked at Melane, eyebrows raised.

"Okay." Josie sat down, letting out a big breath, then arranging herself. "I'm Josie Blevins. A middle-school teacher. I moved back to Two Pan over a year ago. I love it here and want others to find the peace and enjoy the beauty that the Eagle Caps gifts to those who walk her trails. Why don't we say our names and what we want to gain from a trip like this.

"Since Kick is busy ..." She nodded toward the young woman who was hanging over the counter, her feet off the floor, her bottom in the air as she poured coffee into mugs. "I'll tell you that she works at an assisted living facility and volunteered to go on this trip as my aide and to provide basic medical care."

"Is she a nurse?" Samantha asked.

"No ..." Josie see-sawed her head back and forth. "Not exactly. But the Certified Nursing Assistants have taught her a lot and let her do part of their load."

"Really?" Samantha stared as though she were looking over invisible glasses.

"This is a small place. Trained experts are hard to keep around. Everybody pitches in where they can. Kick has picked up a lot and she's eager to help." Josie quickly turned to the young blonde. "We talked on the phone, but haven't met."

"I'm Melane." She gave Kick a quiet *Thanks* as the young woman slid a mug of coffee in front of her.

Samantha immediately exchanged it with her cup, whispering, "You had the cat wearing pants." She tapped the graphic on the side of the cup.

Melane hesitated, seeming unsure who to look at. She finally chose Josie. "I'm a realtor, new to the area, working for Max Buddy Realty."

Samantha Jarmin did a double take. "Really? Where are you from?"

"Bakersfield."

"And *why* are you working for him?"

"Okay." Josie interrupted. "We'll have plenty of time to get to know each other as we trek." Josie's smile got thinner as she nodded and yelled, "Lottie!"

No one answered. A moment passed. Josie yelled again, "We're sharing goals, Lottie. Why do you want to go on this adventure?"

Lottie paused her conversation to yell over her shoulder, "I want to get away from Zimm. But I haven't made up my mind if I'm going."

"How else are you getting a break and discovering who you really are?" Josie called back.

A male voice yelled from the back room, "Please go."

"If I left," Lottie jammed her hands on her hips, shouting toward the other room, "you'd have International Harvester bumpers and a motorboat welded to the roof when I got back. The outside of this place looks like hippies still run it ..."

Kick cupped her hand around her mouth, whispering to Melane, "Hippies invaded Two Pan back in the '60s."

"Why's this town called Two Pan?" Melane asked.

"It started in the gold mining days," Josie said. "Now, Samantha, tell us your goals for the trip."

"Wait!" Melane said. "There's gold here?"

"Dream on, girl. Look around." Samantha Jarmin gave her get-real glance and continued, "Well, I'm going—"

The door burst open so quickly the kitty-bell only made a dull *thonk*. "Is this the meeting?" a short woman called from the doorway. Her brown Carhartt jacket looked new. Her stiff jeans were tucked into unscuffed cowboy boots, and a coontail hung off the back of her black Stetson.

"Yes, Miz Belle." Josie nodded.

"You finally talked me into it." Belle slapped the door closed, the bell banging into the wooden frame. "I'll go, but only if you're not trudging up Hurricane Creek."

"That's the main hiking trail. Jiggs said we'd find plenty of camps and—"

"Oh, hell. Jiggs couldn't find his way out of an outhouse. And that trail is so heavily used by tourists, there's toilet paper under every rock. Besides, it dumps you into the Lake Management area. You can't have campfires there. You like cold camps, do you?"

"No, but—"

"I know where there's an abandoned pioneer cabin. You can explore Earth-Groan Cave. Sift for gold at Crack-butt Creek ..."

"I don't think those are real places," Josie said.

"If it were on a map, everybody would be there. No tourists or hiking in horse droppings. Spectacular vistas. Campfires every night. A million stars. Watch the deer and elk play. Up to you."

"Sounds cool!" Melane said.

With a defeated feeling, Josie looked at the smiling, nodding women.

"Okay." Belle clapped her hands and pointed at Josie. "We'll line out the route tonight. Bring fried chicken home for dinner." She yanked the door open, making the kitty-bell *thonk* again.

"Wait! We're getting to know each other." Josie fanned her hand outward. "Ladies, this is the most experienced rancher and independent woman in the county. Meet Miz Belle Chere."

Belle gave a wave. "It's a hike. Prepare to walk your asses off. I'm goin' to Grubbs." She went out the door, leaving it open.

"Wait! We're talking about equipment," Josie yelled, but Belle didn't turn around.

"Who *was* that?" Melane stared at the coon tail swinging back and forth with Belle's every step.

"She's a bit testy, but she'll be an invaluable guide and mentor. She's been staying with me and I've been working on her for the last few days. You have no idea what an honor it is that she's going. It's like taking lessons from a virtuoso. It'll be challenging, but I'm sure we'll see things we've never experienced because of her knowledge of these mountains.

"Now, what to bring ..." Josie said, and Kick jumped up to hand out the colored notebooks and pens. She held one out to Lottie, who had her hands on her hips, watching Belle track across the street. "I'm not going." She shook her head slowly. "I'd rather stay here with Zimm."

In fifteen minutes the women were cruising the aisles of Grubbs Mercantile. When the two newcomers finished gaping at narrow rows piled floor-to-ceiling with bags of beans, hacksaws, and overalls, they focused on the white enameled deli cases. "Is that homemade jerky?" Samantha pointed at gnarled, fleshy triangles.

"Nope." Belle glanced at the bin. "Dried pig ears. For your dog. Here, if you like pig." She offered the open bag she was snacking out of.

"What is it?"

"Cracklin's." She shook the bag. "Pig skins for humans."

"Thanks, no ... can you recommend other snacks to carry?"

"How the hell would I know what you like to eat? Are you killin' and cookin' along the way or carryin' that dehydrated crap?"

Josie stepped between the women. "Remember I explained you'll be packing your food the first two days, but I'm supplying it. It's included in your fee. You only need to bring your own snacks." Josie held out a hand like a game show hostess, pointing the women down the aisle. "I'd recommend energy bars, raisins, and peanuts." As the women shuffled to look for treats, Josie threw a dark look at Belle.

"Excuse me ..." Samantha Jarmin turned and came back with a frown. "When you say *pack*, do you mean backpack? I thought we were on horses."

"You got a horse?" Belle leaned against a shelf, her elbow resting on cans of beans as she dipped a hand into her bag.

"As a matter of fact I do. Two Tennessee Walkers."

"They ever seen a bear, crossed running water, been on granite trails or narrow ledges?"

Samantha considered the question. "No. But I thought this would be a good opportunity to ride them. My husband says they're expensive and unnecessary. I need to justify them whenever possible."

"Well, one of my mules will be packing in the food for this shindig. You'll only carry a couple days' supply on your back."

Belle's face squeezed up in a squint. "Why don't you earn your own money so you can keep your Tennessee Walkers? Then you can tell your husband to shut the hell up."

"The purpose of our exploration ..." Josie stepped in front of Belle, her voice loud, aiming a stare at the old woman, "is to do inner examinations. The process is enhanced by walking. As I said, we'll hike to the base camp. From there, we'll make longer and longer hikes each day. The work and the solitude allow solutions and ideas to *rise* from within you. Walking is part of each of our journeys."

Belle gave a loud snort.

Josie waved people away. "Everyone! Inspect the camping supplies while I talk to Miz Belle."

"Where are they?" Melane glanced around.

From several aisles away, a woman's voice called out, "All over the store. Just wander around. Move stuff piled on top if you need to."

"Was that the checker?" Melane wore another this-is-weird look.

"Snacks are this way." Kick herded the women down the aisle, pausing once to examine old *Life* magazines and text-books.

Josie leaned close to Belle, her voice nearly hissing, "I'm thrilled you're going, and I know you think this trip is a bunch of woowoo, but it's something I want to do and these women want, or they wouldn't be here. So if you plan to go for free—"

"Damn right."

"Then I'm willing to comp you for your expertise, but those are my only two *paying* clients. I figure that's perfect for a trial run. If you can't be helpful, I'd prefer you not come at all."

Belle didn't say anything, her tongue poking her cheeks, working the crumbs from between teeth. "Okay." She nodded. "I'm sure Jiggs has told you I have a few rough edges. But it's mostly because I have no patience for stupidity. Look at them, they're checking out cans of beans, for Pete's sake. You should make each one of them lug a number two can of peaches ten miles. That'll make even the dumbest person calculate pack weight pretty damn quick."

"Why are you really going?"

"I know you're supposed to keep an eye on me, while Jiggs and the sheriff act like the Hardy boys tryin' to solve the who-burned-the-house-and-barn mystery." Belle rolled the cellophane closed on her bag of crisps. "So you tell him that I'm used to working. I'm bored. What else do I have to do instead of tag along on this wander-about? I have no house. Nothing to maintain. Who knows? Maybe I'll make some new friends in my old age. But if you don't want me to go, that's fine. I'll stay and fix up things at your place while you're gone."

"No." Josie said too quickly, eyeing Belle for discrepancies between her face and her words. "Just don't run off my paying clients. If you do, this trip is off."

"Wouldn't dream of it." They stared at each other like a cougar and a coyote drinking on opposite sides of the stream.

Without glancing away, Belle waved toward the end of the aisle. "You'd better help 'em pick out bug spray. I'm guessing you haven't told 'em the mosquito hatch is heavy this year."

"It is?"

Belle rolled her eyes and walked to the register. She laid her half-eaten bag on the counter.

Cleova Klegg gave her a smile as she punched keys on the old black metal register. "The outing will take your mind off your house. I'm sorry I didn't see the burn sooner, Miz Belle. I was pulling weeds, getting my garden ready to till and noticed a glow over the hill out your way. Clegg and I jumped in the truck and drove. Sure enough we saw the orange light. By the time we pulled in your drive, flames were poking out the barn door. I went in your house and started calling folks on the phone tree while Clegg sprayed what he could." She shook her head as the cash drawer popped open with a *ding*. "I can't believe it's all gone. They say somebody started it. What's this country coming to?"

Belle handed her a five. "You were good neighbors. I appreciated you and Clegg. It was a nice ranch, but not anymore."

"Aren't you going to rebuild? Cliva Spinrad is having a house-shower for you. She figures you won't come, so she's simply collecting goods to give to you."

"Of course she is, that old do-gooder. Tell her I need bourbon and soft bath towels. That oughta set her tail in a twist." Cleova frowned, as though trying to decide if that was a joke.

"You know ..." Belle looked at the rows of cello-wrapped cigarettes. "Maybe I'll take up smoking, too. What do I have to lose, huh? You sell any of those little filtered Gaucho cigars?"

"Oh, Miz Belle, don't start that ..."

"Maybe I'll bum a few cancer sticks until I decide if I like the brand or not. Tell me, who smokes Gauchos around here?"

12

Adventure Is Just Bad Planning
~Roald Amundsen

MOST PEOPLE BELIEVE the distance to a trailhead is long. There's the planning, buying equipment, telling friends, buying more stuff, and trying to pack a mountain of gear into a seven-liter bag. Then the excited hiker travels by truck, train, bus, or bicycle to reach a parking area and a lonely signpost, marking the start of a journey.

For years, folks in Two Pan have watched tourists, hikers, and hunters blow into town, buying batteries and bug spray, chattering like excited squirrels at the idea of pitting themselves against the wilderness.

At the Bar and Grill, they spread maps over the tables, have a last beer, and ask how long it takes to get to a trailhead. Most folks say, "Seven miles." But one or two of the old-timers may smile and tell them it depends on how long it takes to gather up the experiences that brought them there in the first place. Some folks think of adventure in terms of distance; others ponder risk in terms of what they've already survived.

The hikers chalk the strange answers up to living in such an isolated place for so long. But folks in Two Pan have learned the hard way; the trailhead begins each morning the moment they step outside their doors.

And as Miz Belle always says: "The gospel truth of a successful journey is remembering to pack the seven inches of space between your ears."

~*~

Josie drove the Trekkers down the rutted two-track path. The sun was up, but hadn't made it over the top of the mountain to chase away the wisps of clouds. It had been a week filled with phone calls and getting supplies. This morning, she and Kick had picked up the clients. They stopped at the Latte-Da for coffee. Lottie sent them off with a bag of cinnamon cake balls. There was little conversation as they rattled over the rough road to the trailhead.

Cool air tinged with pine scents filled the car when they parked at 5,600 feet. They pulled their gear from the trunk and stabbed hiking poles into the ground. Conversation broke through nervous fidgeting with packs. Every few seconds the topics switched: eye drops, scrunchable hats, or emergency whistles. A buzz of excitement popped beneath their words. Laughter punctuated thin jokes about testing their bodies or changing their lives.

All of them looked up when the Range Rover and horse trailer drove into the lot. "Morning!" Belle yelled as she got out and tossed a tarp toward them. "Dump your packs."

"What?" Samantha said.

"You heard me. Pack check." Belle ignored the women's complaints as she backed the mules out of the trailer, walking each one in a circle before tying it up. After inspecting their feet, she threw a plush new blanket on one mule's back.

Melane groaned, poking her bulging rucksack with a finger. "I repacked this three times last night to get everything in. I don't want to take it apart until I get to camp."

Josie wore a pasted-on smile as she spread the blue tarp. "I'm sure Miz Belle is going to give some tips that'll make it easier." She gave the old woman a stern look.

Belle missed it. She was hefting her saddle onto the mule and adding saddlebags. By the time she tightened cinches, Josie called, "We're ready."

"Carry those boxes to the tarp." Belle nodded at the back of her Rover and pulled a bridle out of her gear box. She fit the bit in the mule's mouth, smiling at the sight of the women lugging the heavy, bulky cartons across the graveled parking area.

Doing a last check of the mule, the old woman made her ritual rub across her brand: a bell with squiggly marks at the top. With two pats, she turned to the waiting women. "Anyone here good at animal husbandry or geometry?"

The ladies looked at each other with puzzled faces.

"Well ..." Belle rubbed her hands together. "You're in for a treat this week. Because you're gonna get really good at it. Here's a little mass-weight problem to start with. Listen up. Your life depends on it. Everybody squat next to your pack."

Putting a boot on the cardboard boxes, Belle pushed each one over, spilling the contents across the tarp.

"You were given a stuff sack." She held up a nylon bag with drawstrings. "You were to fill it with what you wanted, extra clothes, bulky things. It would be hauled to the base camp. This ..." she waved at the trappings spread across the tarp, "is too much shit." She toed a cosmetic bag the size of a shoe. "If you wanna lug around a trunk of moisturizers, that's your business. But you need to know that a mule is one of the smartest beasts alive. This is the only animal that will not sink in quicksand."

"There's quicksand here?" Melane whispered to Kick, who shook her head.

"It's the Ripley's-Believe-It-Or-Not truth, and it's not because mules are lighter than air." Belle waved a hand at the animal that was studying the seated women, its head cocked to the side. "He won't sink because he is so damn alert, he'll never bumble into quicksand in the first place. Winston, here, is a genius. He understands mass and gravity. And he—or Marly—will sit down and refuse to move for any knucklehead who disagrees with his weight calculations. So, ladies ..." she held the stuff bag in the air. "You need to make some choices because neither of these mules will haul all this crap up the mountain."

"But it's all important. I didn't know what to leave out." Samantha Jarmin tugged at her earring.

Belle's face pouted into a sympathetic frown. "Well, lemme help you. Who's your partner?"

"Josie."

"You take the tent and stove." Belle pushed them aside. "Josie takes the tent poles and water filter. You both carry fuel."

"We negotiated something different." Josie gave her a flat smile. "I'm taking those so she can carry some personal items."

"Up to you." Belle shrugged. "I don't wanna hear any bitchin' about it later." She picked up another pack, punching it as she gave it a hard shake to get the tightly-stuffed supplies to drop onto the tarp. "Holy moley. Whatta you gonna do with a five-pound bag of trail mix?"

"Eat it." Melane's tone said it was the stupidest question she'd ever heard.

"Listen, by the end of this day, you'll be cussing those nuts and trying to feed every chipmunk in the national forest. We'll be calling you Munk-girl. The pesky little turds don't need your encouragement. Dump three-fourths of that."

"Anybody else want help with their packs?" Belle looked around. "You were told to split the necessities with a partner. This makes you help your partner get to camp, or you'll be hungry, sleeping in the dirt."

"Isn't it your responsibility to make sure we get to camp?" Samantha said.

"Nope." Belle pointed her thumb toward Josie. "She's leader. Think of me as the naturalist. I tell you how to survive or spot poison oak. Ignore me at your own risk."

"There's poison oak?" Melane whispered to Kick, who nodded.

Samantha began stuffing items back into her pack. "And who's *your* partner?"

Belle simply held up her bread-loaf-size stuff sack. "Sort through your personal effects and fill your bag till it looks like this. You won't see it for two days. If you need something in it before then, carry it with you. Essentials on your back, the rest in the stuff sack. That's all you get to take. Period." She gave Josie a look that would bend iron and circled her finger at the tarp. "Fix this."

"I'll help." Kick's voice was a bit too cheery for the butt-kicking Belle had handed out.

It was another fifteen minutes before Jiggs and Nap drove into the trailhead parking lot. The young man got out and headed toward Kick and Melane. Jiggs opened the door, calling, "Hey, gals. Ready to *find* yourselves?"

Ticked-off scowls swatted him as women put magazines and flip flops in the pile, lifted their packs, checking the weight, then tossed more items into the pile.

"Well, it looks like you've fired up the troops," Jiggs told Belle as she lashed on her bedroll. "Are you riding this mule? I thought I was using both of them as pack animals."

"That was before I decided to go on the trip. I'm seventy-two years old. My old bones don't like traipsing up these passes and jamming my knees on the descent. I'm riding."

"Well I wish somebody would tell me these things."

"If you load right, Tool, you'll only need one mule to pack everything in." She leaned close to him, her fingers lacing the roll in place without looking. "But if you don't think you can handle one mule, then I'll stay here and help you. 'Course your girlfriend will get lost a few times, but you say the word, and I'll unsaddle this mule. I'll putter around your place, helping you. I'm a good ranch hand."

"No!" Jiggs waved her off. "I just don't want you searching for your arsonist. Sol's working a lead on a truck that's been seen on Winn road. He'll probably have someone arrested by the time you get back."

"Hopefully, he'll shoot the devil if he catches him. I would."

"Mabel ..." Jiggs shook his head, searching the blue skies above for help. "Never mind. Be nice. Don't run over Josie."

"Yeah, her backbone isn't fully formed yet. We'll work on that while we're out here. Think you can handle Marly?" She waved toward the mule still tied to the trailer.

Jiggs' hand clenched at his sides. He let out a long breath. "You forget these were George's mules before you got your mitts on them. I've worked with this animal plenty when it had a decent name—Marlboro. What quirky habits have you taught it?"

"If you're such a big mule whisperer, you'll find out." Belle smiled, rolling the culled belongings in the tarp like a burrito. "Put that in your truck and haul it home. The gals decided they didn't need this paraphernalia."

"Yeah, okay," Jiggs said, studying the hand-drawn map Belle had given him with routes to the base camps. "How is it I've never been on this trail?"

"You're in for a treat. Marly knows it. I took the mules twice last fall to toughen their hooves."

"Are we ready, everyone?" Josie called, pulling Kick and Melane away from Nap and a conversation that had the three twenty-somethings laughing. "Gather 'round. Your blue packet has today's map and information about the plants and trees surrounding you. It's a short hike. Five miles. Our first rest will be at an abandoned pioneer cabin. Everybody find the spot." Josie paused, letting the women study their maps. Belle ignored them, as she dug through her gear box. "Miz Belle, did you hear? We'll be taking a rest break, so don't keep going past the turnoff."

The old woman grimaced. "I *know* where the cabin is. I made love in it when I was sixteen. That's why this is called the *great* outdoors."

Melane and Kick spit out laughs, looking at Nap.

Josie hurriedly pushed a camera into the young man's hands. "Go stand over there." She turned to the women, "Time for pictures."

Belle led the mule to the trailhead sign and the ladies squeezed around it. The young man snapped photos with several people's phones. Most of them came out as wide-eyed women being nuzzled by a mule. "Oh for pity's sake!" Belle sneered, scanning the pictures. "Let's get at least one photo that looks like we're gonna survive past dinnertime." The women lined up and gave their best cocksure smiles.

As they prepared to leave, Samantha Jarmin took off her sunglasses watching Belle mount. "Why do you get to ride?"

Belle's focus narrowed on the woman, but before she could speak, Josie stepped between them, holding up Samantha's pack so she could slip it on like a vest. "I need Miz Belle to be the mobile one in the group, who can come and go if we get spread out. Or she can get to help fast if there's an emergency."

"I thought carrying your own weight was part of the *discovery experience*." Samantha tightened her shoulder straps.

"I've carried enough damn weight and discovered all of myself I want to." Belle gave her a silencing look.

Josie shot the old woman a fiery glare. "Okay. okay. Let me remind you, everyone's pace is different. That's why we went over the map, so you'll know where you're going. I'll lead. Kick, try to stay in the middle. Belle, you're on sweep." The old lady gave her a casual two-fingered salute.

"Ladies, look around." Josie gazed up at the canopy of firs. "Try to remember how the light comes through the branches. Listen to the sound of your steps muffled by the duff on the trail. You are going to see miracles. You're about to change your lives."

The mule flicked his tail. His sphincter flared several times as he pushed out balls of dung. "It's a miracle." Belle patted his hip. "Winston feels better already."

Josie turned and took off. The ladies followed, their packs squeaking with each step, hiking poles thudding into the ground.

Belle, Nap, and Jiggs watched until the trail crooked to the right and the women disappeared around the bend.

"Go easy on them," Jiggs said. "Remember they're tenderfoots. I'll see you in a couple of days."

Belle tossed him the keys to the Rover. He juggled the catch, bouncing it hand to hand. Nap reached in and snagged it.

"What?" Jiggs frowned under her gaze. "No warnings? No threats if I put a scratch on your rig or your mule?"

Belle continued to stare for a long moment, her mouth turning down and her eyes softening as though she'd seen a memory come to life. "Nap," she said quietly, "take care of your dad in his old age. You've got your work cut out for you." She gave a single nod. "Goodbye, Jiggs."

With a tug of the reins Winston turned, and they plodded up the trail.

13

Alone On The Trail

"OH ... GEEZ ..." Samantha Jarmin bent over and gasped, staring at the ground but not really seeing it as she sucked in air.

"Brace your hands on your knees, keep your head down." Kick patted Samantha's back. "Don't take off your pack. Focus on your breathing."

"Who ... put this mountain ... here?" Samantha wheezed.

Melane came trudging up and stopped. With her short blonde hair stuffed under a baseball cap, she looked like a boy. "You okay?"

Samantha's dangling earrings jerked as she nodded, still staring at the dirt. Kick secretly waved Melane on. The young woman continued up the slope without a word.

"She's not ... even ... breathing hard." Samantha stayed bent over, her eyes following Melane.

"There's a little more space between oxygen molecules up here. It takes three days for your body to develop more red blood cells to help with the strain," Kick said. "Maybe five days depending on your conditioning and age."

"Oh ... geez. I'm doomed. Are we going higher?"

Kick pulled out her map and pretended to look. They'd been hiking a steady rise for fifteen minutes and had climbed four hundred feet. Most of the trails in the Eagle Caps rose and dropped 3,000 feet. This woman was taking bigger, more dramatic gasps than the patients she worked with at Mountain View Skilled Care. "We'll gain a bit more elevation."

"Oh ... geez." Samantha straightened, her eyes closed, her nose pointing at the sky.

"The trick is to go at your own pace. Don't try to keep up with Melane. You're different body types. And she's twenty-three years old." Kick gave an apologetic smile when Samantha looked at her. "I checked your health forms before I left."

"She may be only a couple years older than my daughter, but I don't want to be left behind with that old Belle-woman." Samantha slung a disgusted look down the trail.

"I don't know Miz Chere very well. I live over in Elgin. Mostly she keeps to her—"

"Damn. Here she comes." Behind them, Belle was leading Winston up the hill. Samantha walked away. As soon as the landscape dipped and she couldn't see the old woman anymore, she stopped, gulping in big breaths.

Kick passed her, warning, "Slow and steady." In a hundred yards, Kick found Melane sitting in the middle of the path, her boot off, her heel lifted up even with her nose.

"Gotta a blister," she groused. "I pressed all the liquid out."

Kick dropped her pack and dug through it for tape. "It's good you stopped."

In a few minutes, Samantha trudged by with only a wave, her focus on her next step.

"I bet she quits tonight." Melane stared at the plodding woman as Kick bound her heel and little toe. "She's had too much creature comfort."

"There. We'll check it at the next stop." Kick stowed the tape and hurriedly slipped her arms through her shoulder straps. "We need to keep moving." She tapped her watch and hiked away.

Melane looked at the trail rising steadily above her. Behind her, Belle and the mule appeared at the switchback, ascending at a pace as constant as a ticking clock.

She jammed her foot into her boot and took off, trying to walk and tie it at the same time. With an *oooof,* she slid on hands and knees into the brush on the side of the trail. It took a second to curse and look around before she recoiled, scrambling backward. Surely this was the dreaded poison oak she'd been warned about. She held up dirty palms, expecting to see red blotches and kernels of pustules sprouting over her hands.

"You're so stupid." She pushed to standing, brushing pine needles and dirt from her knees. She froze. Had she just spread poison oak to another part of her body? Shit. Shit. Shit. A quick glance behind her showed Belle making steady slow progress toward her. Melane took off. "Keep calm and carry on." If it got the Brits through World War II, it would get her up this hill.

In five minutes, she passed Samantha sitting on a log, bent over, sucking in air. "Tag," Melane said. "You're it. You get the horsewoman of the Apocalypse bearing down on you." She hurried on without waiting for a response.

When Belle and the mule neared the bent-over woman, they stopped. Samantha waved them on.

"No rush," the old woman said. "Look at that mushroom next to where you're parked. The one that looks like a white saucer collided with the log. You know what that is?"

Samantha's face squeezed into a *yuk* expression as she mouth-breathed and looked first on one side of her then the other. "This? Is it ... poison?"

Belle's forehead furrowed with thought. "I never ate one. We always used them as punk to light our firecrackers." Samantha gave her a blank look, but Belle's head turned from tree to tree, watching a pair of brown birds flit between the branches. "Can't see the sky under this canopy. We may be in for some weather. Whaddya think?"

Samantha looked directly overhead, then around her, and finally shrugged.

"Birds." Belle pointed. "They get crazy active when a front is coming. It's like people mobbing the grocery store right after the weatherman says a blizzard is rolling out of Canada."

Samantha studied the trees. Now that she looked, there *was* a lot of movement. Wings flittering between the ground and back up to the branches.

They watched for a moment before Belle walked on, the mule following, his reins swinging slack between them.

"Hold up. I don't want to be alone on the trail," Samantha said.

"Push through. It's just around the bend," Belle called back. "Besides, unless you're carrying somebody in your pocket, you're always alone on the trail."

Samantha gave her earring a nervous tug, watching them walk away. She'd keep the ass-end of that mule in sight.

The turnoff didn't appear around the bend, nor the next three bends. At some point she forgot to look for the mule as she watched birds flash across the trail. As she neared the junction ahead of her, she could see the women waiting and talking. Her breathing came in gasps, but her heart wasn't trying to burst through her chest anymore.

"Don't sit down," Josie cautioned. The women were putting on their packs. "Drink. Catch your breath and we'll go."

"Some of us have been waiting fifteen minutes," Melane said.

"Well, good for you, *Munk-girl*." Samantha shucked out of her pack.

"Now, ladies, we're all a bit winded," Josie said.

"I'll lead. Come when you can." Belle swung a leg over Winston. "C'mon, Munk-girl. With super-mule Winston on point, you don't have to worry about snake attacks."

"There are snakes?" Melane watched Belle plod up the trail. "Poisonous ones?"

"They don't attack," Kick said, "unless you step on them."

"You're sure I'm not covered in poison oak?" Melane held her hands up for the fifth time since they'd stopped for a rest break.

"You're fine. But wait a moment." Josie held up a finger, peeking up the trail. The other ladies fell silent, watching her and waiting. "Okay." she gave a single soft clap, her hands remaining together in prayer position against her body. "I'm asking for your indulgence. I'm fully aware that Miz Belle Chere is a pain in the keister, and I'm sorry about that." A couple of the ladies nodded. "What you may not know is that she lost everything she owned in a house fire a couple of weeks ago."

"Oh!" Melane's hand went to her chest. "That explains a lot."

"It was arson," Josie said quietly.

Moans of *Oh*! or *No*! arose as Samantha Jarmin mumbled, "Well, I can understand why." The women stared at her. "Well, I mean … face it. She *does* like to rile people up. And around here, if you do that to people … well … you're taking your life in your hands."

Kick's eye's narrowed. "What do you know about people around here?"

"Ladies," Josie held up a hand. "I only told you so you'd understand what's going on and cut her some slack. She's going through a hard time, and we're on the brunt end of some of her words. This trek is the best thing for her right now. Let her have her space and give her your patience—" She looked at Samantha, "—if you can."

The abandoned pioneer cabin sat in a small clearing. Four log walls stood without a roof. Much of the chinking had been replaced with furry green moss growing between the cracks. "This was a doozy in its day." Belle pointed out. "It had a window."

"I don't see any broken glass here." Samantha kicked around a bush that had taken hold under the opening.

"They wouldn't haul glass up here. They had to tie logs to the back of wagons to slow them going down that hill you just climbed. They would've covered this opening with a hide or greased paper," Belle said. "It'd let in the light, but they couldn't see out. The covering was probably eaten by coyotes or elk, long ago. In the winter, it'd be boarded up so the bears couldn't climb in."

"Are there still bears out here?" Melane asked. Kick gave a loud sigh. "What?" The young blonde threw up her hands. "I'm from San Diego. All of our critters are in the zoo."

"What's the matter there?" Samantha pointed at the mucky paste of yellow chopped grass covering Melane's hands. Chunks crumbled from the buildup lodged between her fingers.

"An old cure for poison oak. I have to leave it on twenty minutes."

"What is it?" Kick leaned down to examine her hands more closely. "Smells like ..." She straightened and gave Josie a disgusted look. "Mule crap."

"Miz Belle!" Josie yelled with the voice she used on kids who liked to punch others on the playground. The old woman was no longer around. "Miz Belle!"

"She handed me two balls of dung," Melane said. "Told me to squeeze them and rub it in. I figured she was putting me on, but what-the-hey. She's some kind of mountain woman. I'd rather try it than break out in blisters. And if it doesn't work, I'll simply wash it off."

"You don't have poison oak," Kick said. "At least, I'm pretty sure."

"I put another two balls on my knees." Melane stood so stiff-legged, her knees bowed slightly forward.

"Go wash it off." Anger simmered under Josie's words.

They found the old woman twenty yards away, down the embankment by a creek, watering Winston. "Did you tell her to cover herself in crap?" Josie pointed toward Melane walking like Frankenstein, trying to keep chunks of her manure salve from cracking off her knees.

Belle grinned. "We should eat. It's one o'clock. This wagon train isn't moving as fast as you thought it would."

"We'll eat at the cabin—after we wash," Josie said. "We'll sit where pioneers once sat. Look at the same view they did."

Belle shook her head, walking Winston to a grassy spot and staking his lead rope to the ground. "You'd best leave those spirits alone."

"I'm having lunch at the creek. Cooling my toes." Kick smiled. "Munk-girl ... you need to wash and cool that blister."

By the time Josie and Samantha joined them at the creek, Belle, Kick, and Melane were sitting on the bank, eating the sandwiches Josie had handed out that morning. Their feet splashed in the water. Squeals of "It's so *coooold!*" carried through the air.

"Are you not eating at the cabin because ..." Melane leaned forward to give Belle a moon-eyed look, "it reminds you of that hot night with that bo-oy?" She drew the last word into a two-syllable question.

Belle didn't answer, watching the clear water burble over stones, keeping her feet submerged for as long as she could stand it.

Kick elbowed Melane, finally filling the gap in conversation with, "Do you know who lived here? Or what happened to them?"

"Why would anyone live way up here?" Samantha shivered at the forest crowding around them.

"Gold," Belle said.

Melane leaned over, her nose a foot from the water, inspecting the streambed. "Here?"

"Only two pans of it. That's how the town got its name." Belle pulled her feet out of the stream, resting them on a rock as she leaned back on her elbows. "The story goes that a group of men were early travelers on the Oregon Trail. They dragged their families out here, looking for riches. There's other cabins nooked around here. This is the only one I know that's still standing. The others have rotted into piles. Trees growin' up through them. Sometimes you can still find the rusty head of a shovel or pick axe."

"What happened to the people?"

"Gold—in California. The men took off, leaving one old man in the area to look after seven or eight families. It was common. They expected to get rich quick and be back. Story goes a mother and four children waited here. The kids walked up and down that hill to get to a woman who offered schooling for the kids in the area. Of course, they didn't make the climb in the winter. With the winds coming off the north side of this mountain, it's twenty below or more. They'd be snowed in up here. They'd end up eating the horse or oxen to get by. Once you lose your animals, there's not much hope." Belle shook her head. "I like to think that as soon as spring melted the drifts enough to make it out, they left for home whether the father was back from the gold fields or not." Belle used her bandana to dry her feet and pulled on her socks.

Samantha shook her head. "After walking half-way across the continent why would anyone turn around and walk back? There were civilized towns around then. Why not move to one of them?"

"A lotta people picked up and went home. Their men died or never came back from California. Their children got choked out by the diphtheria. Their animals froze, were stolen, or got eaten. Over half of them left. Lemme tell you, when you lose everything, it's hard to keep going."

"My family stayed." Kick gave her the knowing smile of sisters of misfortune. "I hear yours did, too."

Belle gave a nod. "There's a grave up there by the cabin." Belle grabbed her boots and pulled them on. "Well, that's the story handed down to me. It sure looks like a grave. It's the only cedar tree that I know of on the mountain. A pile of stones sits at the head of a small sunken spot."

"One of the children?" Melane frowned.

Belle stood, dusting off her backside. "The tale goes that the family's mutt walked the kids to the shack used for a school. He'd growl and bark and let them know if a cougar was stalking them. At the end of the day, the hound would meet 'em and safeguard 'em home. When it started snowing one afternoon, the kids left school early and lit out for home. The dog wasn't around. By the time they got to their cabin, the blizzard was blowing sideways like it does up here. The dog didn't come home that night or the next few days either. They finally made their way downhill and found him, frozen, in front of the shack, waiting for them to come out."

Belle looked at the sad faces. "That's the hearsay of this place." She pulled up Winston's stake, knocked the dirt off, and stowed it in her saddle bag. "As for the grave marker up there ... they say the dog is buried there. And he'll wait until the father comes back from the gold fields. Together, they'll find wherever the kids have gone."

"I want to see it," Melane grabbed her pack and climbed the embankment toward the cabin. Samantha rolled her eyes.

"I'm pulling out. Don't take too long," Belle called as she led the mule up the trail.

Josie checked her watch and turned toward Samantha, "Perhaps you'd like to start now? We've got two more miles to go."

"Are they uphill?" Samantha groaned.

Kick gave the woman a flat stare and walked past her. "I've lived around here all my life. Everything is an uphill struggle." Her stride was long and fast, leaving Josie to deal with her paying clients.

14

She Who Desires Revenge Should Dig Two Graves

~A Paraphrasing of Confucius

ON THE PATH, Belle arranged three good-sized sticks into the shape of an arrow, indicating the turn off. If the women followed the meandering side trail for fifty yards, they'd find a small meadow. A narrow channel of clear water skirted the new grass before streaming down a ravine.

She stared at her "mountain message," hoping Kick hiked in front; she'd notice the arrow. Josie might also, but the other two bozos would kick such an obvious man-made arrangement as they blundered past.

Mounting Winston, she rode for another mile, cutting upward onto a game trail angling across the side of the mountain. When the path narrowed, she dismounted so Winston could keep his balance without worrying about her on top. That's what she told herself. Truth was, she got off because she felt agitated. Winston could tell and kept swinging his head around to eyeball her.

Thoughts roiled through her mind as she walked ahead of him. After fifty feet, the reins pulled from her hand. Winston had stopped. "C'mon." She grabbed and snapped the leather straps. He cocked an ear as though she were speaking Sudanese. "We're gonna check Bald Blowout. We don't even have to ride down into the canyon to see if it's clear. We can look from above. If nobody's there, we'll head back to camp." He stuck his muzzle close and breathed on her. "Not now." She pushed him away and walked ahead. He didn't follow.

"Okay, buddy. You earned a time-out. I'm tying you to this parking meter and going on without you." She looped the reins around a fir, finishing it with a slip hitch. "If it's a cougar that's got you spooked, then kick the guts outta him until I get back. Good luck, you stubborn gluepot."

She picked her way along the path, which became narrower and more overgrown. What had she been thinking, volunteering to go with these women? It had allowed her to buy tack and ride into the mountains without being dogged by the sheriff and Jiggs. But little had she imagined what a bunch of whiners and titsy-fritzels these gals were. Only one night. That's all she had to spend to get them settled. One night, then she'd disappear. It was an exercise in extreme patience.

Josie was so directionally challenged, she didn't know up from inside-out most of the time. Kick was young and eager, but trying to please everybody. Samantha Jarmin would probably tell her husband about the pioneer cabin, and find a way to make money out of it. Munk-girl hadn't shown her character yet. She seemed nice, except for the chip on her shoulder, but Belle wasn't hanging around to find out more.

She ran her hand over her mouth, muzzling herself too late. What was the matter with her? She shouldn't have shown them the lost cabin. Look what had happened when a man found geysers and bubbling mud holes, or another guy had discovered trees that had turned to stone. The lunkheads had dragged their friends to see Mother Nature's art projects. And now there were multi-lane highways into Yellowstone, and part of the Petrified Forest had disappeared because people lugged chunks home for their rock gardens.

She'd traded the cabin so she could alter the route of this trip and find a worthless crawler. He had to be in these canyons if he was spying so easily on her house. Her job would be over if he was in the first—

Belle's boot dropped six inches as the ground gave way. She froze with one foot forward and one foot back, hands out to her sides. Slowly, she looked directly beneath her. The soil teamed as though a thousand worms were writhing under the surface. Specks worked away from her boot. Particles the size of BBs lined into rills and dribbled downhill.

Forcing her eyes up the side of the slope she saw she'd walked across a crevice that had been frozen over and was now thawing. Snow had stayed in the natural cleft longer and melted more slowly, leaving the soil particles connected only by water. The few firs growing above her were small. The ones downslope were—a crisscross tangle of boles and root balls. This area had slid before. And if she hadn't been thinking about sweet revenge, and the amount of traffic in Yellowstone National Park, she would've noticed the ground around her.

Slowly she dragged her foot backward, wobbling side to side as she eased her weight onto her back foot. The dirt dropped from under her another few inches, sliding sideways off the trail. Her feet scrambled to lodge against a sapling as she fell upslope. With her face in the dirt, she could see the tiny pieces of soil jiggling and funneling into larger streams the size of pencils, trickling downhill.

In slow movements she rolled onto her side, facing the way she'd come. She could see Winston, the animal that would never walk into quicksand—or a landslide. What was the matter with her? Griping about these stupid women had made her ignore the best alarm she had. She studied the ground a moment, then rolled onto her stomach, stretching her arms and legs wide.

Her fingers bent into claws. She pushed with her toes. Army basic training had taught her about quicksand: Don't try to stand up. Instead, spread your weight over a larger area. Slow, small movements would navigate the body to the edge, where a person could roll out.

She could do the same, but face down. Except she couldn't tell where the edge was. Each handful of earth she clutched crumbled through her fingers. At times her toes flicked air as dirt shifted beneath her. Inch by inch she moved forward. "Don't grab that, you air-brained birdie!" Her drill sergeant screamed in her mind as her hand took hold of a small tree. "Whaddya wanna do? Pull that sapling up by the roots and set this section rolling?"

Damn! She had hated that woman. How long was that voice going to hide in her brain? But how many occasions had those orders saved her life? One finger at a time, Belle released the sapling in her grip, fighting the need to use the tree as leverage and heave her body forward. "Push through," she whispered.

When her fingers hit soil that didn't give, she didn't stop. When the toes of her boots thudded into hard ground, she crawled ten feet farther. Rolling onto her backside, she sat up. A fifteen-foot section of the trail had slid down the mountain one to two feet. The vertical face of crumbling soil waited for a squirrel or heavy rain to disturb the balance and finish the job. Pushing to her feet, she tramped to the mule and sat down heavily, rubbing her forehead.

How could she have been so stupid? Even her mule had tried to tell her. If the thieves were using that canyon, the trail would've been clearer. What was the matter with her? She was becoming an old, stupid woman.

"Stay in the *here and now*!" her drill sergeant commanded.

Belle's head bent low, her hand covering her eyes. She was losing it. Like she'd lost everything else. What did it matter? It didn't—not anymore.

Winston leaned down and nudged the top of her head. She reached up and patted him, her dirty fingers streaked with tears.

As she rode to camp, relief sifted through her thoughts. Company would feel good after the close call. The emotion surprised her. Unfortunately, they'd want to know what happened to her. That was the problem with hanging around others. They were witnesses to stupidity and cheerfully asked questions about it. She stopped at a creek and splashed icy water on her face, washing away dirt and red eyes. Using a stick, she scraped the caked-on soil from the front of her new jacket and jeans. She smoothed the flyaway hair around her temples and snugged her hat on tighter. Her best defense had always been offense.

Female voices floated out of the clearing. Their steady hum of conversation and laughter made her feel safe. She pushed the feeling down and stamped on it.

The four women, sitting on a fallen tree, greeted her as she entered the clearing. "We were starting to worry." Melane waved.

"Heavens. What happened to you?" Josie stood.

Belle got off the mule, giving them a stern stare as they passed a bag of gummy worms between them. "How long have you been here?"

"About an hour, where have you been? Are you okay?"

"I fell down. Explain to me how you've been here for sixty minutes and no work has been done. You!" She pointed at Samantha. "Start filtering water." Belle turned like a Gatling gun, targeting the women. "You set up tents. You build a fire ring. You collect wood." The ladies stared at her.

"We were resting and doing sensory exercises before starting on chores," Josie said.

"Now!" Belle didn't wait for questions and comments but led Winston toward a grassy spot. "As soon as you're finished, you can lollygag."

As she cared for the mule, Josie appeared. "You want some help?"

"Whatever you see, you can carry." Belle hefted the saddle. "We need to talk."

"I agree." Josie toted the bedroll and saddle bags, placing them between the two trees where Belle pointed.

"I wanna show you something important here. You'll remember this, probably forever." Belle walked into the forest and Josie followed. Belle turned, pinning her against a tree, watching the whites of her eyes grow large, obviously surprised that such an old woman had any strength. "You need to remember two emotions motivate people." Josie stared.

"Fear and desire," Belle continued. "Are you listening?" She gave Josie's shoulder a shake and the woman nodded. "I don't imagine these women are sleeping in the dirt because they actually *desire* this finding-yourself bullshit. I'm guessin' they each have other reasons they're out here. But you're busy selling *desire*. You keep telling them, 'Aren't these woods lovely? Think of other lovely times in your life. What made you happy?'" Belle let go. "For that reason, I'm selling *fear*. This mountain doesn't give a damn that you're here. Everything on it would like to bite you, eat you, suck your blood, or fall on you. Each of those women has to pull her head out of her ass and pay attention or she'll get hurt."

Free of the old woman's grip, Josie straightened her shoulders and pushed away from the tree. "I get that. I've been hiking and camping before. And I don't appreciate—"

"Really? So tell me what a person's supposed to do after they've determined the area is safe to camp in?"

"Turn into a human and talk to her campmates?"

Belle shoved her against the tree again. "A rider takes care of her horse. A hiker sets up shelter and preps camp. Always be making your situation better so you don't get jammed up. You need to decide if you're going to be leader or one of the girls."

"We were resting."

"In less than an hour, the sun will drop behind that peak. Night comes fast and early in the mountain's shadow. I guarantee when we walk back out there, it will be a clusterfob of women bitching and not knowing what to do. In case you hadn't noticed, Samantha has a dehydration headache. Melane and Kick are exhausted because they want to lose weight and didn't eat enough today."

"Okay." Josie made a face. "You don't have to be so nasty about it."

"School teacher, if you want a woman to discover who she is—then teach her to survive in whatever situation she's in. And that means you do what's necessary *first*. You got it? Go take care of your squad."

She let go of Josie and watched her walk away. She wished the woman had pushed back—at least a little. What kind of leader survives if they won't put up a fight? The poor woman probably had never been pushed around or given a Come-to-Jesus talk. Josie would remember this, at least Belle hoped so.

It had worked on her.

15

A Year Of Nightmares

WOMEN'S BASIC TRAINING in 1967 hadn't included long road marches like the men had to make. But her drill sergeant thought short conditioning hikes were good for female stamina. Belle hated marching. Pointless loops. Neat rows, uniform steps. Stupid rules for no reason.

"Private Chere!" Her drill sergeant yanked her out of line and shoved her against a tree. "Can you tell me why you are incapable of staying ten feet behind the person in front of you?"

"I'm not paying attention, ma'am." Belle followed the two rules she had learned the hard way on her first day in basic: Do not look directly at the sergeant. Tell the sergeant what she wanted to hear.

Mostly basic had consisted of six months of rudimentary nursing skills, waxing floors, scrubbing bathrooms, and keeping her locker organized with hangers one inch apart and the left shoulder of jackets and shirts facing outward. Rules. And more stupid rules.

And then she'd been pushed into another tree. Not hard, but solid enough to make her focus on the here and now. "Do I have your attention, private?"

"Yes, ma'am."

"You *will* keep your intervals. Let me hear you say it—loud, so your squad knows they can count on you not to have your head up your ass."

Belle yelled the words, but she got to meet another tree before she was dismissed. "Now because we had to stop and have this little pep talk with Private Chere, everybody gets to double-time to keep to schedule."

Other drill sergeants hadn't been so "military." It was Belle's luck to get the one female expert on base who believed in tree-to-tree counseling. And since then, how many times had the woman's stupid rules saved her life—even today, crawling over a landslide?

Belle walked back to the camp site. Kick sat on the ground, fighting with a rainfly and yelling at Melane. Melane cursed and dragged fallen branches across the tent area. Samantha complained that the "Stupid water filter won't pump."

Belle set up her hammock between two trees. She'd stopped sleeping on the ground years ago. As she secured a pad in the bottom of the sling, she watched Josie trot from one woman to the next.

"Frick. Frick. Frick!" Melane yelled and dropped the branch she'd picked up. "I think I stuck my hand in poison oak again."

"You never had it in the first place," Kick yelled.

"Where's the dung?" Melane asked as Belle headed to the creek with a collapsible water bucket. The old woman pointed toward the edge of the meadow where Winston nipped grass. Melane jogged off.

Belle was dipping the soft-sided bucket in the creek when Josie arrived. "Maybe you could help with the water filter? It won't work."

"Maybe you shoulda started earlier? It's like a student doin' homework. If you don't start as soon as you get home from school, you might run into a problem and not finish it. Right now, I'm doing laundry." She walked past.

After taking a wipe bath, she slipped into her zipleg pants and synthetic t-shirt. As she churned the dirt out of her clothes in the bucket, she listened to the complaints: The tent poles didn't fit where they were supposed to. Munk-girl didn't want to use her hands for twenty minutes after rubbing dung on them. Samantha Jarmin had given up filtering and laid next to the stream, complaining about her headache.

Belle rinsed and wrung out her clothes, hanging them across the rope she'd strung between trees. She walked into the center of camp, next to Melane's fire ring and called out, "What have we learned, today, ladies?"

"Screw you." Samantha rubbed her forehead as she climbed into her tent and zipped it.

"Suit yourself." Belle shrugged. "I'm giving a cooking lesson in ten minutes. If you wanna eat tonight, haul your food, stoves, and little butts out here."

Soon two propane burners roared under pots of water. Belle tossed a smooth, gray river rock the size of a golf ball into each pot. "At high elevation, it takes forever to boil, so add a rock to concentrate the heat. It's not necessary here, but you'll need to do it at the base camp in two days—so get used to it."

As the water heated, the women continued their chores. Melane wouldn't wash off the dung or touch another piece of wood until Belle identified the plants and declared them harmless.

When the water boiled, the ladies added boxes of macaroni. As it cooked, Belle gave a demonstration on how to field strip the water filter.

They added seasonings and flaked tuna in packets to their meal pots. Kick and Melane were too starved to wait for their macaroni to finish cooking. They divided their goo to begin munching hard, half-cooked noodles.

"Crap." Munk-girl frowned at Belle. "I took out my silverware when you made us lighten our packs."

"Oh my! Whaddya gonna do?" Belle cocked an eyebrow as she scooped cheesy macaroni into her thermal cup.

"I'll borrow a spoon when someone finishes."

"Wow! Sounds fun, spending every meal watching people eat before you do." Belle smirked and sat on the tripod stool she'd packed.

"What are *we* supposed to sit on?" Melane looked around, her stare finally landing on Kick sporking her macaroni directly into her mouth from the cooking pot.

Belle fanned her hand around them. "There's a whole world out here waiting to be introduced to your butt." Melane stared.

"What the hell is the matter with you women? You'd think all of you were crouching behind bushes the day God handed out brains. Tell yourself 'I'm in charge of the present situation. I'm the queen of *Now.*' Whaddya gonna do? For the love of the few functioning brain cells you've got ... think!"

"Like Samantha said, 'Screw you.'" Melane grabbed Kick and together they rolled a log closer to the fire so they'd have a place to sit.

Josie had lured Samantha out of her tent with a cup of Gatorade. She stood quietly, sipping her drink and watching the chaotic housekeeping proceedings. Josie pointed to the macaroni. "Fix yourself a plate." Samantha skeptically lifted a lid to look at the food. The bickering ceased as the others settled down to eat.

"Oh no!" Samantha's face squinched as she stared into the cook pot. She pulled the top burner of the stove out of the pot, its knobs covered in cheese goo. "I ... I was trying to move it and—"

"Eat!" Josie declared. "Everybody just eat!" She let out a long breath.

Belle gave her an *I-told-you-so* stare.

*

After dinner, Belle barked orders several more times, making the women bury their leftovers away from camp, instead of hurling them into the bushes. She wouldn't let them wash their dishes in the stream. "Because it's wrong, and because I don't like bears licking my toes."

Josie threw her an angry look. "Stop trying to scare Melane with threats of wild animals."

"Okay, but why do you think we have Bear Mountain, Bear Wallow, and Bear Creek on a map?" The old woman shrugged. "Just do your toilet and bury your leftovers far away from me." She pointed at Samantha. "And you need to drink more."

"It makes me pee, and I hate squatting on the ground."

"Fine. By tomorrow, it'll feel like somebody slammed an axe between your eyes. Your joints will burn and ache ... all because you don't want to whizz in the dirt."

"You don't need to worry about me," Samantha said. "I'm going back tomorrow."

Melane grinned and nodded at Kick, who pretended not to notice.

"What's that smile supposed to mean?" Samantha lasered a stare at Melane.

"She bet you'd drop out tonight," Belle said, whittling on a stick. "You being older and all."

"Well, you're no spring chicken." Samantha squinted at the old woman.

"You're right, Tinkerdink, but I drink a lot of water." Belle smiled, pointing the knife at Samantha. "You want the secret to weein' in the woods?" Samantha nodded. Belle got up and whispered in her ear.

"What?" Melane stared. "We wanna hear."

"I bet you would." Samantha gave the young woman a smirk.

"Nobody's leaving!" Josie announced. "There's only one car sitting at the trailhead, and I have the keys. So that's that." She gave Belle a *see-there* nod. "Now ... on to tonight's activity. I promise tasks will get easier. Each evening we'll explore a part of our lives that influenced us. Tonight, we're talking about mothers."

Samantha moaned and continued eating and cleaning cheese off the stove.

"You can share what you want about how your mother predisposed you: good or bad," Josie said. "No one asks you questions or makes comments. Share only what you want. When you're done, you call for a drink. Each of us will take five gulps of water. I'll count them off." Josie looked around. "Kick, could you start?"

The young woman pulled her ponytail through her fingers and stared at the fire for several moments. "There's not much to tell." She became quiet again, and then shifted on the log, crossing her feet in front of her. "My dad's dead. My mom works seven days a week. I don't see how she's done it. She's inspiring." She went silent again then finally shrugged. "Drink." The ladies sipped from cups, sport bottles, or platypus bags. By the time they reached five gulps, several laughed, coughing and spitting water.

"Anybody want to be next?" When no one answered, Josie began, "My mom had New York tastes in a two-bit town. She hated her life here, and married her way out of poverty. But no matter what she had, she always wanted better. Still does. I didn't think much about it while growing up. Now I'm sorting it out. I'm not quite ready to dig through all of it yet, so I'll simply say, she lives in Florida and we don't talk. Drink."

Samantha stared at Melane. She made a point to take one more gulp than Melane.

Melane stared back. "I'm from California. It's only Mom and me. She's great, considering she had *no help* raising me.

She got pregnant early in life. My father wasn't interested. So I learned from her you have to take care of yourself because no one else will." She raised her water bottle to the night sky. "Thanks, Mom." She locked eyes on Samantha, making a show of drinking more than her. Josie called time, but neither woman quit gulping.

Melane was the first to lower her water bottle. Only then did Samantha stop and wipe her sleeve across her mouth. "Well, I'm the odd-ball in this group. I had an Ozzie and Harriet kind of life. Both my dad and mom were great. They loved all three of us kids and supported us in whatever we wanted to do. I started working in real estate right out of college." She looked at Melane. "We were a middle-class family. I paid my way." She held up her sports-bottle to Melane. "I may be older than you, but I can still out-drink you. Another sip?"

Even after Josie called time, the two women stared at each other and gulped water. They would've continued if Belle hadn't interrupted, "What are you two idiots trying to prove? And what the hell does my mother have to do with sitting in the dark in the middle of the wilderness?"

Kick laughed. Josie gave her a shushing look. "It helps us discover some of the baggage we're carrying and the messages we've been taught by our mothers."

"Oh hell, yes. I know about baggage." Belle nodded. "My mama only wanted babies. At three or four, as soon as we developed enough brain cells to sass her back, she didn't want to mess with us. She'd pop out another kid. Her message couldn't have been clearer. She used a horse as a babysitter. An ancient old nag was tethered in the backyard, and all day long we kids climbed and hung all over it. That ol' swayback never bit or stepped on us. You can't beat a horse for a mom substitute. But what I'm wondering is … so what? If you're alive and sitting here, you learned to survive. If you're still whimpering about it, then you're packin' a load of excess crap. Get over it, because it sure as hell isn't bothering your mothers—if they're still alive. What I want to know is what the hell does any of this have to do with *NOW*, sitting out here attracting bears?"

The fire crackled. The women stared. Finally Melane whispered to Kick, "There are bears around here?"

"Miz Belle!" Josie used her exasperated teacher voice. "This needs to be a safe place to share. Some people are carrying wounds."

"I can see that." She lasered a glare at Josie. "Drink." The women tipped their sports bottles, Melane and Samantha gulped and stared at each other until the blonde lowered her empty bottle with an "Aaaaah," and a snake-charmer smile.

"Good job. Here, Munk-girl." Belle handed the young woman a stick.

"What's this?" Melane examined the end that had been whittled into a flat shim.

"A spoon. *Bon appetit.*" Belle mimed shoveling food in her mouth. "Now excuse me while I hang my food in a tree." She widened her eyes as she looked at Melane. "To keep it from *the bears.*" As she walked away, Melane made a face and tossed the stick over her shoulder.

Josie let out a long, loud sigh. "Also each night, Kick will make a presentation on camp health and hygiene."

Kick stood, holding up a plastic trowel. "Tonight we talk about how to dig a cathole and poop in the woods."

After practicing what they'd learned, the women settled into their tents for the night. Belle stirred the fire and added wood until it threw wavering shadows over the tents. She crawled into her new sleeping bag and hammock and arranged herself diagonally so she lay flat. Usually she set up the rainfly over her sling, but this first evening out, she wanted to feel the night.

The blackness loomed so big, most people wanted to shut it out. Thin nylon walls formed a safe space between the sleeper and whatever the mind imagined was roaming through the dark.

Belle always challenged herself to meet the beast—the darkness. Voices quieted in tents and faded into sleep. The fire died to embers. Owls hooted to each other, their calls getting closer and closer, until they silenced in nocturnal romance.

Stars winked above. The mountains had been her refuge when she'd withdrawn and hidden from people. They had helped her heal. Had new fears allowed old memories to float to the surface? Was she in need of healing again? It didn't matter. The only cure she needed was to eliminate the man who'd stood in the blackness, watching her place burn. But the darkness couldn't cover everything. Half a world away, the nights had been even blacker and the days so bright it had hurt her eyes.

It had still been daylight when she'd stepped off the plane in her heavy olive skirt, jacket, and nylons. The heat swarmed her, sweat making her clothes stick to her skin. The black painted bus carrying her to Long Binh for processing felt like an oven. MPs ordered, "Stay low," when she tried to look out the glass covered with chicken wire. The trip in-country to Cu Chi barely registered. Her brain grogged with the kind of weariness that came from hopping oceans and continents for two days to arrive seventeen miles from the Cambodian border. At the 12th Evacuation Hospital, in a wooden hut, beds lined the walls, barracks-style. A few women had put up bamboo screens for a hint of privacy. That first night, she had no trouble sleeping in a dark heat that pressed and squeezed the moisture out of a body.

The explosion next door awakened her. Corrugated metal plates from the nearby roof slammed against her building, rocking the cots.

Hearing the roar of incoming mortars, she saw women huddled under their cots. She joined them, waiting for the shell that sang their names. Across the open field from the hospital sat the intended targets: the petro dump and artillery battery.

Orange-yellow flames lit the night, their glow wavering through the doorway. The black silhouette of a man appeared. He staggered into the building screaming sounds gutted with pain. Then he tossed an object. *Thump-thump-thump.* It bounced across the floor.

"Grenade!" a woman screamed. Hands over her head, Belle pushed into the planking as though air and canvas cots could shield against death.

Seconds ticked by. The explosion didn't come. One of the nurses crawled from under her cot with a flashlight to investigate. An American soldier lay crumpled on the floor. Blasted from a building, he'd stumbled to the nurses' hut, dropping his pocket watch as he died.

It was the first night in a year full of nightmares. She learned people hung on to strange objects as they left this world. Watches, photos, comic books, letters. She, like the others, learned to adapt, and the scream of missiles or pain no longer kept her awake. It was the dreams that made her sit up. In half-waking moments a man would run into the room, dropping explosives: a grenade, a satchel bag, a bounding mine spraying shrapnel at waist-height. *Thump-thump-thump.*

Alcohol became her sleep aid. And still—she had to be alert and ready to roll when the call came. She stared at the corrugated metal above her, praying the alphabet: A—take me a*way* from here. B—God help the men who *bleed out*. She tried to meet the beast in the darkness, and when she could stand it no longer, she crawled under her cot, joining the other women who needed one layer of canvas for a sense of safety. C—God bless these *cots*.

Now Belle watched the moon come up over the tents. The fire had burned into orange, pulsing coals. Zippers opened. Ladies relieved themselves and climbed back into their tents. *Ziiiiiiiip*. The outdoors was shut out. Belle understood the power of believing in a thin layer of fabric.

In the forest, a stick snapped. Something walked among the trees. She let out a slow breath. When she'd returned from 'Nam, she'd taken comfort in these mountains. She could be sure whatever moved out there wouldn't explode or be a sniper. But now ...

A man had made the night frightening again. She would not go back to that fear. Looking up, she counted the stars, starting with Draco. The same moon, the same stars had shone over Vietnam. Old friends, making pinholes in the grip of darkness. One by one she breathed their names, drifting into sleep.

Until a woman screamed.

16

You Make The Road By Walking On It.
~Nicaraguan Saying

THUMP.THUMP.THUMP. Steps thudded across the campsite like the dull sound of a hammer pounding the dirt. Belle sat up, reaching for her pistol. The Smith and Wesson K38 with five-inch barrel lay holstered in the hammock beside her sleeping bag. Before leaving the trailhead, she had pulled it from the gear box in the trailer and strapped it on. Her long-hipped coat covered it. She'd been surprised Jiggs hadn't asked if she was taking a gun. She was sure he'd made a visual check of her saddlebags before she'd ridden off.

She held the revolver low, scanning the edges of the camp in the direction of the footfalls. No sound came from the tents.

When the world decided to be still, the quiet crept over a body like crawling fingers, especially if a gal was used to city noise: cars honking, people yelling, and neon buzzing. Ranches had their own hum: trucks motoring graveled roads, calves bawling for their moms, squirrels scolding a passing coyote.

Even the battlefield had an incessant voice. The random pop of small arms. Compression waves from bombs brushing the body, rattling supplies. The blades of the medevacs, whopping the air. Men screaming in different languages. When she'd returned home, she'd found the wonder of the woods lay in its silence. Not even a plane engine echoed through the forest.

Only the wind sighing through the boughs and the sound of her own breath.

But if a person was afraid and let the waiting and listening go on too long, the stillness crept up her spine and made her yell just to confirm life beyond the quiet. Belle walked to Melane and Kick's tent, giving it a slap. "You yelled. Are you comin' out to look, or are you hidin' in there all night, gettin' nervous and wonderin' when it's gonna eat you?"

"You check on it. You're the Queen of Now," Melane said.

"Get out here," Belle ordered.

"I can't find my headlamp."

"I've got a light, but you won't need it."

The zipper on Kick and Melane's tent came down several inches. An eye peeked through the gap.

"Dammit. Grow a pair and get out here." Belle yanked their zipper all the way open.

Munk-girl slowly emerged like a gopher inching up from a hole. "I don't see anything," she whispered. When she finally stood beside Belle, the older woman flashed the light on for a second. Two sets of fluorescent eyes glowed back at them. Melane jumped. "Shit! They look like the undead."

"What is it?" Kick hissed from the sanctuary of the tent. Finally she stuck her head out to peek. "Deer?" She stared at the forms at the edge of camp. "They sounded like elephants. Right behind the tent. Actually kicked it."

"Did one of you pee there?" Belle asked.

"I'm not traipsing into the wilderness to do my business." Melane threw a pinecone at the deer. The animals stared at her.

"They love your uric acid. You made a buffet of mineral-soaked grass. I hope you enjoy having deer browse next to your head all night."

"Boo!" Melane jumped at the animals. They spooked and ran ten feet. "They'll come back, won't they?"

"Dig up the dirt and grass. Carry it somewhere else," Belle said, heading toward her hammock.

"I don't have a trowel. But that's your fault. I dumped it when you did a pack inspection."

Belle shrugged and kept walking. "Whaddya gonna do *now*?" She went out to check on Winston, whistling a quiet little tune as she walked so she wouldn't spook him.

When she got back to the campsite, Melane was pouring water on her spot. "I'm washing the grass, will it work?"

"Guess you'll see." Belle got into her hammock and arranged herself, her sleeping bag, and her gun.

"Hey! I can see out here without a light. Who knew the stars were so bright?"

Belle watched the young woman hold up her palm as though she were catching a handful of light. "Your body is adapting. It'll tune in to the world around you, if you'll let it." Belle yawned.

"Can I stir the fire and sit for a while?"

Belle pulled a tarp over her hammock, leaving her head sticking out. "Go ahead, chipmunk. It's your forest."

A wisp of steam curled from Belle's coffee as she stood next to Winston, eating jerky and a hard biscuit with jam. A zipper announced that someone would soon be appearing. Josie, bundled in a fleece jacket and cap, crawled out of the tent she shared with Samantha.

"Exciting night, huh? Thanks for taking care of it." Her breath steamed in the morning chill. "Is that your breakfast?"

Belle nodded, chewing her jerky. "Make it myself. It's tender. Easier on the teeth. 'Course it won't keep as long. And don't start a fire this morning," she said as Josie picked up a stick to stir the ashes.

"Why not? It'd feel nice."

"When there's a fire, everybody stands around. You need to get going. A big storm's movin' in. It's been coming for a day now."

Josie looked at the sky dimpled in white and gray. "It's not supposed to rain. I checked before we left."

"Well, the weatherman in Portland, or wherever he sits in an office and looks at charts, he isn't here to smell the low pressure pushing the scent of pine down on us. Don't build a fire."

"You know," Josie lowered her voice so it didn't broadcast over the camp. "I appreciate your help, but I don't appreciate you treating me like I'm an ignorant tenderfoot."

"Then teach them to survive. They think you're going to protect them from the outdoors. And you're trying to get them to do some kind of loopty-do re-think of their past. If you wanna make a difference, teach them to take care of themselves right now."

"Oh? How'd that work out for *you*? Alone. Without a family. Did all your survival skills make a difference when someone burned down your house and barn?"

"You're right." Belle gave her a hard nod as she mounted. "I'm leavin' to take care of that right now. Roll apart the fire ring. Spread the ashes. Leave-no-trace means you can't tell we were ever here." She nudged Winston with her knee and he plodded forward. "I marked a new campsite on your map for tonight. Kick is good at maps in case you can't find it. Don't stay at the place we planned. It'll be a bog."

"Wait. Aren't you meeting up with us in a mile or so?" Josie called down the trail.

"Enjoy the rain," echoed back to her.

Josie gave her head a fast shake like a dog holding onto the end of a rope. Old or not, homeless or not, that woman made her want to throttle a tree. "Get up." She gave Kick and Melane's tent a hard shake as she went by.

It took an hour to get everyone up and moving. "Do you have anything else for breakfast?" Samantha flipped through the packets of instant oatmeal.

"Add dried fruit. It'll be a gourmet delight. And the coffee's fresh perked." Josie held up the well-used aluminum coffee pot.

"Just a cup of coffee for me, thanks." Samantha Jarmin's smile didn't reach her eyes.

"I thought you were going home?" Melane said, scanning the ground. She bent over and picked up the whittled stick, wiping it on the seat of her pants.

"I feel better this morning. My headache would be completely gone if it had been quieter last night." She gave Melane a look.

The young woman was busy pouring boiling water over the whittled end of the stick and more water into a bowl. She dumped a packet of oatmeal in it and stirred it with the stick.

"No matter which way I moved my sleeping pad, a rock poked the middle of my back." Kick bowed her shoulders forward in a stretch. "Next time do a better job of clearing the area."

"Hey! I did firewood duty. I only picked up the burnable big pieces. You were in charge of rocks." Melane used her shimmed stick to shovel food to her mouth.

"Don't worry about it," Josie said. "We'll switch jobs. Everybody will learn each duty." She glanced at Samantha who was studying Melane. "Be sure to drink often today. And everybody, put your lunch packages at the top of your pack, so you don't have to dig all the way to the bottom when we stop. Now we need to get moving. Miz Belle said it might rain a little today."

"Pffft!" Melane blubbered her lips and licked her stick clean. "She made it sound like a monsoon was coming. I heard her. I can hear and see like Superman out here." Samantha rolled her eyes. "What?" Melane countered as she tucked her stick in her hip pocket. "I'm not kidding, living in the forest is amazing."

"Miz Belle likes to yank our chains," Josie said, "but we still need to get moving. As soon as you're done eating, start packing and breaking down camp." She dumped oatmeal in her bowl, only to discover they were out of hot water.

Another hour passed before the women stood on the path, packs on their backs, going over their maps. "Cool. Not even Sherlock Holmes could tell we were ever here." Melane looked behind them.

"Except for your toilet spot." Samantha tapped her temple and walked on.

They quickly strung out, walking at different speeds. Josie had insisted they stop every thirty minutes and re-group. Kick acted as timekeeper and no one passed her. Josie brought up the rear. They made it a half-mile before Samantha stepped on a rock and rolled her foot.

"We should've stretched before we left." Josie watched Kick wrap the ankle. "But I was in such a hurry to get moving."

"It doesn't look like rain, now." Melane stood with her head thrown back, looking at the sun breaks in the gray clouds. They continued and had barely made a quarter of a mile before they were slapping mosquitoes.

"Crap! They're going for the eyes." Melane sprayed herself and the air around her in a fog of fumes.

"Don't spray your face," Kick commanded. "Do this ..." She whooshed some chemical into her hand and rubbed her forehead while the other slapped themselves like street performers beating on buckets.

"Shit. Shit. Shit." Melane bounced on her toes, fanning her hands around her body. "What's in that spray? Fruit juice? They love it. Look!" she pointed to twenty mosquitoes sitting on her sleeve. "Those little suckers are trying to bore through my shirt. Even the pests have superpowers out here." She began beating herself all over.

"Only the females want your blood," Josie said. "They're getting ready to lay eggs. Everybody keep moving. As we climb, we'll get out of the swarm. Kick, why didn't you get DEET?" Josie said, examining the can.

"It's bad for you." Kick pulled a stocking cap over her head and ears. "Why put poison on your skin and into your system?"

"To kill the damn mosquitoes!" Samantha hurried by, favoring her right foot. She passed Melane, but the younger woman soon ran by, slapping her ears, which she hadn't sprayed, and yelling, "Yiiiiiiiiiiiii!"

"They're going to stumble or run into a tree." Kick said.

"Then so be it!" Josie yelled, covering her face with her hands. She shook her head with an "Aaaarrrgh!" Mosquitoes lit on her wrists and between her fingers, plunging in for breakfast.

A fast-paced mile tracked by before Josie and Kick caught up to Samantha. She had on her rain jacket, cinched at the bottom and collar pulled high, her head hidden inside the coat. She bent over, the fabric writhing as she swatted inside.

"I've gotta get a photo of this." Kick pulled out her phone.

"Leave. Get out of here," Samantha's voice filtered through the jacket. "You're bringing them with you. They followed you here like zombies."

"They came from that swampy lake we passed. Didn't you notice it? There's not as many now, see." Josie slapped her neck.

"I can't see a damn thing. And I'm not coming out." Samantha stood straight, appearing to be only legs extending from a coat.

"Fine. Meet us on down the trail." Josie took off at a brisk pace. Kick followed, batting the air around her head. In a few minutes, Samantha Jarmin passed them at a run, her hood drawn up so tightly, only a five-inch circle of her face could be seen.

As they race-walked, Kick's phone made a *ding*. "You've got cell service?" Josie panted.

Kick pulled it from her pocket and looked. "Not anymore. Every now and then, there'll be an errant signal. I know it's supposed to be line-of-sight to the tower, but it doesn't seem to be logical. I can be in the middle of the forest, thousands of trees all around, and one radio wave will make it between the boles. Sometimes, I step back, and the signal is gone."

"Turn it off and don't let the others know. They'll call for an air-lift," Josie said.

In another half-mile they ran into Melane. She knelt beside a creek, her arms submerged in the icy water, "to numb them." Nickel-sized welts dotted her skin. She had peeled off her t-shirt, exposing bites layered on top of more bites on her shoulders. The sun broke through the clouds making the bloody spots she'd scratched stand out on her skin.

"Let's get some Bite-Ease salve on you." Kick rummaged through her first-aid bag.

"Is this an apocalypse-free zone?" Samantha's whole body turned side to side as the circle of her face looked around.

"There's a few. But nothing like the nightmare by the lake."

"Do you think the mule dung works on bites?" Melane asked and began counting the bumps on one arm as Kick worked on the other one.

Kick let out a sigh, shaking her head. "Mule turds don't help anything but your garden."

"I'd wallow in it if you told me it stops the itch. Twenty-seven bites—elbow to wrist," Melane proclaimed.

"I hate this!" Samantha yelled. "I should have turned left and gone to the trailhead, instead of right and into hell."

"When you're out here, you have no choice but to deal with what's in front of you," Josie said. "We knew there'd be mosquitoes. Now what? We move on."

"You sound like Belle Chere. Where the hell is that old lady right now?" Samantha's voice rasped as she unzipped her cocoon.

"She rode off to scout the next campsite, I hope," Josie scratched her leg as she checked the map.

Samantha let her pack drop to the ground, and sat heavily on top of it. A loud *POP!* made all the women look at her. Samantha's teeth clenched and face hardened with exasperation.

"It was something in your pack," Kick said.

"I *know* that," Samantha yelled. Before she could get it open, water dripped out the bottom. She flung bags and equipment aside, then turned the pack upside down and shook it. What wasn't wet at the top of the pack was now damp as water poured from the opening.

She yanked out the culprit. The plastic liter bag with tubing that she carried for water had blown its lid when she flopped on it.

"Can you believe this?" She held it up. "Everything ..." her hands made circles over her pile of goods, "is wet." Spotting a mosquito on her arm, she slapped herself with the bag. "Crap!" She flung the bag into the trailside shrubs.

No one spoke. The creek chattered and burbled. Kick waited until it felt as though the anger around them had washed downstream. "Ummm ... I'm pretty sure," she glanced at the bag in the bushes, "that's poison oak."

Melane snorted a laugh.

Another hour passed by the time the women gobbed themselves with Bite-Ease, ate their sandwiches, and complained about God's wisdom in creating mosquitoes. Samantha wrung water out of her extra clothes, toiletries, and equipment. She left her water bag hanging in the bushes.

"But we're Leave-No-Trace women." Kick frowned at her.

"If you want it, get it." Samantha waved her permission.

"Pack it in. Pack it out." Melane wagged a finger at her.

"Ladies, let's focus on this." Josie held up the map as the women shouldered their packs. Kick picked up a broken limb and tried to snag the water bag. "Miz Belle changed the camp this morning. The one she marked requires that we go a half-mile farther, then turn off the trail and go another half mile up a canyon. We'll have to hike back out the same way, tomorrow."

"So, she's adding two extra miles to the hike?" Samantha said.

"Looks like it."

Kick peered over Josie's shoulder, the water bag swinging from her stick. "The other camp was closer, but it's by a lake. Could be more skeeters."

"No mosquitoes!" Samantha made a barrier with her hands. "I'm a quart low already."

"I got bitten twice as much as you." Melane squinted at her. "And I'm not complaining."

"Okay. Okay." Josie folded the map. "It's not a competition. We'll go to the closer lake. Miz Belle will have to find us—if she shows up at all."

"What? She's not abandoning us is she?" Medicinal goo oozed through the shoulder fabric of Melane's shirt.

"I can't make any promises about that woman." Josie shook her head. "We're fine. We'll get to camp and have a campfire and a good laugh about today. We know what to do. It'll be so much easier and enjoyable tonight, now that we've got the kinks worked out of our set up. And look ... there's no more mosquitoes."

Melane held out her paste-smeared arms. Not a skeeter or even a fly hummed or lit on them.

"I have to admit the air is invigorating." Samantha drew in a big breath. "Full of pine and fir, like a super-Christmas tree."

Josie and Kick exchanged glances then looked at the sky. "Let's get moving." Josie took off at a brisk pace as the first raindrop pocked the dirt.

17

Into Each Life Some Rain Must Fall
~Henry Wadsworth Longfellow

TWO PAN FOLKS would jokingly call the shower "a foot of rain," meaning twelve inches between each drop. At least, it started out that way.

Kick and Melane hiked for thirty minutes in the drizzle, then waited beneath a fir for the slower walkers to catch up. "I have a problem," Melane said as Josie approached them. "I don't have my waterproof jacket. I think I dumped it when Belle made us downsize our packs."

"Oh," Josie said quietly. Under the shelter of the tree, the dirt was still dry. Wood could still burn. Hikers weren't miserable. Her mind raced through the problems and complaints this weather was going to cause. Maybe Samantha had been right this morning about turning toward the trailhead—and all of them should've followed her. But here they were. "It's snug under this tree. Let's wait for the shower to pass." She peeked from beneath the boughs at the gray skies and the droplets streaking to the ground. Low clouds blurred the mountains where they needed to go.

"Can I borrow a tarp?" Melane asked. "Didn't I see you had a little green one?"

"And I have a garbage bag." Kick dug in her pack. "You can use that."

"While we're working on this, I have something I need to talk to you about, Melane."

"Go for it." She T'd her arms, and Kick held the black bag against her, marking the neck and arms for cutouts.

Josie looked down the trail. "I need for you to lighten up on Samantha."

"What? Everybody's been snarly this morning. Not just me."

"True, but it seems like there's irritation between the two of you. I'm only asking that you make an effort."

"Sure, if you'll have the same talk with her. I don't think it's my imagination that she picks at me. I really wanted to meet her. Get to know Dr. Richard Jarmin's wife."

"You know Dr. Jarmin?" Josie asked.

Melane opened her mouth then closed it and thought a moment. "Not really. I had imagined ... *oooh a doctor's wife. They'll have a wonderful life.* But she sure doesn't act like it." Melane stared at the woman hiking up the trail toward them.

"Try to get along," Josie whispered.

Kick held out her creation. "Put this on."

"Now what?" Samantha said as she neared. Melane pulled the garbage bag over her head.

"You need to rest and eat something. You didn't have breakfast this morning." Josie held out a granola bar. "You won't make it to noon."

"I'm fine." Samantha rolled her eyes, but took the snack as she looked Melane up and down. The corners of the garbage bag jutted over the young woman's shoulders like a space cadet costume. The bag came down to her knees. "What are you supposed to be?"

"Happy." Melane gave her a flat-faced stare.

"How many more miles?" Kick asked a little too loudly.

"Four or five." Josie talked around a mouthful of granola bar as she pulled the tarp out of her pack.

"Well, I'm moving on. I stay warmer that way." Samantha walked away.

"Eat something," Kick called after her. "It'll help you keep warm."

Melane mumbled, "And not so bitchy." She arranged the tarp over her head like an old woman's shawl. "I'm leaving, too. I'm pretty sure it bugs her when I pass her."

"Wait." Josie peeked out from under the tree. "I think we need to buddy-up today. I don't want to search for anybody in this rain."

"Kick, you and me." Melane pointed then gave Josie a Cheshire-cat grin. "And guess who you get to walk with?"

The young women took off, raindrops smacking the tarp like it was a percussion instrument. Josie stared back down the path. If she left now, how long would it take her to get to her car? But more importantly, would the mosquitoes eat her alive if she tried? She turned and followed the women.

Winston muzzled Belle's cupped hand, licking the last of the oats from her palm. "No more. You're on short rations." They stood under a tree, Belle looking through binoculars at the backside of a mountain. Her thief would likely travel the narrow paths the Nez Perce had cut through these canyons. If a cow had a misstep and rolled off a cliff ledge, too bad.

Belle scanned the sloping forest walls. She didn't want to ride down into the canyon. In this rain it'd be slick. Of course, if she did, she could ride out the back way. Good holding spots for livestock had two ways to get into it. All hidden trails led to blocked-off logging paths or dead-end roads like the one that ran to her ranch. She could ride out right now and be sitting, warm and dry, with a cup of coffee in her ...

No. She'd be sitting in a pile of ash.

She scanned the visible parts of the canyon floor. Only a stupid bungler would be down there—unless he was holding stock for shipment. A cagey cow thief would be parked in trees near a ranch, waiting for the storm to dump buckets so owners and ranch hands would go indoors and have coffee.

Belle did one more sweep with her binoculars. The rain dripped through the limbs, carrying a scent so clean, it made the top of her lungs tingle when she took a deep breath. No broken branches. No cows or carcasses. She pushed the field glasses into their soft case as a rumble of thunder sounded to the north. Winston's ears swiveled toward it.

What was she doing out here? Hadn't she been in these mountains, waiting out many a shower with Del? Look where that had gotten her. They'd sat in front of a campfire, making homestead plans and pitying the poor devil who had to make a living in weather like this.

The tempo of the rain picked up, tapping harder on the surrounding rocks. She was out here because almost fifty years later, she was again wishing for a cabin and a safe life. It wasn't right.

She pulled a hunk of jerky from her pack then mounted, her long black slicker covering the pommel and cantle, draping over her legs. Rain dripped off the brim of her hat. What would she have done if her thief *had been* in that canyon?

Winston needed a little extra nudging to get him to leave the shelter of the big fir. He picked his way down the rocky ridge and back to the trail. Belle tried to imagine what she'd be feeling if she were riding away, leaving a guy lying back there. She wouldn't abandon him, wounded and bleeding out. That'd be wrong. He'd be dead. Lord knows, she'd seen enough killing. It wasn't something she wanted, but nobody had stopped that worthless sack of flesh yet.

Dead, he'd simply be another body. She'd dealt with plenty of those.

With her limited nursing skills, she'd been assigned to intermediate care wards at the 12th Evac. But when mass casualties arrived from hot zones and overran the operating rooms, critically wounded were pushed into all wards. Her learning curve had been steep.

Doctors and combat nurses performed triage on the helipads as the dustoffs landed. Some soldiers were flown directly to Saigon or Japan. Others went to pre-op to be stabilized. Those too severely-wounded to survive were the "expectants." In hours or a day, they would be wheeled to Graves Reservation and placed in body bags for transport stateside.

Little of her training or mock trials in the States had prepared her for reality: there was neither time nor resources to save everyone. "Don't talk to them about your home or family," one of the nurses had cautioned her. "Don't make a personal connection. We're minutes from the battlefield, and they come in covered with mud, blood, and oozing through the dressings. If you think of them as individuals, you'll go insane."

Eventually she learned not to look them in the eye or notice the insignia on their sleeves. They were bodies. She tucked their photos, and rabbits' feet, and letters from home into a pocket or stiff fingers. She forced herself to stop thinking how they'd never again have the chance to feel sun on their face or lick ice cream dripping over the side of the cone. They were doing their duty. But they hadn't deserved any of this.

Then there were the survivors. Patched up. Healed. Sent back to dodge more ambushes and trip wires. Tolin, R. had arrived, tagged GSW RLE—gunshot wound of right lower extremity. He was a funny guy, always cracking jokes. Weeks later, he arrived in her ward again. This time with no legs and a hole in his chest. He'd jumped from a helicopter and landed on a mine. He'd gripped her hand until it hurt, his eyes fading into that empty stare. After Tolin R., she'd stopped looking at the block letters of their names above their pockets.

That worthless coward she hunted ... he'd ruined enough lives with his drugs, his thieving, and his burning. He was a body that deserved the bag.

Would she turn herself in after she'd killed him? A misstep over the cliff would be the handiest. She wouldn't have to worry about life's injustices anymore. Jail, home, cattle, getting feeble, or falling out of a tree and lying with no one to find her. All of it would be gone with a misstep. She patted the mule's neck, which was more to comfort her than him.

The rain pounded down, droplets splashing up when they splatted the ground. Water coursed between rocks, cutting channels in the dirt. Rivulets trailed off Winston's mane and down his neck. Belle wondered how far the women had gotten. She pictured them lost, hiding under a fir, arguing about where they'd made a wrong turn. Surely one of them had enough brains to look at a compass and backtrack. But then, none of them knew orienteering. Wherever they were, they'd be in a pickle. "Push through," Belle told the mule. "We've got another canyon to check."

"This might be beautiful—if we weren't in a monsoon," Samantha called over the roar of the rain. The women clustered under Melane's tarp, peeking out at the lake at the base of two small peaks. Around them, trees ran to the shoreline except for a twenty-foot clearing. Old stumps stippled the tiny open area. "No hauling water." Samantha admired the ground leading into the lake.

"But is there enough room to set up tents between stumps?" Melane darted from under the tarp to check.

"Kinda noisy." Kick looked up, holding her hand on her rain hood to keep it from dropping over her eyes. The tops of the firs thrashed as the wind squalled through the gap between the crags.

"Shit. Shit. Shit!" Melane yelled, trying to pull a foot free from the bog. "I'm sinking in this stuff." The duff and dead needles covered the toe bug and two inches of her boots.

"Get out of there, stupid," Samantha shook her head.

Melane squelched her way back toward them, her mouth pulled into an irritated sneer. "Thanks for the help,"

"Good grief ..." Samantha turned her back, "I guess that cute dumb blonde thing isn't an act, is it?"

"Okay. Okay. We've got bigger problems." Josie pulled out the map. "We can't stay here."

"No shit." Melane shook one foot then the other, spattering Samantha with mud. Samantha glared.

"Ladies, do you feel like walking a mile to the camp Belle marked on the map, or do we want to scout around here and see if there's another spot?"

"Oh ... give me a break!" Samantha threw up her hands. "Will you friggin' figure it out, so we don't have to stand in the pouring rain, experimenting with ways to die."

"Have you eaten anything today beside a granola bar?" Josie eyed her.

"Ugggh." Samantha closed her eyes and shook her head. "Screw you." She turned and walked down the trail.

"I'm getting as far away from this deathtrap as I can," Melane shouted and ran past Samantha.

"Where are they going?" Kick asked.

"They don't know, and they don't care." Josie watched them disappear into the haze of the rain.

"Well ... " Kick smiled. "This is going well, isn't it?" She turned and followed them.

The neon-pink strip of flagging tape tied on the bush whipped in the wind. Melane walked past it. A few minutes later Kick stopped. She examined the eight inches of plastic.

Nothing was written on it, but the sticks in the trail caught her eye. It could have been an arrow that Melane kicked apart. She probably hadn't seen the pink marker as she hunched under her tarp. Kick looked around but didn't see any side trail.

The other women weren't coming yet. She grabbed the sticks and jammed them into the mud, creating an upright X across the path next to the pink tape. She took off after Melane.

Josie had tried to walk beside Samantha, who was keeping her head down, staring at the ground, water dripping off the short bill on her rain hood. Josie didn't have a bill; water ran off her chin. For the last twenty minutes, she'd followed Samantha because the trail was too narrow and the rain came in gusts, making conversation impossible.

Now Samantha suddenly stopped, pointing at sticks barring the path. "What's this?"

"Someone set up this X. I'm guessing it was Kick." Josie leaned over, inspecting the mud. "But her bootprints go beyond and up the trail. At least, I think it's her tracks."

"Melane is in such a hurry to be out front, she probably ran right past this."

"Could you two not pick on each other so much?"

"She's not stupid." Samantha leaned back, her hand sheltering her face from the rain as she eyed the hillside. "And she's not the sweet thing you think she is."

"Why do you say that?"

Samantha said a word, but it dissolved in a rain gust. "What?" Josie pulled the side of her hood back, exposing an ear. Samantha pointed up at the boulders and slabs of granite laying in a forty-five degree jumble up the side of the hill. "What?" Josie leaned closer.

"Another marker under that little pile of rocks. And there's another one farther up."

Josie squinted through the rain, spotting the tapes. She looked at the piece of pink plastic flicking water as it twisted on the bush. She shook her head. "Surely Miz Belle doesn't want us to climb those rocks. What could be up there?"

"Knowing that grizzled old harpy, she's saying, 'If I can do it, so can they.'" Samantha stepped on top of an eighteen-inch boulder. Some stones were flat-faced, others rounded, all were uneven. With arms wide for balance she stepped to another rock. Cupping her hands around her mouth, she yelled, "What the hell? We're all gonna have to be rescued from here." She wobbled across two more stones, then turned and shouted garbled words, giving a *c'mon* wave.

Rain pelted Josie's face as she stared at Samantha warily hopping rocks. What was Belle Chere thinking, making them climb the side of a mountain in a downpour? If the old woman were here right now, she'd receive *both* a tree counseling session and a straighten-up-and-fly-right speech.

Samantha had reached the second cairn of rocks and flagging tape and was looking down at her.

Crap! Now the group was strung out along an unmapped trail that led to who-knew-where, and one of them was boulder-hopping up the side of a mountain. She grabbed more sticks and arranged them so the arrow pointed up the side of the hill.

Using her hiking poles, she leveraged herself onto the same tall boulder Samantha had used. With arms wide for balance she stepped up to the next boulder, and then the next, thinking there'd better be a Hilton on top of this ridge.

She was surprised the rocks weren't slick. It was a bit like climbing steps of an uneven, warped staircase with dangerous crevices that you could wedge your foot into and break your leg. She reached the first cairn and looked down. No sign of Kick or Melane, so she continued.

After she'd made it to the second cairn, she collapsed her poles and strapped them to her pack.

"I can't find any more flags," Samantha yelled when Josie caught up to her halfway up the hillside.

"I see a little rock pile there." Josie boulder-stepped upward; Samantha followed. They stopped several times, panting, rain running off their bent-over backs. "Don't look behind," Josie warned. "It'll make you dizzy and you might fall backward. Look at me." Samantha nodded, her eyes on Josie as she huffed air. "Look for the cairns—human-stacked piles of rock. The pink tape has disappeared. Ready?" Samantha nodded again.

High on the hill, they finally reached a fault line. The cliff had slipped, leaving a nine-foot smooth wall rising above them. "Now what?" Samantha braced herself on her knees, catching her breath.

"There's a cairn on the ledge." Josie pointed. "We go up right there. But I don't see any handholds."

Samantha's whole body wagged side to side as she shook her head. "I can't."

"We're almost there. Just over this rise."

"Bullshit." Samantha straightened and looked at the clouds, her arms wide. "Stop it, dammit! I'm tired of this friggin' rain. Enough already." She kicked the rock wall, losing her balance. Josie grabbed and steadied her.

"Why is everything so damned hard? Every-frickin'-body lies. Every-damn-thing is just 'a little bit farther' or 'around the next curve in the trail.' Bullshit! It's all bullshit." She launched into a scream fest that reminded Josie of a fifth-grader's meltdown, except eleven-year-olds didn't use the same language.

The wind carried her curses up the hill. The rain still came down. And they were still stuck on the side of the mountain.

After a minute Josie asked, "Ready?"

"How did that old bat do this?" Samantha slowly straightened her shoulders. "I want whatever vitamins she's taking."

"Forget her and weave your fingers like this." Josie shoved her hands together, making a stirrup. "You're going to cheerleader-me up there. You crouch. I step in the stirrup. You stand, and pop me up."

"I wasn't a cheerleader."

"Here's your chance."

"I hated all of them." Samantha could only heft enough for Josie to finger-grip the ledge. Then she pushed on her rump and feet until Josie heaved herself over the top.

Samantha waited. "Hey! You okay?" The wind gusted her shout up the hill.

After several moments, Josie's face peeked over the edge. She extended her hand. "I'll pull you up."

Faint shouts from Kick and Melane carried up the slope. Below, the girls were climbing the boulders.

"Look who's finally showing up." Samantha grabbed Josie's hand.

"Let go!" Josie screamed as the top of her shoulders slid back over the edge.

18

Some Are Weather-wise, Some Are Otherwise

~Ben Franklin

"I CAN'T HOLD you up much longer." Samantha balanced on the boulders, her arms shaking as she pushed above her head. Josie hung over the ledge, staring into her face.

"Help's coming." Josie's body bent like an L, her legs on the ledge, her hips and torso hanging down, supported by Samantha. "Just a bit longer."

"Bullshit." Samantha looked down so the rain pouring off of Josie's hood would stop hitting her in the eyes. "That's what they always say."

"Here." Melane arrived, breathing hard. She put a foot on the boulder next to Samantha's, grabbing Josie's right hand. "You take that side. We'll push her back up."

"Don't you think I've tried that?" Samantha yelled. Josie squawked a gasp when Samantha let go and put both hands on Josie's left hand.

"Bend your legs!" Kick shouted as she hopped toward them.

"No. Pull her forward," Melane ordered.

"We have no footing," Samantha growled into Melane's ear. "If we pull her down, she'll head-plant on these rocks and take us downhill with her."

Kick climbed onto the boulders with the women, pushing them slightly apart and shouting into Josie's face hanging above them. "Bend. Your. Legs!" Her index finger curled upward to demonstrate. "Do it! NOW!"

Josie screamed, "My foot!" Her body jerked back slightly. Melane and Samantha gripped her harder. Kick slapped their hands, trying to make them let go. With one violent jerk, Josie slipped from their grip and disappeared over the ledge.

Melane, eyes wide, the wind drowning her voice, mouthed, "Bear?"

Kick shook her head and stepped downslope, pointing uphill. Before the women could follow her, a lasso coiled through the air, whacking Kick in the face, half looping her shoulder.

Belle Chere stood on the ridgeline, the rope attached to Winston. Kick rubbed her cheek as she gave a tired wave and stepped back to the wall. Stepping into the loop so it wrapped her foot like a sling, she gave the rope two tugs. In a moment, she rose up the face of the rock.

The same procedure lifted Melane and Samantha. "I scraped all the skin off my knuckles." Melane whined at the top, licking the back of her hand.

"Well, me too." Samantha held up her bloody hands.

"Didn't you use your foot to push away as the mule dragged you over the edge?" Kick dug in her pack, looking for ointment.

"Thanks for telling me now." Samantha rubbed blood on her rain jacket. "If I'd known Mule Dragging was part of this trek, I would've brought gloves."

"Patch them up later," Josie said, picking up a branch that Belle had tossed down. "We need to get through at least ten feet of blackberry brambles to get to the top."

"*How* did that old woman get up there?" Melane sucked at her knuckles, watching Belle point at the sheer canyon wall, rising on their left.

"I think there's a trail here," Josie said, using the branch to push thorns away from the cliff face. She picked her way upslope, heaving back vines.

Kick followed, but Melane rested heavily against the cliff wall. "What a relief to be out of that wind. It's much quieter here. It's like my body relaxed the moment we stepped out of that gale."

"Could you keep moving?" Samantha's hood, still drawn tight around her face, showed five inches of frustration. "I want to fall down somewhere. But not in these stickers."

At the top, they climbed into a small flat clearing sheltered by the cliff. Instead of the wind that had been in their ears for the last five hours, a hissy fit roared in front of them.

"*Why* in God's green earth would you *ever* think I wanted you to come up that way?" Miz Belle looked to be more formidable than her opponent, her black slicker covering her boot tops, her top cape broadening her shoulders, and her hat pulled low.

"Because you flagged it with pink tape!" Josie shouted. Her hood partially covered her eyes. Her other hand plucked at her waist where rain had run under her jacket as she hung upside down.

"Do I look like a *pink tape* kinda gal?" Belle slapped her lariat against her leg. "It was probably left by climbers. Maybe last summer or longer. I didn't see it or I woulda taken it down. It's supposed to be pulled by the last person in the group. Judas priest! Why didn't you simply hike up the trail? It's overgrown in a coupla places, but even you could've found your way."

"Ha!" Melane thumped her chest. "I was right. I'd found the correct trail."

"You didn't have a clue where you were going." Samantha pushed past her, heading for the fire snapping and hissing in the rain.

Melane turned and pulled up her pant leg. "I got this trying to help your weak-ass arms." A bloody line of missing skin streaked down her shin. "Slid off a boulder."

"Medic," Belle called, giving Kick a nod. "You've got another patient."

"Do *not* call me that." The young woman grabbed her dock bag and walked past Belle, giving her a hot-eyed glare. "Ever again." The old woman's face wrinkled into a frown.

"Geez!" Josie said. "Imagine that. You've managed to piss off the only unpissable person in the group."

Belle stepped close to Josie, the brim of her hat almost touching her face. "You need to step up and take responsibility. It's not my fault, you can't follow a map. And I can't help it if you let your unit climb a mountain in a downpour and didn't keep them together so they could help each other. However, I *will admit* that I am responsible for getting here early and establishing a base. And when I heard screaming in the wind, I rescued you. It *is* my fault for moving everybody to a campsite that's out of the wind and not thigh-deep in muck. And I apologize for having a fire going and hot water boiling in case anyone has hypothermia with your stupid stunt.

"All my life, I've seen it over and over. Hell! I shoulda known better. You do something nice for a horse or a mule, you've got a friend for the rest of your life. You do something agreeable for a man, he might thank you. But you do something kind for a buncha women, and they'll bitch about it to the whole county. I shoulda kept riding." Belle grabbed Winston's harness and led him away, leaving a trail of mule dumplings as he walked.

No one spoke. The rain continued to peck the ground as the women separated to clear spots and set up their tents. Belle had hung a tarp between trees, creating a sheltered cooking area. Kick mixed up a couple of hot drinks, using the flat rocks

Belle had placed there so they didn't have to set stoves and utensils in the mud.

On the other side of the clearing, two trees grew out of the canyon wall where Belle had set up her shelter. "Where's Winston going to eat?" Kick called to the old woman.

Belle held the mule's front foot on her knee, inspecting it. "I'll take him down the trail to graze. And haul up water. This is a dry camp." She spoke without looking up, prying small stones from under the mule's hoof with her pick.

"Here. I'm sorry I was rude." Kick approached and held out a cup of hot chocolate. "I ... I ... ever since—"

"Don't worry about it." Belle straightened, taking the cup that she recognized as Melane's. "I don't need to know the why. Heaven knows I've got plenty of why's I haven't figured out, but they irritate me just the same."

"I don't have anything for Winston." Kick watched the mule's ears rotate at the sound of his name. "To thank him for helping us."

"He likes to be scratched here." Belle noodled her fingers between his ears. "And if you breathe close to his nose, it's like saying, 'We're buddies, aren't we?'"

Melane wandered over to tell Kick, "I've got the tent set up and our packs under the rainfly. Do you have any dry clothes I can borrow? That trash bag didn't do such a good job." She glanced at Belle.

"You want your cup?" Belle held it up.

"Later. I wanted to thank you for rescuing us." She kept nodding as though the head-shaking would fill in for the rest of her words. After several seconds she shrugged. "You're a pain in the ass, but you came through. In my life, I've discovered that's what actually counts."

Belle lifted her cup to them. "You both were trying to fix the situation. Good job." She drained the mug, handed it to Melane, and tapped Winston's leg. He obligingly lifted his foot.

"This is quite a set up. Why didn't you put this up last night?" Melane inspected Belle's small plastic house four-feet wide and eight-feet long hanging between two trees. Long zippers in both ends allowed the walls to be extended outward to make it into a sheltered portico. Currently the sides were zipped together and tethered to the ground, creating a tent.

"First night on a trail, I like to see the stars and get used to the dark," Bell said.

"Can I look inside?" Belle nodded as she checked another hoof.

A large hammock was suspended down the middle. Socks and a headlamp hung from the rope line above. Her bags, saddle, and tack lay on plastic on the ground.

"You can stand up and get dressed in here," Melane said. "I hate that about our tiny tents."

"Dress in the wild. Who cares?" Belle studied the iron-gray clouds scudding across the sky. "Ladies, I appreciate the visit, but since you're the only ones talking to me, I need you to secure the camp. We may be in for more weather. Tell everyone to tie down their tent and rainfly. If they can't drive a stake into this ground, knot the lines to big-honking rocks. And I hate to tell you this, since your tent is up, but you'll want to turn it to face south. You'll sleep better."

"Is this any good?" Samantha held up a foiled, vacuum-sealed package of dehydrated lasagna.

"I don't mind a boonie-rat diet." Belle poured hot water into her package of dried rice and beans and stirred it. "As long as it's not for more than three days." Melane threw another limb on the fire; the wind pushed the flames at an angle as the rain spit on them.

"Why are you wasting wood? Nobody's standing over there," Samantha said as she added water to her packet.

Belle sealed her food bag and stuck it under her shirt. "Because anytime you're in a bad situation, you keep trying to make it better. Every action helps, no matter how little. I told Melane to keep the fire going. A good fire warms, dries, and throws off light. I find comfort in that." She tapped her temple. "It keeps this calm. Provides a feeling of *doing something* about a problem."

Josie glanced at her. "Is that why you're out here? You're doing something about your problem?"

Belle shrugged. "Whatever it takes to make me feel safe. Works in regular life like it works in outdoor survival."

Samantha looked back and forth between the two women. "Are we still talking about food?"

"Go incubate your packet." Belle waved her away, ignoring her squeamish-look.

Shortly, most of the women had foil bags under their jackets as they stood around the campfire. "Feels toasty," Kick patted her midriff.

"Here. Gestate this baby for me." Samantha gave her package of beef stew to Kick. "I saw a nice log down the trail when I used the restroom facilities." Melane raised an eyebrow, glancing at the other women, but soon Samantha returned, dragging several dead limbs behind her. She dropped them by the fire, staring at Melane, who was raking food into her mouth using a stick.

Melane stopped and held up her utensil. "I call it a *stoon*. I whittled some improvements. It's not finished yet." The stick had a slight cupped depression in the flattened end, and she'd peeled the bark off the handle. "You want one, don't you?"

"I'll wait until you finish testing the beta version." Samantha opened the food packet Kick handed her and then looked at Belle. "I have to admit, the fire *is* a comfort. It makes a hard day a lot better. How you got it going when everything is sopping, I don't know, but thank you."

Belle nodded. The women glanced at Josie, the only one who hadn't apologized yet. The flames sputtered and hissed as the women ate.

"Tell us a story," Kick said as she scraped the inside of her bag with her stoon. "How did you know about this place?"

Belle looked at the trees over her tent. The boughs swayed and shook as the wind streamed overhead. She let out a long sigh. "A boy showed me."

"The same bo-oy as the cabin?" One side of Melane's mouth teased upward. "Does this place bring back memories?"

"Bad ones." Belle flattened her empty packet, running her thumb over the press-close bands on the end. "I have memories of only two good men. My dad ... and one other fella."

"Who and where is the *other* fella now?" Melane said.

"Gone. Ox Woolsey was stubborn and cranky and if he said he had my back, I could take that to the bank. They don't make 'em like that anymore."

Samantha's eyes widened with a recollection. "That was the name on the brass plate on the bench in front of the Bar and Grill. He made that?"

"Are you talking about Jiggs Woolsey's father?" Kick said.

Belle nodded, staring at the flames. "The timing never worked out right ... and it doesn't matter anyway. I'm too much of a loner."

"What *is* that?" Melane squinted, cocking her ear, trying to pick out the thin-pitched wail floating on the wind.

"Coyote." Belle cupped her hand to her mouth and howled back.

Melane grinned and laughed. "Why's he baying? It's still daytime. Isn't it?" She scanned the black ribs on the clouds.

"He's a sentinel. Lonely. Looking for his friends."

Melane leaned back and howled. Then putting both hands around her mouth, she howled again. Kick began barking. Belle tilted her chin to the sky and joined the cacophony, yowling into the gusts.

A chorus of yips answered them.

"Geez!" Melane turtled her head to her shoulders. "We've stirred things up. Are they going to kick our butts for being in their neighborhood?"

"No, they're in a hurry. They're moving." Belle walked to the cooking area and began taking apart her stove.

"How can you tell?" Kick asked. The yelps and yips seemed to be coming from no special direction, but floating everywhere.

"I've spent more nights riding fence and sleeping in these mountains than you've lived."

"With your special fellow?" Melane got up and stirred the fire.

A tender memory crossed Belle's face as she stowed the stove and fuel canister in its bag. She looked around, picking up trash and tossing it in the fire. "That was then. This is now. And *now* our problem is the same as the coyotes'. We need to put everything away. Make sure your boots are under your rainfly, everything is tied down, and everyone has taken a leak. Settle in."

"The coyotes told you all that?" Melane asked.

"The mule." Belle walked toward Winston.

Belle led the mule next to her shelter and tied him to the tree. Unzipping the south end of her tent, she gave him enough slack to stick his head inside. Her watch showed 5:30, but the skies were as dark as seven. She lay in her hammock for a cat-nap. Just a short one ...

*

The silence woke her. The sough of the winds in the branches had faded. Belle peeked out to see gray-green clouds hanging low and not a bird in sight. Not a fir needle moved. She took a deep breath as she watched the fire. It had died to a single flame skittering across the top of the embers as though happy to have them all to itself.

The coals should be banked. They'd be easier to get going again. Instead, she pulled her head back inside her tarp tent. She grabbed Winston's halter, speaking in low, slow tones. She waited.

The sky lit up followed by a *BOOM*! Compression waves slammed into the mountains. The mule side-stepped, threatening to pull the tent with him. Belle hung on as she was being dragged out the end, still speaking in a low, slow voice.

The sky flashed brilliant white from pole to pole again. Another explosion split the air. Winston flinched, but didn't try to jerk his head from the woman, her hands on either side of his halter as she prayed the alphabet.

"I'm not staying here," Melane shoved her feet into her boots. "We're like bags of lightning bait in a metal dome."

"The poles are carbon fiber." Kick grabbed her arm. "We're okay. The storm's moving fast. The thunder and flash popped on the north side, now it's more to the south."

"It's the overhead part that I can't take." Melane unzipped the rainfly and peeked out. "You know, I was right about which trail to go on. My body is becoming one with nature and Mother Nature is telling me to get the hell out of here."

Kick watched her run ten feet to Josie's tent, unzip their rainfly, and duck inside. "How is that any better?" she shouted, but the first wave of rain had swallowed her words. Like pages tumbling in the wind, white sheets of water billowed then dispersed, pushed by the next sheet behind it. Kick chewed on her thumbnail, looking around the tent. The lightning cracked open the sky. The fists of water beating on the nylon worried her. She jammed her feet into her boots and pulled her rain jacket over her head.

The zipper ripped open on Samantha and Josie's tent. "Coming in!" Kick yelled. Water dripped from her elbows and hood as she shucked out of her jacket.

"This is only a two-woman tent." Samantha quick-brushed water off her sleeping bag. "Go to Belle's."

"When the lightning flashed, I saw someone standing next to her tent."

Josie straightened, suddenly alert. "Was it her?"

"I couldn't tell. It's like being doused with a fire hose out there."

"Who else would it be?" Samantha asked. "Bigfoot?"

Josie shouted, "Miz Belle?"

"She can't hear that!" Kick unzipped the rainfly and stuck her body, up to her shoulders, out of the tent. When she pulled back in, she looked as though she'd plunged her head in a tub of water.

"Watch it!" Samantha pulled her jacket away from the water dripping off Kick's ponytail.

"No one's there now."

"I wish I weren't here either." Samantha gave a shiver. "Who would be out in this weather?"

"No!" Kick glared. "I mean neither the person nor the mule is there."

"But the tent is?" Josie asked.

Kick nodded. Josie shrugged. "She probably hauled that mule inside her tent. She's got all kinds of mojo in dealing with animals. She used to keep a raccoon as a pet. She'll be fine."

"Hey!" Melane nudged Samantha's foot. "What'd the ol' gal tell you was the secret to peeing in the woods?"

"She told me to stop wearing underwear." Samantha barked a loud laugh and the others joined in. "What's going on with her? Where does she go while we're climbing mountains and getting lost?"

Josie chewed her bottom lip as she looked at the tent's doorway. "I told you her house burned down ... well, I'm not sure, but I think ... she's out here, looking for the guy who did it." She quickly held up a hand. "The sheriff and Jiggs are sure the guy is in town. He knows too much about everyone's schedules. Why she's searching out here ... I don't know. And she'd deny it, if I asked."

"What's she think she's going to do if she finds him?" Kick asked.

"He shot one of her cows and burned her house down. She says she'll shoot him," Josie said. "She already hit him with a load of shot when he cut her fence."

"Oh, good grief." Samantha's face scrunched up.

"Well, I can see why she'd do it. Not everyone has deep pockets." Melane stared at Samantha. "Some people work two jobs, seven days a week to scratch out a life that's nothing special, but it's all they've got. So when it's taken, you can't even imagine what they've lost. I can understand a woman like Belle going after anyone trying to hurt her. I would."

"But threatening to kill a man?" Kick said.

Josie held up her hands again. "I don't know that's true. I'm only making guesses. We're perfectly safe. She's not a socio-path. She doesn't socialize much, but she's certainly not stand-offish. She shows up at a few social functions. A round-up. Community calf-fries. Fourth of July dinners. She brings presents to weddings, but doesn't stay. I wouldn't call her a mingler."

"Somebody ought to check if she's okay." Kick looked at Josie. The others stared, listening to the rain pound the tent and the hum of a freight train traveling through the skies.

"What's that?" Melane squinted as the sound grew louder.

The nylon walls began to shimmy and pop. The gales lost their high-pitched dree and rumbled into a pulsating roar. Melane grimaced, grabbing her ears. Kick flattened, lying on the tent floor, her arms over her head. Josie pushed the other women down.

"What's happening?" Samantha screamed, but no one heard her.

In less than ten seconds, the growl of the freight train ebbed southward. The women didn't stir until the tent stopped flapping and shaking. The sound of a steady rain pattered around them.

"What *was that*?" Samantha pushed to her elbows, pulling her sleeping bag off the top of her head.

"I'm pretty sure we just survived a tornado," Kick said.

"Here? In the mountains?" Melane gave her a big-eyed stare.

Kick nodded. "It happens." She put her hand on the zipper. "I'm afraid to look." Slowly, she worked the zipper down and peeked out. "I can't tell for sure. It got dark."

"Is the tornado coming back?" Melane threw an *oh-shit* look at Samantha. "Do they loop back on themselves? I know they spin."

"What do I look like? A meteorologist?" Samantha clutched her sleeping bag, watching Kick lace her boots.

"They probably didn't teach that at Vassar, or wherever you went to school," Melane said. As soon as Kick left, Melane stuck her head out, waggling her hand behind her. "Hey Miss Vassar, hand me that flashlight I saw in your corner."

"For your information, I went to Washington State." Samantha slapped the Maglite into Melane's palm.

"Excuse me. I haven't had the chance to go to college." Melane threw her a sour look and flashed the light around the camp. "Well ... my tent is gone." Samantha let out a groan. The young woman pulled back inside, squeegeeing water off her face. Samantha threw her micro-fiber towel at her.

"Miz Belle?" Josie asked.

"Couldn't tell."

They waited, listening for voices outside. The rain tapped a staccato rhythm on the nylon. The longer they waited, the less frequently they glanced at each other, and the more they fidgeted.

The z-z-z-z-z-r-r-r of the zipper made them look up. "I found our tent. It's caught in that thicket of blackberries over the side. Everything else is pretty much in place, except Miz Belle. Her hammock and tent are there. But not her or the mule."

"Go, Melane." Josie ordered as she crawled to the tent door. "Go help Kick free your tent."

"How are we supposed to do that?" Melane frowned.

"C'mon, Samantha," Josie pulled on her boots. "Help me find Miz Belle."

"And how are we supposed to do that?" Samantha sighed.

Josie scratched on the door of Belle's tent. Getting no answer, she unzipped it and shined her headlamp inside. Clothes, tack, and gun were all neatly hanging from the main rope line running the length of the tent.

She whipped the light back onto the holstered gun. Belle hadn't mentioned she was carrying. Folks often took a weapon into remote areas like this. But in Miz Belle's case, it meant she planned to act on her threat.

It seemed unlikely the old woman would leave without taking her gun. Josie scanned the area, looking for footprints, but the rain had beaten dimples into the thin layer of dirt covering bedrock.

Curses and shouts drifted through the mist. Josie followed them to the hillside where Kick tried to free their tent from blackberry bushes while Melane beat the vines and threatened fire if they didn't let go. It took the four women fifteen minutes to rescue the tent. "Well at least I got all my mosquito bites itched." Melane shoved up the sleeve of her wet shirt, showing long scratches trailing elbow to wrist and bleeding. Her garbage sack raincoat looked as though she'd been in a fight with a cat.

"How do you do that?" Kick asked as they carried the tent back to its original spot. "I've used over half my medical supplies on just you."

"I take risks." Melane shrugged. The young women were inspecting rips in the nylon when Belle led Winston into camp, wet from head to toe as though they'd been swimming.

"You're here!" Josie cheered. "We checked up here and were about to start walking. We thought the wind had taken you to Oz. Are you okay?"

"Yep." Without looking at them, Belle tossed her hat inside her tent. She leaned sideways and used one hand, starting at the base of her neck, squeezing water out of her braid trailing over her shoulder.

"We were worried. Where'd you go?" Josie watched her.

Belle took off her slicker and hung it on a broken branch, folding the corduroy collar inside so it would stay dry. "You wouldn't have had to look far, if you had tried. I huddled a hundred feet down the trail, standing in the blow with Winston's head snubbed between trees."

"I wish you would've told us you were leaving. We were all in one tent."

"It sounded like your party was full, laughing and having a grand ol' time. So Winston and I made do with our own soiree. Now, if you'll excuse me." Belle ran her hand down the mule's nose, turned, and stepped into her tent. "I feel like hammered dog shit. Good night." The zipper traveled back up to the peak of the tarp.

Josie's shoulders sagged as she looked around. Samantha stood in front of their tent, her light off watching the exchange. Without a word, she kneeled and climbed inside. Josie clicked her own light off. Somehow the dark felt comforting. Like throwing a blanket over the ripped spot on a couch. She walked toward Melane and Kick's headlamps, the mist making white slashes in their beams. They were jury-rigging two ripped pieces of their rainfly together, using dental floss as thread. "Everything going okay over here?" Josie asked.

Kick looked up, brushing water off her face. "I shouldn't have left her out here alone. Never leave a man behind." She turned back to their project. Josie stared, unsure if those had been tears or raindrops that Kick had brushed away.

19

A Perfect Night For A Ride

ON THE OTHER side of the mountains, past the valley, beyond Two Pan, the rain blew across miles of pasture. Lightning zagged to the ground. It was a prayed-for drencher, needed for hay and grazing. Electric bolts shooting out of clouds weren't requested, but sometimes petitioners got more than they asked for.

It's said that there is always a light on in Two Pan, but truth-be-told, folks mainly scanned for lights that were out of place—fearing a fire or shenanigans.

For that reason, the truck sat idling without its headlights on. Of course, the young man had driven to the back door like any countryfied person would. He'd waited for somebody to realize he'd parked there. After a while, he killed the engine, got out, hunching under a rain poncho as he dashed to the door. He shook off the water and stood on the covered porch a few minutes, allowing the folks inside to get up and turn on the yard lights. After the appropriate amount of courtesy time, which was long enough to get pants, shirt, and boots on— longer if the residents were old and slow, or recently kicked by a bull—he knocked.

The lights remained off.

He knocked again. Harder this time, although the sound didn't carry through the blowing rain.

There being no response, he trotted back to his truck, started it up, and drove slowly toward the barn and stable. He cussed when he stepped out of the cab to open the gate. He knew he'd get wet, but cussing made it more tolerable—like looking at a pay stub; a fella knows they're taking out a chunk, but complaining about it makes him feel better.

As he drove through the gate and parked in front of a new building, he looked around. Sometimes the hired hand stayed over, but his truck wasn't here. Well, who could blame him on a night like this? Nobody got paid enough to work in this kind of weather.

He opened the door of the stable and breathed in the scent of hay and horse. Nickers and snorts greeted him. He haltered the gelding in the first stall. When he gave the animal a little slice of apple, the second horse banged the partition between them. Quickly, he put a lead on the other gelding and rewarded him for being sorta patient. They were both good animals. Before leading them into the trailer behind the truck, he gave them a second slice of apple. With a little flake of alfalfa in front of them, they should be cooperative about traveling on a night like this.

Back in the tack room, he hefted a saddle on each shoulder and carried them out. He grumbled with the third trip. The poncho leaked like a sieve around the neck; his drenched shirt leaked into his pants. Gathering up halters and bridles, he loaded them in the truck, along with bales of alfalfa that would anchor the tarp over the whole shebang.

He paused for a moment, finally deciding to be safe rather than sorry. Using the yellow nylon rope looped on the stable wall, he zig-zagged a couple of hitches across his load. With a final look around, he shut the stall and stable doors, so the water wouldn't blow in.

Outside, the storm had picked up. As he drove up the lane, the treetops wagged and twisted like snakes. He got out and closed the gate behind him, water leaking down his neck and between his shoulder blades. Shutting gates had been bred into him as the right thing to do. He still cussed about it.

The rain came at the truck sideways. Even if the headlamps were on, he doubted he could've seen far. Motoring slowly, very slowly, he avoided veering into the fancy fencework along the drive. One of the horses nickered. He slowed even more. He didn't recognize which one was calling. He hadn't worked with them long enough to recognize their whinnys. They were both well-tempered animals with breeding papers made of platinum. It'd be nice if he could have one, but his dad would insist that they both be sold. Unless they cut off their tattooed lips, they'd be too easy to identify.

The wind roared overhead and the water poured down, beating out his tire tracks. Barely able to see beyond twenty feet, he scanned up and down the farm road. No lights. Nobody was out tonight. One of the horses nickered again. "Hold on, boys." He wheeled out of the driveway with Samantha Jarmin's prized Tennessee Walkers.

20

After The Storm I Dream Of You

BELLE CLOSED HER eyes. Sleep refused to come. Rain wasn't a regular visitor in the Eagle Caps. More often she heard snow pecking her metal roof—the roof she didn't have anymore. Now droplets tapped her tent "Not everything that falls from the sky is bad," she whispered to herself. "Good things fall, too."

The mantra had begun in 'Nam during random artillery rounds for harassment and interdiction. The H&I fire sporadically blasted through the night to erode enemy morale. Then, some sapper would hit a trip wire, setting off foo gas on the perimeter of whatever hill nineteen-year-olds were told to hold. It seemed the firefights came in the thin hours of darkness, as bright and frightening as the lightning that had crashed over her head less than an hour ago.

Miles away, in her hooch, she'd hear the explosions. She'd been part of something then. A group trying to put pieces of men back together. Sometimes the nurses climbed on top of the roofs, watching the helicopter gunships, Sharks and Cobras, spray the ground with bullets. Then the Puffs followed, every few rounds of canon fire had tracers, painting green lines on a black sky.

When the lights had dropped from their brightest, loudest, and most ghastly beauty, usually the phone would ring. "Wounded." If she was in bed, she was dressed in boots and fatigues in two minutes, her flak jacket flapping as she ran to her ward.

Tonight's thunder had been as loud as the shell that missed the petro dump and landed near the nurses running to the OR. It knocked several of them in the air, but not her. Not this time. She had kept her interval and not bunched up in a group. It had become instinct. Her drill sergeant would've been pleased.

They weren't supposed to bomb hospitals, but there was a thin margin of yardage between the target and the rest of the world. They weren't supposed to fire at the dust offs either. But bullets and rockets flew at them like any other helicopter. The big red crosses plastered on all sides meant nothing. And women weren't supposed to be flying into hot zones, keeping soldiers alive en route. But sometimes they had to. The men had been pulled to the field.

It seemed a sick kind of logic to classify women as non-combatants, protecting them from battle. Instead, the ladies were handed the bloodiest horrors: faces blasted away, bones and flesh hanging by ligaments, blood leaking from holes made by bullets, shrapnel, and punji sticks.

Maybe it was old age and nearing life's end that was making her mind spit out these hidden horrors. Usually, she could blank it all out—except for the smells. The exotic flowers, rotting vegetation, sewage, the scent of blood in the baking heat, and the brief, cool rains. Almost every night, the skies lit up with death. And many nights the rain pattered down, promising life. At least that's what she told herself as it tapped the roof of her hooch.

"Not everything that falls from the sky is bad." And that's what she whispered tonight, when, for some reason, the thunder rolling to the south made the memory of soldier after soldier ghost through her mind.

*

The next morning, Josie scratched Belle's tent. "You okay in there?" No one answered. It was past seven o'clock and neither she nor Samantha had seen Belle. Melane and Kick weren't up yet. Samantha led Winston down the trail, taking him to graze. She'd volunteered to haul water back to camp.

Josie scratched the tent one more time. "Miz Belle?" After several seconds of silence, she pulled the zipper. The inside was warm and dry and dark. Josie snapped on her flashlight and poked the plumped-up sleeping bag. The hammock swayed slightly. Unsure if anything was inside, she mashed on the bag.

The old woman sat up, startled and blinking. "What is it?"

"It's Josie. I didn't mean to spook you."

"Get that damn light outta my eyes. Is somebody hurt?"

"No."

"Then why are you wakin' me?"

"I touched you, but you didn't move. I thought you were dead."

"Shit." Belle flopped back onto the hammock. "I am dead. I was up most of the night, with a hammerlock on a mule, telling him a twister wasn't gonna eat him and he didn't have to run home. 'Course, my argument kinda fell apart when it got so loud he couldn't hear me."

"You're such an early riser. I was worried because I hadn't seen you yet. Are you okay?" A wet sock hit her in the face. "All right." She let out a huff of air. "I'm glad you're fine. Can I bring you anything?" Expecting a *Go-to-hell* answer, she began zipping up the tent.

"Uh ... yeah ... a cup of hot coffee would be dandy."

Josie let out another long breath. "Well ... my stove doesn't work, and the water bags fell over and leaked out last night."

"Now ... whaddya gonna do?"

"Now ... you can simply dream of a cuppa joe." She threw the sock back.

Walking to Melane and Kick's tent, she scratched on the nylon. "She's okay."

"We heard," Kick said, then lowered her voice. "Did she say why she cried out early this morning?"

"No," Josie whispered. "Probably a dream."

"That'd be a hoot to learn …" Melane murmured. "What do old ladies dream about? The boys of their youth?"

21

If A Tree Falls In The Forest …
Deal With It

THE SUN PEEKED over the mountain. Water sparkled and gleamed, dripping from branches. A morning breeze circled the crisp, fresh-washed air from the peaks, carrying it toward the valley. With hands on her hips, Belle watched Samantha lead Winston back up the trail. Shortly after Josie had disturbed her, she'd broken down her hammock and tent. "Thanks for taking care of him." Belle nodded.

"This is a good animal." Samantha leaned against the mule's neck, watching the old woman heft the saddle chest-high. Belle grimaced and lowered it quickly with a grunt.

"You're hurt?"

"I fell on my shoulder some time ago. Pulled it again last night."

"I'll do it." Samantha exchanged places with Belle. "Maybe I shouldn't be saddling for you. I've heard you're riding off to look for trouble."

"Trouble already found me. I can bareback Winston if I have to." Samantha looked at her, and twisted her mouth into the same face she wore tromping through blackberry vines. "Yeah," Belle agreed. "I don't really wanna do that."

"Why not teach me how to arrange the saddlebags and bedroll so they don't rub?" Samantha asked.

"And when you're finished there," Melane said, walking up, "teach me how to get a fire going when everything is wet."

"Then I'll have coffee ready in a few minutes," Kick announced.

Belle looked from one woman to the other, a quizzical frown on her face. She scanned them again.

"Go with us today," Kick said. "Please?"

"You'll be fine." Belle nodded.

When Samantha finished tying on the gear, Melane held up a map. "Tell us about this mine you marked on today's route."

"Pay attention to where you put your feet, Munk-girl. You'll do all right." Belle checked the hitches and then led her mule away.

"What time do you think you'll get into camp tonight?" Kick called after her. Belle kept walking.

A hundred yards down the path, Josie stood in the middle of the trail, her hands on her hips. Belle acknowledged her with a quick nod. "The sooner you get them packed up and hiking, the better it'll be."

"They've been through a lot. They're tired. So are you."

"Take a bad situation and keep making it better. Moving forward will help."

"I know what you're doing out here," Josie said with an icy evenness. "You're riding the canyons, looking for your arsonist. I saw your gun. That's not part of this trip. You don't give a crap about this discovery journey or these women. You think that's their lot in life. They made the choice to live with cocksure husbands or soul-sucking bosses or people who look down their noses and think they don't measure up."

"No. That's exactly the kind of jackasses they should avoid."

"We can't avoid them. That only works if you live alone on a ranch, miles from anyone, and shoot the finger at everyone who passes by. The rest of us live and work in the real world. We're in the herd, trying to watch out for each other."

Belle flipped the reins over Winston's head. "That's a good start. I respect the spine you're starting to grow. And I'm trying to keep your girls alive, but I'm not playing tour guide to a group who can't tell coyote scat from their own. That's your job." She swung a leg over the mule. "Now kindly step aside." She arranged herself in the saddle and gave Josie a smile. "But I have to say, I'm encouraged by your attempt to keep me in line."

"What are you going to do if you find this guy?"

"Make a bad situation better." Belle nudged Winston, pushing Josie off the trail, wet socks flapping behind the bedroll as she rode away.

As Winston trod by the pink flagging tape, Belle leaned over and yanked it off the bush. Her chin rose, tracing the upward route through the boulders the women had climbed yesterday. They must think she was really something if they imagined she could haul herself up that. And what would she have done with the mule? Morons. She could barely lift her right arm this morning after wheeling around a lariat.

She concentrated on loosening her jaw. Anger simmered and popped below the surface of her thoughts. It was a dangerous feeling, but she didn't know what to do about it, except "Push through." She'd seen it happen to the men in the medevac. They suffered and wondered who to blame. Magazines, music, or the simplest topics could become "fighting words." She rubbed her shoulder, which she'd been careful not to do in camp or they'd bug her about it. The ache ran from her neck to her elbow and half-way down her back. A sickly fear was brewing in the pit of her stomach. Outdoors, her life depended on working body parts. An injury could be dangerous. But what did it matter, she reminded herself, stuffing the dread deeper in her guts. She wouldn't live through this ordeal anyway. It was better to go out like she wanted than waste away, alone, in some old folk's cubicle.

The sun on her shoulders helped push her thoughts to the back of her mind. She passed the boggy lake. A sheen sparkled across the saturated ground. She rode for forty minutes on a path rising to the ridge trail. Around a bend, Winston stopped.

Trees had been ripped from the ground, and then tossed and dropped in a seventy-foot circle. Not a trunk remained standing. Boles, two-feet in diameter, lay broken and jammed in every direction like a thrown-together burn pile.

Belle tied the mule to a branch and explored to the east and west. The ground dropped away sharply from the ridge. She returned to Winston, who'd found green shoots poking through the trailside moss. She pulled a tube of peanut butter out of her saddle bag and squeezed a dollop into her mouth, following it with a bite of pilot bread. "Breathe." There was a way out of every situation. She simply had to decide what she had to give up to get what she wanted.

The ninnies she was with would try to walk across the top of the downfall to reach the trail on the other side. All it would take was for one log to shift. Her alternate path would take them right by the canyon she wanted to check out, but she didn't want them near such a guy. She stared at the jumble of trees balanced on top of each other like a game of jackstraws. Crap.

Finally she turned the mule around. "C'mon Winston. We gotta save their damn lives again."

Belle lay stretched out on a log in a dreamless nap, her cowboy hat over her face. Winston chewed grass nearby. Melane poked her with a stick. The old woman lifted her hat an inch, her eyes sliding sideways.

"I know you have a gun, so I didn't want to scare you," Melane said.

"You gals sure gossip. Am I your main topic?"

"No. I try to make fun of Samantha every chance I get."

"Well, pull up a log." Belle dropped her hat back down. "What happened to you?"

"These?" Melane touched the tiny ripped up pieces of duct tape dotting her eyebrows and temples. Her arms were covered with larger patches. "I was scratching my skeeter bites so much, Kick taped them. It kinda helps the itch. Don't you have bites?"

"Yep. I don't scratch 'em."

"I didn't expect to see you today." Melane took off her pack and lay on a nearby log. "Josie told us about the guy who burned your house." Belle didn't answer. "I understand about defending what's yours. When I was twelve—"

"I'm tryin' to sleep here," Belle interrupted. "A sunshine nap after a bad night. Try it. Knocks the spiderwebs from your dreams."

Melane sat up, looking around. The sky had cleared into blue. Mountains rose on either side of them with a stream running through the narrow valley. "It really is beautiful. This seems like the first moment I've looked around. Usually my chin is resting on my chest because I'm so tired—"

"Shhhhhh," Belle breathed.

Melane took a deep breath and let it out loudly. "I think I made a mistake coming here ..."

"Shhhhhh."

"Although, I *have* enjoyed the fierce, raw beauty of ..."

"Then *you're* gonna *love* what's on this afternoon's agenda."

"Why?"

"You're just the chattiest little thing, aren't you?" Belle slowly pushed herself up. "The others are coming."

"How can you tell?"

"Sound travels a long way in a valley. Quit gabbing and you'll hear it. If all else fails, check Winston." The mule stared down the trail, one ear forward and one ear pointed at them.

As Kick came in sight she yelled, "Holy smokes, what're you doin' here?" and jogged up to Belle.

"Bad news and great news, ladies." The old woman waited for the others to gather around. "The tornado that came through last night was a 'skipper.' Unfortunately, it landed right in the middle of our trail on one of its bounces, and we can't get through. But that's good news because I know a shortcut. It means less distance you hafta walk today and more fun."

"How fun?" Josie asked.

"Your choices are to go my way or go back. If you wanna get to base camp, then this is the way."

"How will Jiggs pack our stuff in to us?" Josie said.

Belle waved her doubt back at her. "He'll be comin' another way. We're on the scenic route." She rubbed her hands together. "Okay. This is like an amusement park. First ... the water crossing."

Since last night's downpour, the stream poured over the tops of boulders and frothed in eddies. The ladies scouted up and down the run for a quarter mile, looking for a shallow passing. "I think this is as good as it gets." Belle surveyed a wide spot before the banks narrowed and the water roared between two boulders.

"This is the only way?" Josie made her voice heard over the rush of water.

"No." Belle rubbed her backside as though warming her hands. "There's a bridge north of Two Pan. The stream's bigger and faster by the time it gets there, but you can hike back to your vehicle and drive over it without getting your feet wet. That's your alternative." Belle sat on the bank and pulled off her boots and socks.

"I'm all for hiking back," Samantha said. "Why does everything out here involve the possibility of dying?"

"That's the pioneer spirit. Put anything important in your waterproof bag," Belle said.

"Well, I don't have a ..."

Belle left Samantha mid-sentence. She tied her hat to her saddle, then yelled for everyone to gather 'round. They leaned in, their heads together in order to hear. "The rocks are gonna be slick and the current fast. Don't lift your foot and set it down like you're picking your way across a lot filled with cow shit. The current will knock you sideways. Try to skate your foot close to the bottom. If you're wearing shoes, make sure they're tied tight and the laces stuffed inside. Put your cell phones in Josie's dry bag if you didn't bring one—mine's full. Use your hiking poles, wide on either side of you. It's like another set of legs."

"My poles!" Samantha covered her mouth. "I left them at the boulders."

"Well, the outdoor credo applies here. 'If you don't have it, you don't need it.' Go get you some sticks. Everybody, undo your belts and chest straps. Your packs are small. If you slip, you can probably get up, but if the current sucks you under, shuck out of your pack, you're less likely to snag on the bottom. Okay ..." She gave a clap. "Who wants to be first?"

"Are you friggin' kidding me?" Melane stared.

Belle studied the stream. "That smooth strip in the middle looks like a channel or a hole. Try not to bungle down into it too deep. Swim across on top. C'mon, c'mon." She held up the rope tied to Winston. She was hurrying them, the less time they stood, gulping at racing water, the more courage could fire up in their brains.

"We'll go." Kick nodded to Melane.

"Nope." Belle put her hand out. "One at a time. Tie this on." She handed Kick the rope, then tapped Josie's shoulder. "You come with me." They moved down stream twenty feet where the banks began to narrow. "Can you handle this limb?" Josie nodded. "Have it ready. If Kick goes in, stick it over the water, she may be able to grab it. Hit her with it if you have to, but don't let her pull you in."

"You're sure there's no other way around this?" Josie held the branch by the end, but couldn't keep it lifted; she scooted her hands down until she leveraged a manageable grip.

"You wanna go forward or back? You're the leader. It's your decision."

Josie stared at the water cording into currents as it split around boulders and topped others. She gave a tiny nod.

Belle cupped her hand to her mouth. "Kick!" She whipped her other hand sideways as though starting a race.

"Go slow!" barked Josie.

"She can't," Belle yelled. "Her feet'll go numb." Kick stepped into the river. Proving Belle's point, her mouth squeezed into an "Ooooh" then flattened into an "Eeeeeeeeee!" as the water climbed mid-calf.

The women watched her shuffle to middle. She moved at a good pace, but stopped, staring and prodding her poles in front of her. Each stab jerked sharply downstream.

"Come back," Belle yelled. "Don't risk the current."

Kick ignored her, walking upstream, ten to twelve feet, stabbing the bottom. She looked up, and nodded to Josie, who held out the rescue limb. Belle, feeding the rope, gave a wave. Kick stepped; the water jumped past her knees. She jabbed her poles, violently trying to find the bottom of the next step, and fell forward, her arms windmilling as she splashed in. Her head disappeared. A couple of seconds later, she popped up seven feet downstream, drifting toward the opposite bank, too far away for Josie to reach with the branch

Suddenly she stood, her legs wide, water cascading from her pack and ponytail. She wobbled until she got her balance then sloshed to the pebbled landing. "Whooo!" She shook like a dog then threw her arms overhead and did a little dance.

"Kick!" Belle yelled, rolling her hands around each other as though she were hog-tying a steer. The young woman untied the rope and hitched it to a tree. "Josie. Drop that branch. You're next."

Josie trudged more slowly, keeping the rope under her arm as though hugging a banister on a stairway as she inched across the stream. When she reached the deep part, she tried to dive and grab the rope at the same time. She came up empty-handed and sputtering, but made it close to shore, where Kick pulled her in.

Melane serenaded everyone through her crossing with shrieks and a "Squeeeeee!" each time icy water splashed her. She stepped off into the deep water as though it were a surprise. For several seconds only one hand stuck above the current, gripping the rope. Spitting like a wet cat, she finally surfaced. Hand over hand, she pulled herself to the waiting women.

"All I could find were big limbs. I can't find any walking sticks," Samantha looked around.

"Then go with me. We've got a mule." Belle untied the rope and signaled Kick to pull it in from her side.

"I don't think I can do this." Samantha shook her head.

"You've already climbed a mountain." Belle flipped the saddlebags up and tied them so they'd stay on top of Winston. "If Munk-girl can do it. you can."

"She's stupider than me."

"No." Belle gave her a chiding glance. "She's more willing to take risks."

"I take risks." Samantha's chin jutted slightly.

"Then stay on the upriver side." Belle pushed Winston's reins into her hands. "I'll be in front. He'll follow me. Do not let go of him or grab me. He'll make it to the other side. His will to live is stronger than mine."

Before Samantha could croak out a word, Belle grabbed the mule's halter and waded into the water. She sweet-talked him as they shuffled across, the splash rising to their knees. Winston stopped. Belle yanked on his halter. On the opposite bank, the women called his name. He looked up and down the channel as though considering the process too slow and the stream too damn cold. Without warning, he jumped forward. Belle stumbled backward, sinking under water. Samantha hung onto the reins screaming, "Whoa!" He kept going.

His hooves plunged into the deep current. Ears forward, legs paddling, he swam toward the women on the bank. When he climbed out of the shallows, Samantha stumbled next to him, still clinging onto the lead. Belle, coughing, had a tight grip on his tail as he dragged her across the sand and rocks.

When everyone was checked over and nothing was lost except their dignity, Samantha and Josie hugged the mule and each other. Melane sang Superman's theme song, "Dat—da-da ..." and hopped around, shaking her fists in the air.

"Why the hell did we roll up our pant legs?" Samantha held up her pack, water dripping off the sides.

"Well, now you can check 'fording a stream' off your bucket list." Belle coiled her rope. "Ladies, wring out your underwear, while I squeegee the mule. We need to keep moving." Samantha helped scrape the water off Winston. The shivering women checked their packs, thrilled at what stayed dry and moaning over what was wet. Following Belle's lead, they changed and hung wet clothes on the outside of their packs. In ten minutes, Belle hollered, "Push through!" They left the stream, shirts and socks flapping in the sunshine as they walked.

The clean feeling of an icy bath didn't last long. Belle led them up a ridge onto a game trail. When a downed tree blocked the path, they humped over it. Bark scraped the tender insides of their thighs as they straddled it, then it scruffed their rumps as they threw a leg over and slid down the other side. The next fallen tree had too many limbs to climb over, so they dropped to hands and knees, crawling low in the dirt under the trunk to reach the path on the other side.

Belle bushwacked around the barriers, riding Winston in longer circuitous loops to rejoin the trail. One of her detours took her by Skiptail, though that name didn't appear on any map. She leaned against a tree, rubbing her shoulder, scanning for humans. To her relief, the area hadn't been used lately. When Winston pushed a path through scrub brush and trees to return to the group, her reaction surprised her. The previous day, she'd been disappointed each time she'd found an empty canyon, but this time … maybe it was for the best. She didn't want these women around when she had to do what she came for.

As Belle rode up, Samantha spread her arms. "Look at me. I look like I've been wallowing face down on the trail. I was clean this morning."

Melane gave her an exaggerated frown. "Aw … poor princess, this is probably the first time in your life you've been really dirty, eh?"

"No." Samantha's eyes narrowed. "I've mucked my horses' stalls."

"Quit'cher damn pecking," Belle dismounted, then flashed a smile at them. "More great news, tenderfoots."

"Lunch?" Melane said.

"No. We'll save that for the gold mine. Now, we get to cross *back* over the river to get on the trail we left on the other side."

Groans broke out among the women. "Shit!" Samantha said, then covered her mouth. "I'm sorry." Her shoulders sagged as she shook her head. "This trip has been hard on my vocabulary."

"Learned that at Washington State?" Melane smiled as she passed her.

"For that, Munk-girl," Belle pointed, "you get to be first in the water."

When they reached the stream, most of the rainfall had already flowed down the mountain. Belle rode straight across, and the women followed, the water rising only to mid-calf.

"We're stopping," Josie yelled. Belle turned to look. Behind her, a couple of the ladies had already stripped out of their shirts, bending streamside in sports bras, rinsing their clothes and arms. Kick was pulling the water filter out, offering to refill everyone's bottles and bags. Belle smiled and rode on. They'd be able to find the trail and make their way from there.

When the ladies arrived at the mine, Melane climbed the eight-foot pile of granite rubble and white quartz tailings to reach the adit. "Does this really lead to a gold mine?"

"It's a hole in the middle of nowhere. What else do you think it could be—a root cellar?" Samantha dropped her pack next to a small fire. "Where's Belle?" She looked at socks on a line between two saplings. Winston grazed nearby, staked to the ground.

"Oh, good grief." Josie's eyebrows shot up as she turned away. "She's down by the stream, naked."

"What's she doing?" Samantha watched the old woman flick a stick forward, wait a moment, then flick it again.

"Fishing." Kick said as she carried her wet clothes toward the clothesline.

"Is it just me, or is that weird?" Samantha wore a puzzled gaze.

"If you hadn't noticed, Belle's packing really light. She probably only has one extra set of clothing." Josie scanned the entrance to the mine, then shoved clothes into Samantha's hands. "Hang mine, too. I've got to see where Melane went."

The young woman had traveled into the mine until she couldn't see. Josie scolded her back out. Fifteen minutes later, Belle walked toward the group, wearing only her cowboy hat and boots, and carrying two fish. She stopped at the clothesline to slip on her shirt and pants. "Josie, you got an extra plastic bag?" Belle held up her trout. "I'll cook these later."

"Wow! A person could live out here. Fish when they're hungry. Wear clothes when they want," Melane said.

"They were called trappers." Samantha's voice underlined her condescending glare.

Ignoring it, Melane continued, "Teach me to start a fire. My boots got wet."

Belle let loose a long sigh. She pointed to the young woman's arms. "What happened to your duct tape?"

"Most of it came off in the water, but it helped with the itchies. I'm doing it again if Kick doesn't run out of tape."

Kick shook her head as she stood up. "Miz Belle, can I borrow your fishing pole?"

The old woman handed her the monofilament she'd tied to a stick. "Look under the rocks for a grub worm to put on the hook." Kick took the stick, but Belle didn't let go. She rubbed a finger across the small caduceus tattoo on Kick's arm, and stared at the two serpents winding around a winged staff topped by a cross. "I'm sorry." She gave the tattoo a soft pat. "Truly sorry." Letting go of the fishing gear, she looked away. Kick walked silently to the stream.

"Sorry about what?" Melane's eyebrows furrowed.

"Munk-girl, we've got plenty of space to spread out—like a million acres. And yet we're all bunched up like gopher town. Why don't you go find dead fir branches, the inside of bark, a few dried pinecones, and you can earn your fire-starting badge."

Josie watched Melane begin her search beneath trees. "I've been thinking about getting a tat. An outline of Oregon with a star in the corner for Two Pan. Do you have any ink, Miz Belle?"

The old woman stared across the mountains and over the ocean, watching nurses rub salve on lesions and ulcers of jungle rot. When it healed, it often left the skin a different color. And the Napalm victims. Puckered skin, peeling and hanging in strips. Even if they survived, the new skin was angry red, as though raging at the atrocity it had gone through. "No," she said quietly. "I've seen too many scars. I've come to think of smooth, unhurt skin as a real blessing."

"You didn't ask me," Samantha said. "But I don't have any tattoos, either."

"Nobody figured you did." Melane plunked her collection on the ground, adding. "I need to borrow somebody's matches. Mine are wet."

Belle made Melane arrange her tinder into an airy pyramid. Shaving thins layers from Belle's magnesium striker, she tried igniting the bits with a spark. Twenty minutes later, with a lot of huffing and striking, a tiny flame finally licked her pile of broken sticks and needles. "That's a cool little tool. I need one of those." Melane handed the striker back to Belle. "Now I need your flashlight so I can explore the mine. My flashlight is wet. It won't work."

"You've got a fire to tend." Belle frowned at her.

"Samantha can watch it. She won't go."

"I'll thank you not to speak for me." Samantha pinched her earlobe as though checking to see if her earring had fallen out, even though she'd stopped wearing them. "Besides, you're out of luck, everyone's lights need to dry out."

"Now whadda ya gonna do?" Belle looked at her with wide eyes.

The women ate lunch and worked on toasting their equipment by the fire, turning their boots often so the soles wouldn't melt.

"We figured it out!" Melane announced after lunch. She fanned her hand at Kick, who held a flat round stone. "Let there be light." A pinecone burned in the center of the rock. "And I've got plenty of fuel." Melane patted her pockets, which stuck out like jodhpur britches, the hips filled with pinecones.

"You're determined, aren't you?" Belle sighed. "All right. Pull me up." She extended her left arm to Samantha. "You're goin', too, Tinkerdink." Samantha blinked at her, then gave a firm nod, as though making up her mind, and helped Belle to her feet.

"I'm staying out here," Josie said. "So I can tell them where to look for the bodies."

22

We Carry Thorns Within Us

"DON'T GO SO fast. I can't see anything back here," Samantha's voice bounced off the uneven granite walls.

"Keep up," Melane whispered, even though the women were within elbow-gouging distance from one another. No debris or fallen stones littered the floor. No rafters hung loose or slouched with distress. When their light dimmed, the ladies stopped and lit another pinecone on their rock platter.

The mine seemed level until Kick looked behind her. The opening was higher than they were. They continued slowly walking downward as the walls narrowed and ceiling dropped to five feet. Crouching, the women finally gathered at the end.

"This is all of it?" Melane ran her hand over the rough-cut back wall. Her jaw worked to pop her ears.

"What'd you expect? Nuggets lying around?" Samantha brushed a cobweb from her face.

"This is a modern-day mine," Belle said. "Not the charm of those old death traps, huh? Factory-milled timbers. Galvanized bolts. Machine cut surface."

"It's not part of the pioneers and gold rush?" Melane's voice carried disappointment.

"No. Fifteen years ago an outfit found a little color and worked the quartz until they hit granite. There may be some gold in the crystals in the pile out there. They'd only keep big pieces. It wasn't worth their time to pick out little traces back then.

"Around here, the tailings are where people find gold. After the rush was over, the town nearly died. People moved on to California and Arizona. Those who stayed tore most of the old cabins apart to reuse the wood and nails. In one shack they found hundreds of dollars of gold dust that had sifted through the floor boards. Mostly they'd find it in the piles by the door where the sweepings and stove ashes were dumped. The stuff is fine, especially if you're trying to work it into a poke. It's caused nothing but trouble and brought lazy-assed people who wanna get rich quick."

"You wouldn't be saying that if you had a working claim," Melane said.

"Hush!" Belle had her finger to her lips.

A low groan, barely within hearing decibels, whispered around them. The quieter they were, the more it filled the air, pressing on their chests. It came through the dirt, pushing up on the soles of their feet and into their bodies. Behind them, the white light of the adit, seventy yards away, was only as big as a half-dollar.

Melane barely breathed the words, "What is that?"

"The mountain talking," Belle murmured. "Everything out here is alive."

The women listened to the hum, like a 747, far beneath them with the whispers of vibrations brushing over them.

"I don't think it likes us here." Without another word, Melane ducked and headed for the exit. Kick followed, holding the pine-torch high for the rest of the women. The trip out was twice as fast as the trip in had been. When they stepped into the sunlight, Samantha turned her face upward to drink in the brightness.

"How was it?" Josie called.

"Spooky. In a sobering sort of way," Melane said quietly. "I think I'll sort through some of these rocks." She squatted, her fingers clawing chunks of milky crystal. "Wouldn't that be cool if we found a nugget? Even a little one?" Kick nodded and bent to help her.

Belle retrieved her clothes and packed them into saddle-bags. She led Winston toward Samantha, who was leaning close to Josie in a huddled conference and whispering of a "gold digger."

"I'm off," Belle interrupted as she swung a leg over the mule. "Take down my clothes line when you're done gossiping."

"Oh!" Josie looked up. "Uh ..."

"The gals know what they have to do now. The weather's pretty good. Jiggs is bringing up steak and chocolate. You're safe." Without discussion, she kneed Winston onward, past the tailing pile where Kick and Melane squatted. "You girls rich yet?"

"No. These crystals cut up my fingers." Melane flicked stones from her with a stick.

"More duct tape," Belle called as the mule ambled away.

Belle rode, relieved she was missing out on whatever soap opera Samantha Jarmin was sharing. Being with these women had reminded her of being with her hoochmates. She missed intelligent conversation and the camaraderie. She did not miss the drama.

Winston trudged up a faint trail on the high ridge. They stopped at a small circle of firs pressed around a cliff face. A strand of barbed wire bounded the trees, creating a corral. Del had put it there long ago. Belle ran her fingers across the rough bump in the tree where the bark that had grown over the wire. Who could've imagined life's passage between then and now?

Next to the cliff face, a two- to three-foot ledge angled up the wall. In a few places, handholds had been carved by the ancients long before white trappers had stumbled into the mountains. Facing the wall, she stepped along the ledge, testing her footsteps before she put full weight on stones.

Twice, she chickened out, imagining how she'd bounce off at least three outcroppings before hitting the bottom. "Push through," she ordered. When she was younger, she'd run up this ledge. It hadn't seemed dangerous at all.

Squeezing between granite slabs, she entered a flat space the size of a twin bed, edged by boulders. Del had called it the Lookout. No doubt that had once been its purpose. With binoculars, Belle saw her group at the mine. They should be disappearing into the next valley soon.

No hiker or rider appeared on the trails. She sat back, feeling the sunshine on her skin. Two dusty, blue-speckled cups sat in a cleft. She'd forgotten all about them. Her and Del's. How could a place exist where she'd set down an enameled mug and returned fifty years later to find it dusty and still there? She didn't touch them, lest Del should come back. Too many ghosts had been visiting lately.

After a year in 'Nam, the ghosts had accompanied her to the Real World to finish her duty assignment. At the base hospital in Missouri, they watched her deal with tonsillectomies and broken arms. They asked her what was the purpose to living. They helped her drink.

When she finally returned to Two Pan, her status had changed. She was no longer a thief, but a veteran. People wanted to know about the war, anxiety scratching the underbelly of their questions. Their son, cousin, brother, uncle had received an invitation from the U.S. government to join the fight. What was it like? What was happening?

She'd shake her head, refusing to talk about the dense, triple-canopy jungles or carousing with Boom Boom girls for a dose of V.D., or constantly dreaming of home or calling for your mother in your sleep.

They'd find out soon enough when artillery fire lit up the sky. It would also show a hundred VC crawling up their hill to cut the barbwire. She didn't mention the superstitions for staying alive: Use matches sparingly. One match to light two cigarettes. Never be the guy to take the third light. Pay attention to your bad premonitions.

She didn't tell them. They wouldn't understand. All she advised was, "Don't go beyond the barbwire." There were no "fronts" in 'Nam. Medevacs couldn't be placed in safe rear positions. There were only barbwire perimeters.

And then she'd fled to the mountains where there were no questions, trip wires, or booby traps. Not even the ghosts wanted to be there. One by one, they faded away. There was only silence. A place where a person could lay down, and not be disturbed for centuries.

Belle awakened and rubbed her eyes. A quick look at the sun told her she'd been napping for over an hour. She stretched, wincing and rubbing her shoulder. She felt better. Strange how a bit of sleep made the world a little more hopeful. She should try sleeping all day sometime.

She glanced around. Was she becoming sentimental, visiting the haunts of her youth? No, she'd come to scout the area, but for sure, this would be the last time she'd ever be here. How many years before anyone discovered it again? Carefully, she climbed down to the mule, took the snips out of her saddlebag, and cut the barbwire from the trees. Boundary lines meant nothing to good or evil. It was time to remove the past. She worked a trench in the soft soil and buried the wire. It would rust into nothing. She couldn't do anything about the sections that had embedded in the bark. She patted a fir. "We all carry

thorns within us. The best we can do is try not to snag others."
She mounted and rode away without looking back.

Winston plodded along a well-used game trail until Belle pulled him to a sharp stop. A doe lay under a pine. It had been shot twice, once in the neck, once in the shoulder. Small caliber. Sloppy. No telling how far it had run before it died. Rain had beaten out tracks and blood trail. The coyotes and vultures would soon clean up the carcass.

Belle scanned the woods. It wasn't hunting season; the does were birthing now. Besides being a bungler, the hunter had either been too stupid or fat to follow the deer and put it out of its misery. This was the worst kind of predator. Somebody who shot for sport, just because he could. She was getting closer to the kind of low-life she was searching for. And it made sense: a person who knew the passes could weave through several of these canyons and reach her ranch in seven miles.

She scanned the bushes, looking for broken limbs and clues. It'd be dusk in a half hour. Too dark to trek across ridges or hump up the sides of the mountain. Besides, the doe could've run from any direction to get here. She mentally kicked herself for falling asleep earlier. *Whaddya gonna do now?*

Belle patted Winston who was upwind of the deer and seemed unconcerned about anything but the clump of grass at the base of a tree. "C'mon." She mounted. "We're gonna spend another night with the ladies." She rode the half mile to their base camp.

23

Fear Makes The Wolf Look Bigger
~German proverb

BELLE RODE THROUGH saltbushes dotted with tiny yellow flowers. When the sound of laughter floated from a hillside, the mule pointed his ears and followed it until he found women, sitting on a fallen log, splashing their feet in the stream.

"Well, look what Winston dragged in." Melane pointed her finger like it was a six-gun and fired at Belle. The old woman rode past, putting a boot on Melane's back and giving a hard push.

With a shriek, Melane grabbed at the others, but they pushed her forward. She plopped into the stream. Screeching and cussing, she arose, her clothes plastered to her body. "What the hell is the matter with you?"

"I told you that you'd be first in the water."

"That was back at the mine."

"One stream's as good as another. Besides, you needed to wash your hair. You're lookin' a little greasy."

"And you're not?" Melane flicked water toward Belle.

"I am. Is that a kettle I hear on the burner?"

"It is," Josie said.

"And I built a fire for your mean old ass," Melane said. "I want my merit badge."

Josie pushed Melane's hands down as the young woman continued to flick droplets at Belle. "Kick filtered drinking water. We've got your clothesline hung with our laundry on it. Samantha set up tents. She even cleared a spot for your hammock. Let me show you." Josie took off across camp. Belle dismounted and followed.

"I'll get you back," Melane shouted.

"No you won't, Munk-girl," Belle said without looking at her. "Good job on camp-set up, everybody."

As soon as they reached the small grassy area, Josie stepped close to Belle. "I didn't want to say anything in front of the others, but Jiggs hasn't been here. We don't have supplies."

Belle took the bridle off Winston, snapping a lead to his halter. "Well, that's kinda hard to keep secret. I'm sure they all know it."

"I told them he'll be here later." Josie watched the old woman undo cinches and pull strings.

"Reach up and pull that saddle off."

With a grunt, Josie hefted the saddle down. "What do you suggest we do?"

Belle caught the blanket as it slid off. "Hold that a minute while I get the rest of my stuff. As for Jiggs, I'm guessing he ran into another roadblock the tornado stirred up. He'll damn sure try to get here. He's probably coyote camping ..." She looked at Josie's confused face. "He's dropped wherever he is. He'll ride in tomorrow. Remember, he's leading a loaded pack mule. He's gotta be careful about cutting across rivers and ridges." As Belle talked, she slapped bags and bedroll on top of the saddle until only Josie's eyes peeked over her loaded arms. Belle waved for her to follow.

When they reached the camp spot, Josie unceremoniously dumped her burden on the ground. She turned her back to the women, who were still at the stream, and lowered her voice. "So ... what should we do?"

"Well, hell …" Belle stared at the sky. "Whaddya *think* needs to be done?"

"I kept everybody busy. The camp's in good order. I'm not sure what to do about food."

"You want me to kill somethin' and we'll eat it?"

"No. I bagged your fish from lunch. You rode off and left them. But there's only two, and there's five of us."

"I can't multiply loaves and fishes. I only kill things, re-member?" She gave Josie a cocky look and handed her the running end of a rope. "Tie that as high as you can around that tree."

Josie stood on her tiptoes, knotting a loop around the bole. "I can't believe I'm saying this but … teach us to fish. Kick tried. She didn't even get a nibble."

Belle looked at the sky again. "They should be bitin' about now, but I've got chores." She held up the loose end of her hammock. "Unless you'd be willing to set up? And if Samantha would curry Winston and check his hoofs?"

"Give it." Josie wore a resigned look, holding out her hand.

Belle stepped close and lowered her voice. "You need to keep the gals close to camp. No wandering around—"

"What's going on over here?" Samantha walked up. "It looks like you're planning a conspiracy."

"I … uh … " Belle looked at the ground as though her thoughts were scattered there and she needed to select which ones to pick up. "I wasn't gonna say anything, but if you can keep a secret, I'll tell you two. I saw a cougar pawprint near here. Big one. It'd be best not to wander around exploring the area or go for an evening walk. I'll scout it tomorrow."

"Don't tell Melane," Josie moaned. "We just got her to go wee in the woods. Now she won't get three feet from the tent at night."

Belle placed her hoof pick into Samantha's hands. "Clean up Winston for me. I gotta see a river about some fish. I'll take Kick and Munk-girl to keep them out of trouble."

"What about the ..." Samantha looked around, lowering her voice, "... the kitty cat?"

Belle patted her hip and kept walking.

"Damn," Josie whispered. "I suppose that means she's wearing that gun. I was helping her set up so I could find it and take it away."

"Frankly, I'm relieved she has it. I feel safer." Samantha took the hammock and tied it up.

Josie unfolded the tent canopy. "It really bothers me that she's searching for someone every day. I know she's a tough old broad who hunts animals, but a man? If something happens, I'll blame myself that I didn't stop her."

"I wouldn't worry about it ... " Samantha shook her head. "I suppose we've all got to do what we think is right, but she's not in good shape. I think it's all bluster."

"Then you don't know her." Josie shook her head.

In an hour, the fishing expedition had returned to camp. "I earned my fish-gutting badge!" Melane beamed a smile at Josie. "Did you know fish can see you if you stand on the bank? So Kick had to crawl on her belly to a pool and throw in her hook." Kick held up two cleaned trout. "We are mountain women!" Melane turned her face to the sky and gave a howl.

"Stop it!" Samantha yelled from the meadow. "You're scaring Winston." Melane gave her a sourpuss sneer.

"Give me those. I'm fixing fresh trout." Josie stepped close to Belle, her voice low, "You make sure they're occupied. Try to keep Melane and Samantha separated. They're really at each other today." She headed to the cooking rocks then stopped. "And don't scare them to death with cougar and Bigfoot stories."

Belle rolled her eyes. "Everybody's on their own. I'm wash-in' my hair. My head itches." By the time she'd loosened her braid and walked to the stream clothed only in her shirt and boots, she'd gained an audience. The women cat-called from the banks as she slipped off her boots, waded into the middle of the flow, and squatted down. Clear water cascaded over her back and shoulders. Her teeth clenched, her face went white as though drained of blood. She tried to stand quickly, stumbling and catching herself against a boulder.

"Cold ain't it?" Melane called. "At least no one *pushed* you in."

"Freezing!" Belle's teeth chattered. She put her hands against a rock, trying to balance as she stuck her head in the arc of water flowing off the top of a boulder.

"Good grief." Kick pulled off her camp shoes and waded to-ward her. "You're gonna kill yourself." She steadied the old woman, helping her walk to the bank. The smart remarks stopped.

Long gray hair hung tangled around her face, her lips blue. Her shirt stuck against her body, revealing a small, bony woman. She shivered and goose bumps peaked across her skin. Without her hat, and boots and big coat, she suddenly looked old and worn out.

"I used to do that all the time." Belle's voice quivered as Kick herded her to the fire. "Guess I got used to taking wipe baths." Samantha ran to get her microfiber towel. "The water's gotten colder. Must be that global warming crap." She opened her hand, revealing a tiny plastic bottle. "Here." Kick took it and squeezed liquid into Belle's palm.

"Gimme some of that, too." Melane held out her hand. "I was told I looked oily." She threw Belle a look as she vigorously fingered soap into her scalp.

Belle used only her left hand to rub her head. "You missed a spot." Samantha took over. "Does your shoulder still hurt?"

"What'd you do to your shoulder?" Kick looked up from briskly rubbing the old woman's legs with the towel.

"Nothin'!" Belle's mouth puckered. "Quit'cher fussin'. I've been dunkin' myself in a stream long before any of you were born."

"At some point you're going to have to admit you're getting too old for all of this," Kick said.

Melane elbowed Kick. "Hey, Miz Belle ..." Her voice lilted with a change of subject. "When does this shampoo suds up? I can't tell if it's working."

"It's peppermint soap, dammit." Belle's head leaned over as Samantha worked on her, but her voice rose up with bitterness. "You don't use suds out here unless you wanna screw up everything like they do in town. Hell's bells! Just mix some of that hot water with the cold and pour it over my head, would ya? You'd think this was a beauty salon. Let's be done with this."

The women exchanged glances. Shortly, Melane and Belle were rinsed out. The old woman sat on her stool, griping about the braid being worked into her hair. Samantha leaned so close, Belle felt her breath on her ear as she spoke, "I have a whole married life of someone saying one thing, but really meaning another. So you can bitch all you want, but I know your shoulder hurts, and you won't admit it. So sit still because ..." She stood up straight, her voice loud enough for all to hear. "This is how I braid my horses' tails. So you can just live with it."

Belle relaxed into a slouch, looking straight ahead, blinking away the wetness trying to overrun her eyes. She tried to think of the last time anyone had touched her with kindness. The mules had kicked her, the raccoon had pawed her and nibbled her fingers, the cattle butted and stomped her. It had been over a year since Ox Woolsey had died. The last kind touch she could remember.

When the braiding party finished, she mumbled her thanks and went to her tent. The rope lines were tight. The knots held well. Josie had done a good job. Why were these women nice to her? She sure as hell hadn't been nice to them. It had been like that in 'Nam, too. The women had quarreled. A couple even rolled around in a catfight, but they covered for each other. They all knew being touchy was a safe way to get rid of the fear and exhaustion poking their thoughts.

Belle looked around. Kick and Melane were dragging a log next to the fire. Samantha and Josie were using Melane's trail mix to create trout almandine. Belle blinked at the sight. These women were all in this adventure together. But she hadn't really been a part of their experiences. She'd participated begrudgingly, only when their sorry asses needed saving—which seemed like all the time. She had her own mission to complete. She shouldn't have gotten involved. Tomorrow. When Jiggs came. She'd ride her own way, and he could lead these women out of here.

"Miz Belle!" Josie yelled. "What're you doin' over there? I called you twice already."

"I feel human again." Melane stretched her feet toward the fire, rubbing her stomach. Dusk had faded into darkness. The surrounding forest had grown black as the first stars winked in the sky. "Who needs supplies? I'm clean. A tasty meal. I've learned how to walk in the rain, do laundry in a bucket, take polar baths, pee in the woods, and I made my own stoon." She held up her stick which she'd whittled to resemble a rough narrow spoon. "What more could a woman want?"

"To keep animals out of the camp," Belle said. "Gimme your fish bones and skin. I'll bury 'em away from here."

From the meadow to the west, the mule let out a bray. Belle stood up, her tripod stool falling over. In four quick steps she was in her tent then back out. She hurried away, carrying her gun. Behind her, Melane gasped, "Why is Miz Belle going to shoot Jiggs?"

Winston was staring across the grass into the woods. The area slanted down a forested hill, angling into the valley below. She patted the mule, walking around him, making certain he was okay. Winston's ears remained pointed to the north. Belle took off in that direction.

"You want a light?" Footsteps thudded behind her. "The mule seemed restless when I combed him earlier," Samantha whispered as she followed even though Belle pushed the flashlight away.

Belle elbowed through a grove of wild rhododendron bushes. She held her hand up, signaling 'halt,' which Samantha ran into. "Shhhh!" They froze, scanning the darkness. "The mule has low-light vision. I don't know if he saw something or smelled it. Leave the light off. Our eyes will adjust. Look for any shape that moves."

Silence spread out before them. Their eyes slowly scanned the area. They circled bushes and downed trees, and soon determined too much forest and night crowded around them to do any good. "Whaddya think, Tinkerdink?"

"You're asking me?"

"You have horses. You talk to them."

"I think there's something out there." Samantha stared into the darkness.

A *snap!* sounded farther downhill. "You got that right," Belle whispered. "A branch broke."

"Would a cougar step on a stick?"

Belle waited for the next sound. When it didn't come, she breathed, "It'll probably be gone by the time we crash through the woods, looking for it. C'mon, let's get back. I'm gonna move the mule to the patch of grass behind your tent."

24

A Few Of My Unfavorite Things

DURING THE WORST of the thunderstorm Gil and Boxer Gedding collected two horses and twelve head of cattle. The cows had been harder to load. For one thing—they were stupider. If the gate was locked, it required cutting the fence. Rattling a feed bucket usually brought the dumb animals like a cat who hears the can opener. The real chore required matching calf and mama.

When they'd squeezed as many animals as they could into each of their trailers, they drove to a deserted logging road butting into the forest. A padlocked gate barred the entry, but that was for show. Long ago, they'd cut the lock and replaced it with their own.

The trucks bumped across open meadow and off-loaded in a make-shift corral out of sight from the road. Usually, they only took a few animals at a time so they wouldn't be noticed. And so far their plan had worked, but Belle Chere couldn't leave well enough alone. When she'd shot Gil's dad, she'd started a shitstorm.

~*~

Previously, Gil had listened to the folks who came into the feed store talk about "checking out some suspicious ol' boy sittin' in his truck," or how many times they'd gone out to count their stock. The cattlemen had even hired Frank Helker and his helicopter to scout around once a week, "lookin' for cagey activity." But there was controversy about Frank's effectiveness. He always flew on Tuesday afternoons when he'd finished his deliveries across the area, so he was easy to avoid.

Bright and early this morning, customers at the Feed 'N' Seed yapped the big news of Samantha Jarmin's missing horses. Her hired hand had reported it, and Gil had acted as stupefied as everyone else. The main guy was supposed to stay there and take care of things. Served him right. That's what he got for not doin' his job while Mrs. Jarmin gallivanted around in the mountains.

Gil didn't say any of this when Sherriff Meyers dropped by to interview him. He'd told the truth—pretty much: He hadn't worked at the Jarmin place all week. He didn't think Jess, the hired hand, liked him. As a matter of fact, it seemed very few people in town liked him, but he got along with Mrs. Jarmin. She was always nice to him. She was the one who'd given him a job. All of which was true.

Where was he last night? Home, alone, playing video games. *Which ones?*

He was going say Grand Theft Auto, but that might bring up ideas he didn't want the sheriff thinking, so he'd said, "Portals of Blood."

What's your dad doin' nowadays? The question had surprised him. "How the hell would I know? He lit out long ago." Part of that rang true. His pa *had* abandoned the family. Unfortunately he'd secretly showed up again. Gil felt good that he'd added a decent amount of righteous anger to his voice and had backed the law off. He'd done a convincing job. He wouldn't tell his dad. His old man would feel it necessary to take him down a notch for bein' cocky.

Later that night, Gil rode one of Mrs. Jarmin's horses along the forested trail. He called him Paint, not because the horse had the marking, but because he'd always wanted a smart horse named Paint. Behind him, he led a calf, a rope tied to its neck, yanking him forward each time it planted its little hooves and refused to go farther into the darkness.

Last night, they'd penned the cattle in the makeshift corral. His dad didn't want to drive them along the hillsides during a thunderstorm. Of course, the old man didn't help tonight either. He busied himself making arrangements for a truck big enough to haul this batch. As usual, Gil herded livestock alone. But tomorrow night, all of this would be over. The cattle would be out of here. Lock. Stock. And stolen barrel. "I'll lay low for a while," his old man had said. "You act normal. It'll all simmer down. Ranchers will lighten up. And we can start over."

Bullshit. Once Gil got his money out of this enterprise, his old man wouldn't find him again. Hell, if he'd wanted to look at the ass-end of cattle as a career, he'd work on a ranch. Gil gave a humorous snort; he *did* work on a ranch—part time.

Trees lined either side of the narrow trail. He gave the rope another tug, jerking the calf forward. Its mother obligingly followed. They were herd animals. They'd stay with him unless spooked, but there were a hundred things that unhinged cattle.

As they neared, another ridge, he smelled smoke drifting downhill in the evening chill. He heard women laughing, high-pitched, like bird twitter. He slowed, his mind racing.

It must be that Trek group advertised all over town. What the hell were they doing in this valley, far from the usual hiking trails? What if the calf bawled? All it took was for the little idiot to get startled. Gil liked calves. They were easier to manhandle, and anyone could brand them with their own iron and raise them as their own. He and his dad had been careful to always take mother and calf. It took longer to sort out the herd, but it eliminated the chance of taking a cow and leaving the calf bawling like a siren.

He patted the neck of the Tennessee Walker. He hadn't wanted to steal the horses, but his dad had said, "It's a rich man's farm. The wealthy should stay home and take care of their stock if they don't want 'em to walk off. It's their own damn fault." Gil had to agree. It was like the folks who tossed a wallet or phone on the dashboard because they didn't want to sit on it. If they left it there, they were asking for it to be stolen.

The other Tennessee Walker didn't think much of the cattle or the dark or being riderless. The gelding took a couple of steps upslope, snorting and shying from something. Gil worked his way back through the line of animals. He had figured the horses were going to be trouble. They weren't used to the woods. Probably never been on a trail ride. While most equines were cautious, these horses acted as though dinosaurs would run from the woods and gobble them up any minute.

"You're okay. Let's go," he whispered. He'd seen rocks move faster. High up the hill, he could see a glow above the trees. Probably the women's campfire. He pushed the cows along at a slow, ambling gait. When he'd made it past the camp, he blew a long breath from puffed cheeks.

Above him, a mule brayed.

Shit.

He picked up the pace slightly, worried that one of the horses might answer. Then what? They were leaving prints in the soft ground. If someone came tramping down the hill they'd discover them. "C'mon, c'mon." He pushed closer to a cow. She jumped ahead. A stick snapped. That scared her even more. She ran forward, bumping into the other cattle, making them run up the trail several yards. The sound of their hooves thudded the dirt. To him, it broke the quietness like a stadium of people stomping their feet.

He was spooking them. That was the last thing he needed, having them dash ahead. He'd driven enough cattle along this trail to know its bends and wide spots. It was narrow and beat down, but the storm had blown branches over it. Patches were slippery where weather had poured across the path and down the hill. He couldn't have them darting around like blue-assed flies.

"Shh...shh ..." he hushed, though he didn't know why. Cattle didn't understand the sound. He hummed a tune, slowly making his way through the line until he rode at the front. The scent of the smoke drifted the other way. He paused, listening. No one thudded downhill, cracking through the brush ... yet.

"Ride off," his old man had always said. "If someone sees you, turn and ride any direction you don't think they'll follow." Gil picked out his escape path. It ticked him off he was the one out here pushing stolen stock through the dark, while his dad was arranging for a truck. Tomorrow, the old man would show up, stinking of alcohol and weed.

Shit. He hated this work. He hated cattle and their need to drop cowpiles wherever they went. Slowly he herded the animals around the bend, thinking of all the things he hated, yanking the calf behind him.

25

Some Truths Do More Than Set You Free

"WHAT WAS IT?" Melane asked the moment Samantha and Belle walked back into camp. "Josie told us you saw cat tracks this afternoon. I don't know why you thought you couldn't tell me. I'm not gonna freak."

"I'm sure you won't," Belle said without sarcasm. "Cats are curious. They like to look at what's in their territory. You'll rarely spot one. Maybe glimpse its tail as it disappears. We didn't see anything out there."

"Could it be watching us now?"

"Nope. Don't worry. Winston would let us know. Super Mule sees well in the dark and picks up vibrations through his hooves. I'll stake him behind your tent tonight, if that's okay with you."

"Fine." Kick emptied the pot of dishwater on a bush. "It'll keep Melane from peeing back there."

"I don't do that anymore. I can go in the woods like a big girl, even with the threat of cat whiskers tickling my butt." Melane flexed a bicep. "I don't need no protectin'."

"Since when?" Samantha's voice grew sharp. "Isn't finding protection your goal? Particularly if he's a rich man?"

"*What* is your problem?" Melane squinted at her. "And look who's talking! You've got a rich man taking care of you."

"And you need to back off, missy, unless you want me to go Belle Chere on you."

"Okay." Josie stepped between the two women. "I think we're all tired. This is big, unfamiliar country, and we've been bunched together for the last three days. We need a little space from each other."

"Aww ... let 'em loose." Belle sat on a log next to the fire. "They've been nippin' at each other like horses setting the bossing order in a herd. Let 'em get it over with. Besides, I'd like to see what a Belle Chere fight looks like." She eyed Melane and Samantha. "Keep in mind I *do not* pull hair or use fingernails."

"I'm sure this is simply a misunderstanding." Josie waved toward the log. "Let's sit. One person talks, while the other listens. Then we'll switch." She glanced at Belle and Kick. "Could you ladies give us some privacy?"

"*Hell*, no." Belle frowned. "We've put up with this drama for the last few days. Now that it's finally comin' to a head, why miss out? You want privacy, go out in the dark with the coyotes." She pulled out her knife and picked up a stick, settling in for a craft project. Kick climbed into her tent.

Melane stepped around Josie. "Don't use your schoolteacher crap on me."

"Oh good grief ..." Samantha watched Melane's every move. "It's *obvious* what you're up to. You haven't exactly been subtle. It doesn't fool me, and it won't fool these folks." Samantha waved a hand at Belle. "They're smarter than you think."

"We are?" Belle looked at Josie. "Are we being hornswoggled somehow?"

"Max Buddy brought her in. She's all cute and bouncy and blonde." Samantha waved up and down at Melane's figure. "But tell me this ... if she's supposed to be convincing old men to sell their land, why would she be on this trip full of women?"

All eyes looked at Melane, waiting for an answer. The young woman opened her mouth then closed it. Crossing her arms over her chest, she stared at Samantha. "I'm not talking about work. I'm on vacation, and you're continuing to ruin it."

"That's a good one! You've been here, what? Two weeks? And you're taking a vacation? Before I married, I was a realtor. Now I'm getting my license renewed. So ... Miss California, I can tell you for a fact that sales are made by calling on clients, not stumbling through the backwoods. If you're really too stupid to know that, why did Max Buddy let you join his firm? Oh, let me guess." Samantha waved at Melane's body again.

Melane's face screwed up. "For your information, I did my homework. Miz Belle and Josie both own land that would make attractive sites for any buyer."

"I notice you didn't mention me. I have a ranch. But then you already knew my land wasn't for sale. Didn't you?"

"I *know* how to talk people into buying and selling. So what are you doing out here, Miss Wanna-be Realtor?"

"That's *Mrs. Jarmin,* and you'd do well to remember it. I'm meeting people. I'm an ambassador for my husband's enterprise. He truly believes he can bring a new economy and prosperity to this area. I'm working to let people know we're part of the community. I've done public relations for several organizations. I *know* how to change opinions."

Josie exchanged a glance with Belle as she sat down next to her. The old woman called across the fire, "Whaddya public relating to out here?"

"I'm learning the culture! I've talked to each of you, woman to woman. How else can I learn that it's not uncommon here for people to name their kids with the same letter: Mary, Mick, Max, Monty ..."

Belle's forehead wrinkled as she mumbled, "Is that the Abbots?"

"The Crons." Josie leaned close, whispering. "I've had Max and Monty in my class."

Samantha continued, "Only in Two Pan do you meet a lawn mower, a tractor, or a horse on the street as frequently as a car. And I swear I saw a bicycle leaning against the feed store with a shotgun buckled to the side of it."

"Leon Capper," Josie spoke from the side of her mouth, her head cocked toward Belle. "He lost his driver's license on a DUI."

"Again?" Belle whispered, watching the zipper on Kick's tent slide down several inches and eyes peek through the opening. "He always was a worthless boozebag."

"And do you know ..." Samantha said, "everybody has the same chicken casserole recipe. I couldn't get a copy."

Josie picked up the pokey stick and gave the fire logs a couple of hard jabs. "So both of you are studying and using us like lab rats."

"Not me." Melane held up both hands. "I only came to analyze her." She hooked a thumb toward Samantha. "Meeting both of you ladies was a bonus, and if you ever want to sell your land, please contact me. I came mostly to find out what's so special about *this* woman." She looked Samantha Jarmin up and down. "Sadly, I've concluded, not much."

"You may have a perky little ass and big eyes, but stay away from my husband."

"Whooo! There we go," Belle said as Josie gasped.

Melane's shout razored through the voices, "Is that what you think?"

"Everybody has their motives. You're more transparent than you know." Samantha sneered. "Max Buddy hired you because he botched Richard's project. He probably thought bringing in a sweet, young thing would make these old ranchers open their doors and talk. That'll make Mr. Buddy look great. He'll redeem himself with Richard and make a fortune.

"But that made me wonder why a young woman would want to hang around podunk and talk to old men in overalls? Sure you'd get a commission, but there's no guarantee. This isn't a market with a lot of sales. You've got your eyes on a better prize. If you broker enough property, you think you can make my husband happy. Very happy. Because he would get to do his project. You don't fool me. That's how *I* met him. You and your boss can eat your plans. Because I'll handle any realty requirements."

"Your husband hired me," Melane said.

Samantha stared, her eyes wide then narrowing. She poked the young woman's chest. "You do not want to test me." The poking became hard enough to move Melane's body with each stab. "If you keep *trying* to get into my husband's *pants—*"

Melane batted her hand away. "Richard Jarmin is my *father*. He dated my mother twenty-two years ago while he went through med school."

The hard lines in Samantha's face flashed into a round-eyed stare. Her lips opened slightly as she drew in a breath. Silence unreeled around them, the fire making popping sounds.

"When Mom told him she was pregnant, he dropped her like she was Ebola." Melane's voice grew strained as she spoke through a partially clenched jaw. "She had to sue and get paternity tests to get him to take any responsibility. That's right. You just keep staring at me and do the math. I'm not lying."

Samantha's eyebrows were starting to pinch together. Her posture deflated with slumped shoulders.

"You go on about how your parents are so nice and whoop-te-do. Well, the only dad I've known is a check every month. A very tiny one because his attorneys were better than my mother's. Mom's the one who worked to make sure I had what I needed. And for a reason that now seems completely idiotic to me, I wanted to meet the man who was my father. I didn't even know he was a cosmetic surgeon. Mom won't talk about him. The checks were issued by an attorney. He didn't even sign them.

"I tried contacting him through his lawyers several times. And when I graduated high school, the checks stopped coming. I let him know I was somebody he could be proud of. I'd gotten my real estate license. But nothing. He never replied.

"Then out of the blue he called. I couldn't believe it. He invited me to Portland, and we met. I was shocked by how handsome he was. Finally! Here's my dad in front of me, looking at me, accepting my existence. He even has a job for me. If I can buy land around here—enough of it—he'll send me to college, and I'll also have the opportunity to make a tidy commission. At last! He's acting like a father. So I came. I thought he'd be here. I thought I'd get to know him, but's he's not around. I'm told he's only working out of his offices in Portland right now.

"I was supposed to steer clear of you, but I went on this trip to get to know *you*. I needed to see why he picked you over my mom." Melane gave Samantha a look as though she were something stuck to her shoe. "It doesn't matter anymore. I'm not sure who got justice. My mom—because she's not with a jerk like him. Or him because he ended up with a bitch like you." She turned and strode down the trail into the night.

Without looking at anyone, Samantha stormed toward the meadow.

Josie's head turned back and forth, watching them hurry away in opposite directions. Her voice was thin and accusing, " 'Let them go at it,' you said. 'Let them work it out like horses do.'"

"Hell's bells, why would you take advice on relationships from a social butterfly like me?" Belle stood and threw another log on the fire. "Well ... we can't let 'em wander around out there. Your discovery thing is going too damn well, isn't it?"

26

Don't Ask Questions In The Dark

BELLE STOOD IN front of a tree so she wouldn't be profiled against the fire. As her eyes adjusted to the darkness, she could see Samantha leaning against the mule, crying into his shoulder. Winston U'd his neck to enfold her.

For Belle, horses and mules possessed an ancient wisdom; they understood inner thoughts. When Bonnie, the old broomtail that babysat her died, Belle had bawled for a month. But when her mom ditched the family, she hadn't cried a tear. Belle stayed with her father. Folks said that's why she'd turned out wild like she had, but that wasn't the reason. She was wild because she didn't give a shit. You had to care in order to follow rules.

Winston picked up Belle's scent. He snuffled a couple of times, calling her to come help him with the wreck clinging to his neck. Hell, she didn't know what to do with it either.

Obviously the lie about wild cats sneaking around hadn't been enough to keep the women in camp. She weighed the idea of telling them to be cautious of two-legged animals in the forest, but they'd had enough upset tonight. She'd let them know in the morning when Jiggs arrived. Fears had a harder time stalking you in daylight.

As she crossed the meadow, she announced her presence, calling, "Winston really likes you. Animals are like that. I used to have an affectionate calf—nuttier than a hunnerd-year-old granny. I could tell her anything. She'd make me laugh."

Samantha wiped her face. "What happened to it?" she sniffed.

"I knew a fella. He needed her more than me, so I gave her away."

Samantha's voice broke, her words squeezing together. "What am I doing here?"

"You're asking the wrong person." Belle stroked Winston's nose. "I've never figured out why any of this shit happens."

"My horses are the only real friends I can trust. Does that seem strange?"

"No. I've spent many-a night talking to mules and raccoons. But then, people think I'm eccentric. So you got that to consider."

"My husband controls everything in my life." Samantha's voice carried an ache. "Now I find out he has a daughter. A daughter only a couple of years older than our own. Why didn't he ever mention it? He simply ignored her. What other lies is he carrying around?"

"He must be pretty desperate if he's pulled her in now."

"He mortgaged his practice, and then several of his investments went belly up. Our debt load is quite substantial. He's determined to make this mountain development work. I wouldn't be able to keep my last two horses if I hadn't come to Two Pan. Now I have to make buddies and change opinions so he can get land from old-timers who don't trust him. He's given me six months."

"Sounds like you need to take your horses and go somewhere else."

"You know how I knew Melane was telling the truth? The moment she mentioned his attorneys. She's right. He controls the money. Well, he and his lawyers. I have the lifestyle I wanted because he has money. And the more involved I am with the people who count, the better it is for his business. I'm tired of it. Unfortunately, I've grown accustomed to living ... a certain way. I'm not sure I'd even have friends if I left him. They'd be busy with their fundraisers, and I'd be ... eating TV dinners. When it gets bad, I ride. My horses listen. They don't judge. They get me through. I play his game because I want to keep what I have."

"And now you have to rethink what's important." Belle fell silent, staring at the ground, not sure what she should say next, so she didn't say anything. Finally she pointed to the west. "Looks like a few clouds rollin' in. Don't stay out here long. I've learned, it's never good to bide your time in the dark after licking your wounds. I'll be by the fire. Bring Winston when you come. We'll stake him in the camp tonight. I think everybody'll feel better if he's near."

Belle busied herself, securing the camp: checking tie-downs in case the wind came up. Putting the trail mix, left on the table, in Melane's pack. Hanging the pack on the line with the others so the varmints wouldn't get it during the night.

Samantha led Winston between the tents. "I can saddle him for you in the morning. I know your arm hurts."

"I'll be moving out early."

"I doubt if I get any sleep." Samantha shrugged. "Let me do something for somebody. I feel so stupid and pointless and ..." Her words faded.

"Hey!" Belle prodded her arm. "Stake Winston. Do you know how?" She nodded. "Put my tack under your rainfly so you can get him ready by five. Give him a small treat tonight." Belle pointed to the bags hanging on a big fir.

"Thanks." A tear slid down Samantha's cheek as she walked away with her hand on the mule's neck. Belle felt sure the mule was doing the leading, not the woman.

When Samantha finished, she retrieved Belle's gear and stowed it. Belle told her rituals and tricks to keep a mule still while she saddled him. They really weren't important, but it would help Samantha focus. Years ago, as blood gushed from a soldier's thigh wound, it had helped when a doctor said what to do. She transitioned from staring to doing. Doing helped keep one's sanity.

" ... I should wait up and talk to her?" Samantha was asking.

"No," Belle said. She hadn't been listening, but it didn't matter. Darkness wasn't the time to pose questions that had no answers—and that's mostly what people did at night—wrestle with thoughts bigger than they. She checked the sky. Broken wracks of clouds were beginning to gather. What they needed was a gentle rain. It washed the explosions out of the air. It drove everyone to huddle beneath something instead of going after each other. Its drumming would lull them to sleep.

The stars glinted through the blackness, unconcerned with anything below. "Everything looks better in the dawn," Belle said. "I guarantee it. Go lie down."

Samantha had gone to bed only ten minutes earlier when the other women returned to the camp. Without a word, Melane went into her tent. Kick and Josie walked to the campfire and sat down next to Belle, who was rubbing her pistol with an oily rag. No one spoke.

Finally, Josie lowered her head, rubbing her temples. "Do you have to do that here?"

"Yep. I don't do it in the dark."

"It's just that ..." Josie's sigh stuttered into a groan. "Oh, never mind. You're going to do as you please. This adventure sure went belly up, didn't it?"

Belle frowned. "Why'd you create this Trek, anyway? Didn't you find a buncha of old coins in your grandparents' attic? Don't you have enough cash?"

"I thought I'd start a business." Josie sighed. "Hire local help. Save Two Pan with home-grown enterprise. Maybe others would do the same. It'd help keep us from selling out to Samantha's husband and carpeting the area with vacation condos. Besides ... I took all of my grandparents' hoard and created a college loan for Two Pan kids—one each year. If they come back and work here after they graduate, they don't have to pay it back."

"That's decent of you. Here, Kick." Belle held out bullets. "Take these for a minute."

The young woman shook her head. "I'm not touching them." She pulled her bandana from her head and laid it in Belle's lap. "Put them there. It's clean."

"You obviously know something about gun maintenance." Belle assessed her with a sad smile. "And we've seen your talent for healing. You ever thought about being an R.N. or a doctor?"

"I've looked into Oklahoma State's pre-med program. I can stay with an aunt there, but I don't have enough money for tuition."

"Join the military; they'll pay for your education if you'll commit a few years of service after you graduate."

"No!" She shook her head.

"Your dad?" Belle patted Kick's arm where she'd seen the tattoo.

"He was a medic. In Iraq."

"I'm sorry," Belle murmured. "I can tell he taught you a lot. He'd be proud of you."

"Maybe ... the truth is ... I haven't been honest about this trip." Kick studied the ground. "Josie, I volunteered to assist you on the Trek to get that loan-grant you mentioned."

"Have you sent in an application?" Josie asked. "I've received a number of submissions already."

"Hell's bells," Belle hissed, her face puckering. "Are you gonna spend a week in the woods with every applicant so you can find one who's more dedicated than this gal? Who else would come on a rainy trip with a bunch of whiny, bossy women? She's probably the only one of you who doesn't need to find her inner self."

"There are other applicants. I've got to be fair to everyone."

"Bull-loney." Belle shook her head and looked at Kick. "My house is burned down, and I'm not sure if I'm going to live through this adventure—so I don't have a good handle on my finances right now, but I can promise this much, honey. If I make it, and you get into school, I'll buy your books for as long as you're there. And unlike Miss Stick-up-her-butt here, I don't need an application."

"All right. All right. I'll consider this later. I've got enough to deal with tonight. Like what I'm going to do about those two." Josie nodded toward the tents.

"Not tonight." Belle slid the bullets back into their cylinders. "It'll look better in the morning. Get some rest."

Josie let out a long, weary breath then stood. "Maybe you're right." She circled her finger. "You'll close up here?"

"Sure."

Kick got up, too. She squeezed Belle's arm with a "Thanks."

Belle watched the women go to their tents, relieved that the chat session was over. Zippers closed. A few voices filtered through the nylon walls, then lights snapped off. Belle pulled out her pocket knife and sat, chipping pieces from a branch. Stillness edged in from the forest.

A tall, skinny crane began to form on the stick she held. Whittling kept her busy until tiredness could swamp her racing mind. She focused on retracing possible routes for the dead deer, recognizing which canyons were closest. After the third yawn, she snapped her knife closed.

A tent zipper opened. Samantha climbed out and walked to the fire.

"I was just going to bed." Belle gave her an apologetic frown.

"It's all right. I only wanted to sit." Belle nodded. The old woman used the pokey stick to turn the logs and stir the embers. She threw a broken limb on top; fiery flakes twirled into the air. "Well ... good night," she said as she headed to her tent.

"How'd you get so tough?"

Belle stopped, her eyes squeezed tight. She lifted her hat and put her hand to her forehead, smoothing the tiredness over her skull, all the way back to her braid. "I learned it. It's what I had to do."

"How? How did you grow to be resilient? I missed that lesson."

"Being pretty doesn't help. You think it does because you get more attention. Guys give you stuff. Girls are jealous. None of it's real. Believe it or not, I was once pretty."

"I can see that. So what toughened you up?"

Belle let out a long sigh. She stared at the ground a moment before coming back and sitting on the log next to Samantha. Neither of them spoke for a while. "In my twenties, somebody should've boxed my ears and showed me how senseless I acted. It would've saved a lot of misery. As it was ... I landed in the military."

She pushed the topic away with her hand. "I don't talk about it, so don't ask. I'll only say that's where I learned the difference between important pieces of life and what didn't count. We're animals who form packs. We were meant to watch each other's backs to survive. That mattered."

"You don't operate that way now."

"I've forgotten. When I got out, I spent time by myself. And then the young men around here were being drafted—or signing up. So I did their jobs, hired out as a ranch hand. I thought it would keep me busy. I was used to being part of a unit, so I worked as hard as any of the men. I thought I was really helping out. One ol' boy always gave me a big hug. He'd stand there with his arm around me, talking about chores, how much he missed his son, what a great gal I was, and how he couldn't keep his ranch if I didn't help. I was a 'godsend.'

"Honest to Pete, those were his exact words. And I stood there quiet, while he's making me out to be the savior of our way of life, and all the time his thumb was rubbing the side of my breast. I can still remember his damn thumbs. Up and down real casual.

"I thought, surely it was an accident. After all, I'd known him since I was a little girl. He was respected. He must not have known what he was rubbing. So when he got near me, I kept my arms glued to my sides. Sometimes it worked. Sometimes I thought I'd imagined it. Other times that old bastard actually wiggled his thumb, trying to dig it past my arm. One morning I worked in his barn, fixing a stirrup, and he comes in with a couple of other ol' boys. They're goin' to lunch. Why don't I join 'em? He's buyin'. And before I could squeeze up, he got his arm around me. The others can't see his thumb, and he's rubbing away—or maybe they can, and he's showing what he pays for in a hired hand.

"I don't know what came over me. Like an explosion it dawned on me—I didn't have to put up with shit like that. I grabbed what was handy, which happened to be a branding iron, and proceeded to beat him, threatening to machete his thumbs and stick them up his ass if he ever tried to feel me up again."

Samantha's face froze, her mouth open.

"The other fellas pulled me offa him. He denied it, of course. It didn't take long for word to get out that I was crazier than a run-over dog. Some people wouldn't hire me. I suppose it would sound strange to girls like Kick and Melane. They're warned about that sort of thing. Back in the day, I was told I had to put up with it if I wanted to keep a job or ... " she gave Samantha a dark glance "if I wanted to keep my horses."

"Oh." Samantha shook her head. "I don't think I could ever do that."

Belle nodded, crossing her legs at her ankles, snugging her hands between her knees. "But you asked about being tough. And I'm saying part of having a spine is learning there are people you can trust, and a few you can't. And it's up to you, *not them*, to set what you tolerate and what you don't. And you can't worry whether they like you or not. It's like training a horse. The same technique works on husbands and kids."

"You can't really mean that."

"Too bad you never met Ox Woolsey, Jiggs' dad. Now that man held himself accountable. He often ordered people around like he was a general, but I'd call him on it. He respected me for it."

"You had nothing to lose."

Belle stared at the fire, her voice dropping into a wistful sigh. "If you say so."

Samantha shook her head. "I need to toughen up. Put on my big girl panties and talk to Melane."

"In the morning." Belle stood, shielding a yawn with the back of her hand.

Samantha stared at the other tent. "That poor girl. This isn't her fault. All this because Richard didn't have the guts to be honest."

"Like *you've* been honest about your marriage?"

Samantha gave her a tired look. "Do you have any friends at all?" She got up and went to her tent.

Belle threw her head back with a quiet groan. Why had she even tried? She knew better. She used to believe in community. Helped people. Told them the truth, not just what they wanted to hear. Sometimes they actually made changes. But that was rare. Most people would rather live with the lies. They'd slander you to pieces if you made them face facts. And why the hell did she care? None of this mattered. She didn't need these women as friends nor as an excuse to be in the woods anymore.

Doing a final sweep, she shined the light around the perimeter. When a pair of eyes glowed from the forest, she gave a little jerk of surprise, and then she stomped with a, "Git!" The owl bobbed his head at her.

Shaking away the jeebies, she stoked the fire until its light pulsed past the trees. As she walked to her tent, a glance over her shoulder confirmed the harbinger of death still watched her. Okay, then. If she wasn't leaving this canyon, then she'd be taking a low-life with her, because she'd worked out which hole he had to be hiding in. And it wasn't that far away.

With one last glance around the camp, Samantha's words echoed in her mind. *Do you even have any friends?* No. Would anyone even miss her when she was gone? She stepped into her tent and zipped it against the owl's stare.

The stars of the Seven Sisters had traveled across the sky and settled in the west. Darkness blanketed the camp; the coals had died to black. Melane emerged from her tent. She stood outside, pulling on socks, pants, and shirt, then wiggling her feet into her boots. She paused long enough to tie them. Walking softly, she retrieved her pack from the line. Slinging one strap over her shoulder, she hurried down the trail.

A half hour had passed when Samantha got up and dressed. Sleep had been scratchy. A light mist fell, but she stirred the coals, coaxing two small flames to appear as she rehearsed what to say when Melane got up.

She went to the packs to get the coffee pot. Melane's blue pack was missing. Samantha cracked the zipper and peeked inside the tent. Kick lay sleeping; the other half was empty. She hurried to Belle's tent. With her hand on the zipper, she glanced at the mule, his head low in his half-sleeping stance. In a moment, the whole camp would erupt—which was crazy. This should be between her and Melane.

Samantha pulled the mule's stake. With whispers and nuzzles, she led him down the trail and tied him. She returned for the tack.

Shortly, she swung a leg over his back, waiting a moment to see if he would fuss. He twitched his ears, his head low, still holding onto the last remnants of his sleep. "Melane won't have made it far," Samantha promised him. "We'll be back before the others get up." They headed through the mist toward the smudge of pink lining the eastern horizon.

27

Before The Sun Comes Over The Mountain

GIL GEDDING LAY half-asleep by the small campfire. He would've never heard the rock skitter down the canyon embankment, if it hadn't landed on a cow. She spooked, letting out a *Muuuuuhh* as she took a big-eyed lunge against the canyon wall. Several animals around her moved away, making the herd of thirty cows and three horses shift closer to Gil.

He sat up and listened. Someone was coming. The path followed a cliff ledge overlooking the valley. It dog-legged left as the cliff shot upward and the track dropped into his niche. When the rock face had fallen centuries ago, it dropped seven foot slabs, creating a high, misshapen circle. In the few gaps between giant boulders, ancient fences of woven sticks finished off the holding pen.

On the south side of the enclosure, Gil stood up, trying to see through the ash-gray of dawn. Another stone skipped off the rock face and thudded in the dirt. Mountain goats or man? If it was human, he wasn't trying to be quiet. It couldn't be his dad. Even cross-eyed high, the old fart could walk the ridge without moving a pebble.

Gil visually followed the sounds descending the trail. In a few minutes, someone would be at the log that served as a gate to the corral. He hurried to the other exit, a cleft in the wall wide enough for two cows. He quietly lifted the branch that lay diagonally across it and stepped into the deep shadows of the slot canyon. His heart tried to push its way through his chest.

His short breaths pulsed in his ears as he peered back at the corral. His dad would beat him until he bled for letting the place be discovered. Shit. In twelve more hours they would have been out of there. Letting out a long slow breath, he shifted as he tapped the side of his leg, deciding to risk another peek.

Two women and a mule stood at the gate. They peered over the heads of milling cattle. Only two lost women. He willed them to leave. To head back the way they'd come. His dad would never find out. For shit's sake, how did they get on this trail? What were they even doing on this side of the mountain? Please, please do not let it be those Trek women.

"Hello?" The brunette stood on her tiptoes, calling and looking around. He leaned his forehead against the rock wall. It was Mrs. Jarmin, his employer. His guts told him to take off running. His brain told him to act like a man.

"There's a campfire over there. Maybe they're asleep." A young blonde leaned over the log barring her entrance. It shifted with her weight, rolling off the two boulders it balanced on. With a heavy *thud*, it hit the ground and rolled into the lot. Cattle pushed to the opposite end, a few jumped with tails in the air.

"Great. Fix that." Mrs. Jarmin's voice sounded peeved. "If there's one thing I've learned, it's that ranchers get really ticked off when you mess with their fences or gates."

"How am I supposed to lift that?" The blonde snapped back.

"Grab the other end, Melane." Mrs. Jarmin bent over the log.

"I don't want your help. I want to be alone. That's why I left."

"And that's why you're lost."

"You have no idea where we are either." The two women grunted and heaved, but dropped the log. The *thud* and Melane's squeal echoed across the lot again.

"Crap." Mrs. Jarmin straightened, holding her back and looking around. "Hello? Anybody?" A calf bawled.

Gil leaned against the wall, his eyes closed, cussing silently. If that stupid woman got one calf going, the others might join in. Not because they were hurt or lonely, but because they thought they should. Damn. He hated cattle. Pulling his hat low on his forehead, he stepped from the shadows. "Whaddya want?" he growled two octaves lower than usual. "And talk soft. They're waspish as it is."

The cute young blonde whispered, "I think we made a wrong turn."

"*You* made a wrong turn," Mrs. Jarmin interrupted, "and dragged the mule and me with you."

Gil's words piled on top of each other so fast it was hard to tell them apart. "Go back. Back across the ridge. First trail junction, turn left."

"Would you have any first aid supplies?" the blonde asked.

"No."

"I slipped—"

"No!" He growled louder than he'd intended.

"Well, pardon us for waking you." Mrs. Jarmin gave him a disgusted look as she circled the mule to go back up the trail. "Are you from around here?"

He looked at the ground, the brim of his hat shielding his face. "No. Back-track then left." He fanned a wave, shooing them away. The women took off, grumbling.

Gil hefted up one end of the gate-log, then the other, setting it across the boulders. He let out a slow breath. The women didn't seem to know what they'd walked into. Stupid city people. And even if they figured out that this wasn't one of those back-to-nature ranching projects, it would take most of the day to walk out and tell anybody.

A rock bounced down the cliff face, hitting three times before landing in the lot. He estimated the women were about half-way up the trail when a familiar voice floated down.

"That looks like it hurts like hell."

"It does." The young blonde sounded pouty.

"I've got stuff to put on that, if you think it'll help." Gil's muscles clinched, locking his feet to the ground where he stood.

"You know what? That's all right, sir." Mrs. Jarmin's voice sounded strained. "We know where we made a wrong turn. We'll be on our way."

"Now, don't worry if my son was rude. He ain't none too sociable in the mornin', but he knows how to pour peroxide over a wound. And you're bleedin', honey."

"I fell over a tree root in the dark," the young woman said.

"Well, we'll fix you up, and you'll be on your way before the sun comes over the mountain."

Gil's breath made a whistling sound as he exhaled between gritted teeth.

The women and mule came walking back down to the corral. Boxer Gedding limped behind them. His hair was pulled back into a ponytail. His beard had a three-day growth and his face looked like he'd been using it to soften fists.

Boxer tugged the mule's reins, and they slipped from Samantha Jarmin's fingers. "I'll hitch your ride to the gate. Good brand." He rubbed his hand over the Flying Bell. "How is it you gals have this fine animal and are travelin' before daylight? Kinda suspicious. You steal it?" He threw a slipknot around the log.

"Oh, no, no," Samantha said. "I borrowed it. There's quite a few of us—and men, too. Melane and I were first out of camp this morning. Riding point—that sort of thing. Everyone will be coming along soon. We should be on our way."

"Have a sit. We'll get'cha fixed up." Boxer waved toward the webbed aluminum folding chairs near the fire. "Does it hurt?"

"Like crazy. I washed it in a stream, but—"

Samantha's gasp cut her off.

"What's the matter?" the young woman looked at her.

"Nothing." Samantha gave a quick headshake, pulling her stare away from her horses, standing behind the cattle. She took Melane's arm and stepped past Boxer Gedding. "But we're late. We really need to push on."

"That's not very hospitable." Boxer grabbed Samantha's wrist, bending it backward. "I'm not a violent man unless forced." She grimaced, jerking to a stop. He looked at Melane. "You wanna force me?"

"Let her go. If we're not back, they'll come looking for us," Melane said.

"I'd love to let you go, honey, but women can't keep their damn mouths shut. Are you the gals on that Trek trip I see advertised ever'where?" Samantha turned from his sour breath. Boxer bent her wrist farther. "Are ya?"

"Yes!" she shrieked, close to tears.

"Hikin' to find yourselves, huh? That's what's nice about the outdoors. But I doubt if you gals can find your asses even if you used both hands. 'Course, I could help." He cupped Samantha's butt and gave it a hard squeeze.

"Stop it! We found you, you piece of shit," Melane yelled.

Her jaw popped and her head swung sideways as he hit her across her face. Samantha shrieked.

"Shut up!" Boxer twisted her wrist again.

"Pa!" Gil yelled. "Leave 'em alone. We'll be outta here soon."

"Bring the rope." Boxer leaned close to Samantha. She pulled back, then stopped, giving him a hard stare. "There's only one person comin' after you lyin' little bitches. Belle Chere would never lend out her mule unless she went with him. Thanks for the warnin', ladies." He turned to his son. "You crawl to the top. Call that truck and tell him to get here as soon as he can. We ain't waitin' till midnight."

"What do you need this for?" Gil held up the rope.

"Hog tie 'em. Tight." He picked up his whip. "I'll be up on the trail with a surprise for Belle Chere."

28

A Horse Is Worth More Than Riches
~Spanish Proverb

"HEY!" BELLE STUCK her head inside Josie's tent. "My mule's missing. Where's Tinkerdink?"

Josie pushed to her elbows, wearing a bleary look. "Restroom?"

"According to Kick, Munk-girl is gone, too." Belle zipped the flap open all the way, allowing the morning breeze to swirl inside.

Josie flopped flat, burying her face in her sleeping bag as she gave a loud groan.

Belle poked her shoulder. "Get dressed."

In a few minutes, Josie stepped out of the tent, interrupting Belle and Kick's fireside chat. "Why aren't you out tracking them?"

Belle stood with one foot on the log, one hand on her hip, the other hand holding a mug. "Do you want all of us runnin' in circles, wavin' our arms, and screamin' their names? Get your coffee, sit down, and listen to what we've figured out."

"They wouldn't be who-knows-where if you hadn't insisted they fight it out last night." Josie glared and dropped onto the log, her feet together, her hands on her knees. "This is your fault. You should be finding them."

Belle stared as though inspecting Josie for leaky brains. "You think *now* is the time to assign blame? But we can switch subjects and talk about that if you want."

Josie shook her head, staring into the fire.

"Melane's pack is missing, but Samantha's isn't," Kick said. "I remember hearing Melane get up and go to the woods. I don't know what time it was, but still dark. I slept hard after that, probably because she'd left. She tosses and turns a lot."

"Samantha knew how to handle Winston," Belle said. "And because her pack is still here, we can assume she took the mule and planned on coming back. She probably went after Melane—"

"But where? Can't you do your hoof-print thing? You find cougar tracks and other clues."

"About that." Belle scraped her boot on the edge of the log as she chose her next words. "It wasn't a cougar. It was a dead doe, shot for no reason. I didn't want to scare everybody last night, but there may be an ... asshole travelin' around here."

"Good grief! As in the human kind?" Josie flung her arms up. "You didn't think that was important to mention last night?"

"You sure like to blame instead of solve problems," Belle said.

Josie started to speak, but Kick interrupted, "So what do we do now?"

"Good question." Belle lifted her cup, saluting her. "Kick, you hike north toward the trailhead. I'll mark a map. Stay on the trail. If Jiggs had to detour around downed trees, he should be bringing our supplies the way I've marked. When you meet up, he can tell you if he passed the women on their way out."

"Josie," Belle turned to her, "you'll go southwest to the lakes. You announced we'd be hikin' there today. Maybe Melane headed out early."

"And what're you doing?"

"I'm back-tracking, looking for Winston's hoofprints, though from what I've seen already, that little shower last night pocked them out."

"What about this guy in the area? Is he your arsonist? Are we safe?" Kick squeezed her coffee mug between both palms.

"I don't know. If he's the one who tried to kill the doe I found, then he can't shoot worth a damn. If you two wanna travel together, that's fine. It'll take twice as long to check these areas, though."

Kick pulled out her phone. "I'm calling someone." She frowned, holding it up. "No service."

"You still don't get it," Belle said. "Out here, *we are* the someones." She tossed the rest of her coffee on the fire. It hissed and smoked as she walked away, calling, "Rise to the situation. Push through, girls."

Belle scanned the cliff face with her binoculars. She'd been walking twenty minutes to get to this valley where the face of the mountain had fallen. Even with field glasses, the ledge trail on top couldn't be seen. But from that path, a person could watch up and down the valley. It also led to a small canyon with a natural corral. Del hadn't liked to use it. "Tight-feeling," he'd said. The boulders and cliff towered over them from all sides. He'd felt like a mouse in a box.

She was thankful for Melane and Samantha's drama. It kept everyone out of her business. But she needed her mule to avoid a lot of useless walking. Belle turned and headed back. Jiggs would be there soon, and he was bringing her solution.

At camp, she had breakfast and another cup of coffee. Josie and Kick had dropped everything and left. Belle busied herself, building up the fire. They'd be chilled when they finally wandered in. She broke down the tents so they'd be ready to go.

Within an hour, Jiggs and Kick hailed the camp—both were walking, leading Jiggs' horse, Curly Dogs. Marly trailed last in the line, her sides bulging with bags.

"Mabel." Jiggs gave a nod. "Kick told me what happened. The ladies didn't go for the trailhead. Even if they'd stepped off the path to avoid being seen, the mules would've called to each other."

"Okay. That eliminates that option. Did the twister cause you problems?" Belle poured mugs of coffee for Jiggs and Kick and listened to the detours of his trip.

"I'm starved," Kick said.

"That's right!" Belle sounded as though she'd made a scientific discovery. "You rushed out of here without food. Sit. Eat." She pushed Kick's shoulder, forcing her to take a seat on the log.

Jiggs frowned. "Why are you being so ... caring?"

"I'm not with you. Just with Kick. *You* go get Josie. She should be coming back from the lake by now. She needs your help to make a plan. The poor woman is beside herself. She won't listen to me."

"I wouldn't either." Jiggs gave her a sharp look then drained the last of his coffee.

"We'll take care of the animals. Marly's easier to unload when she's got a buddy."

"That mule has a mean streak. I've had to give her several lessons about biting. I bet if you tried to ride her, she'd jump off a cliff just for spite."

"I'm so sorry, and thank you, Tool. She can be a rascal. We'll wait here in case Melane and Samantha wander back. I'm guessing they're around here, talking things out." Belle pointed. "Josie is just over the hill."

"I *know* the way to the lake." Jiggs gave her a funny look as he walked away.

Belle watched until he disappeared down the path. She hurried to Curly Dogs and checked his feet and shoes. Untying the rope, she shoved the mule's lead into Kick's hands. "Unload and water this animal."

"What about breakfast? What're you doing?"

"I came out here for one reason. Unfortunately, it got side-tracked. I'm leaving now to finish it."

"What about Melane and Samatha? Is your search for your arsonist more important than them?"

Belle unbuckled the case beside the saddle. "It's what I came to do. I don't expect you to understand. If I don't see you again, tell Jiggs he's going to need this." She pulled a long leather case free from the straps and shoved it into Kick's hands. The stock of Jiggs' scoped .30-06 stuck out the top "Tell him to look on the ridge of Blank Wall."

"Wait! What are you saying—" Kick grabbed at the reins as Belle kneed the horse and rode away.

Jiggs had gone a half mile when he heard footsteps pounding the trail behind him and his name floating through the air. Birds fluttered off of limbs as Kick ran up the path, gasping, "Miz Belle took your horse!"

"Why?" he yelled.

"She said she had something to do." Kick stopped next to him, panting. "She's ... been looking for someone ... every day."

"Craphouse crickets! I *knew* she was being nice for a reason. You get Josie. I've gotta get back to camp." Jiggs broke into a trot. He didn't get far before he had to stop, breathing hard in the 3,000 foot elevation. After a few minutes, he took off again at a slower pace.

When Kick and Josie reached camp, they found the carefully packed boxes that had been on the mule were thrown in a pile. Marly was drinking from the creek.

"What can I do to help?" Kick asked.

"Just stay here." Jiggs was tying a rope to both sides of the halter to make reins. "That's the problem with search and rescue. You send out rescuers, then you have to search for the rescuers. You're the base camp."

"I could hike around. Try to get a cell phone signal."

"And tell them what? That two women walked into the wilderness to compare notes about a jerk? One old lady stole my horse and rode off to possibly find more jackasses? What are they supposed to do, except bring cameras and film the whole thing for TV?" Jiggs led Marly to a stump, stepped up, and climbed onto her back. The mule sidestepped, her ears lying along her head.

"You are *not* going anywhere without us." Josie planted her hands on her hips. "This is my Trek. Kick and I aren't going to sit around and 'hold down the fort.'"

"Then try to keep up."

"Miz Belle said if you came after her, you'd need your rifle." Kick called over the *Whoa's* Jiggs yelled at the side-stepping mule.

"Her threats don't scare me." He twisted one of the mule's ears.

"I don't think she was trying to bully you. She seemed sad when she said it."

"Okay." Jiggs glanced at his .30-06 leaning against a tent as Marly stilled for a moment. "Get the gun, Josie. I'm not gettin' off this mule unless she throws me."

Kick slid her arms into the shoulder straps of her pack and checked the level of her water bottle. "She said she was going to Blank Wall."

Jiggs let go of the ear. The mule didn't move. He patted her neck. "Where's that?"

"She makes up names for places. None of this," Kick waved her arm, "has been on a real map so far. Are you going after Miz Belle or are you finding our ladies?"

Jiggs kicked the mule's flanks. Marly jumped forward. "I'm going after my horse."

29

I Wasn't Finished Talking Yet

CURLY DOGS DIDN'T want to turn onto the steep game trail climbing up to the ridge. Belle checked her surroundings. It was always a warning if a horse didn't want to go somewhere. She got off, scanning the firs and rabbit brush. She waited as though she were hunting for deer, her hand on her Smith and Wesson, unmoving, barely breathing. Eventually the deer would decide everything was all right and amble on. In this case, it was Curly Dogs. He took a step to nip the trailside grass. A squirrel cursed him for several seconds before disappearing behind a tree.

Belle's shoulders relaxed. She bent to inspect the ground. If Samantha had given Winston his head, allowing him to lead, he'd veer around the boulder as big as a car. He'd been here before. Belle thought for a moment, then pulled the pink flagging tape she'd yanked off a bush out of her pocket. She tied it to the tip of a branch so it dangled over the trail. If she didn't come back, this would help them know where to look.

Behind the granite boulder, the rough game trail cut straight up the slope. Back in the fall when she'd taken the mules riding to toughen their hooves and work on balance, this trail had been partially hidden by brush. It was still overgrown, but more defined. Someone had been using it.

Under the canopy of firs, she found one of Winston's prints in the soft dirt. Damn. She'd hoped the women had gone on any path except the one she was on.

She mounted and kneed Curly Dogs. He threw his head once, then obliged and climbed the hillside, topping out on a curved ledge running parallel to the valley. In the north, the tail-end of the rain shower worked its way across the sky, tinting the space beneath the clouds lavender. To the south, the peaks diminished until they faded into brown flatland.

Curly Dogs wasn't as sure-footed as she'd hoped. Jiggs should have had him out more. The three-foot wide trail had a narrow margin before dropping into nothingness. In a few spots, trees on lower ledges might break the horse's roll if he went over the edge. In other places, he'd learn to fly, at least for a second or two.

She let Curly Dogs take his time and pick his footing, re-minding herself it did no good to hurry a worried horse. Her eyes focused ahead where the ledge widened to ten feet. She'd sat there many times in her wild youth, watching the world go by.

She'd hoped the women would be there. That's where she'd be if she were keeping watch. The spot was empty except for rocks and a couple of trees growing out of the base of the cliff, their trunks curving upward in a "J."

Belle got off, keeping herself between the horse and the ledge. She examined the dirt, looking for scuffs. Curly Dogs fidgeted, his ears twitching as he stamped one foot then the other. "You're okay. I'm between you and danger. You're not used to bein' this high, are you?" She pulled out her binoculars and leaned against him, both for warmth and to give him comfort. Below her in the valley, there was no sign of Melane or Samantha. A rock skittered down the slant-face wall above her. The horse jerked. "Whoa, whoa." She patted his neck, peering up under his head. Nothing moved on the cliff face. She scanned for a long moment, looking for elk or bighorn sheep. Nothing.

Her stomach had been talking to her for the last hour. She pulled a hank of jerky out of her saddle bag and leaned against Curly Dogs, peering through the binoculars once more.

Three feet from her head, the air sliced open with a loud *pop*. A man yelled, "Hell-o Belle Chere!"

Curly Dogs crow-hopped backward. She pulled the reins, keeping him from the edge.

"Goosey horse ya got there," Boxer Gedding shouted, limping toward her from behind a tree, waving his hands and whip above his head.

"Stop it, you sonuvabitch!" She hung on as Curly Dogs sidestepped one way, then the other.

The man dropped the whip and grabbed one side of the halter, helping control the horse. "It's a privilege to finally meet you. I'm Boxer Gedding." He grunted each time Curly Dogs threw his head up.

"I've got him. Get away." Belle kept both hands on the horse, skewering Boxer with her elbow.

Boxer held on. "Damn! I'd hate to see good horseflesh go over the side. You're tougher than boiled owl, just like my daddy said."

Belle's voice quieted in an attempt to calm the horse, but it was still scorched with loathing. "Who gives a shit what you or your relatives say?"

"You got him now?" Boxer asked.

"Back off."

He held up his hands as though he were surrendering, took two steps back, and picked up his whip. "My pa said you were wild and hot to trot." He gave a shabby laugh. "Guess you got old, huh?"

Belle ran her hand over Curly Dogs' muzzle, talking softly to the horse. "What sorry stock do you think he comes from?"

"Why, I'm Del Harkin's boy. All grown up and moved back. You ain't heard of me? Cuz my pa used to speak pretty fondly of you."

She squinted at him. Indeed, there were traces of Del around the eyes, but that was all. "I didn't even know he had a kid. Your name's wrong."

"Well ... 'round here people judge you by your name. So I picked a different one."

Holding onto the horse's head with both hands, Belle studied the hardness etched on the man's face. If he spoke the truth then, but for the grace of God, he could have been her son. She shook her head. What had she ever seen in Del?

"We lived down south, but when Pa needed to hide out, he and me stayed in these hills. Pa's no longer with us, maybe you heard?" Belle stared at him. "No? Guess you didn't keep up. We had a little hiccup in a cooking accident. The feds visited a kitchen he had down south and *Boom*. He decided to take a few with him as he jumped into his grave. He always was generous thataway."

"How about you followin' him quick-like?" Belle said. "I know you burned my house and barn. Why're you here?"

"Damn, woman! You shot me. What'd you expect? And I didn't mean for your cabin to go up in smoke. That was bad luck. I'm just sayin'. I'll be out of your life in a coupla hours. You leave this horse and walk back down that trail."

"You think that's gonna happen?" Belle fussed with the reins, inching behind Curly Dogs as she slowly pushed her coat back behind her holster.

"I do, 'cause I got a couple of your city girls. I'm takin' that little blonde with me to make sure you don't follow. She might have to travel in the back of the cattle truck, but she'll go."

"Why would that make me head down the trail?" Belle rubbed the horse, her right hand inching lower, toward her gun, with each stroke. "You're stupider than a big sack of shit."

Boxer lunged, swinging at her face. Curly Dogs stutter-stepped and kicked. His dance knocked Belle to the drop-off. She tottered on the edge, rocks and dirt breaking into pieces. Her body swayed backward. Curly Dogs' neck stretched forward, his legs braced, his head low, anchoring her as she hung onto the reins.

With a grin, Boxer neared the horse and gave it a flat-handed smack. It stumbled as it tried to kick.

The edge crumpled. Belle threw the reins, slamming them into the horse's face, yelling "Git!" as she dropped from sight. Curly Dogs skittered sideways, hitting the cliff wall.

Boxer grabbed for the halter. The horse landed a hoof against his bad leg, knocking him over. With another kick Curly Dogs dashed past him, up the trail, and stopped after twenty feet—as he'd been trained, his reins dangling on the ground.

Boxer Gedding lay on his back, cussing and holding his leg. After a few moments, he rolled to his stomach and inched to the drop-off, peeking over the side. Sixteen feet below, Belle lay on a ledge. "Shit. You just won't leave me alone, will you?" He watched her. "Hey! You dead?" Only the wind answered. He cleared his throat and spit. "I wasn't finished talkin' to you."

Slowly, he pushed to his feet and picked his whip out of the dirt. Limping to the edge, he raised his arm, but felt the dirt shift under his feet and stumbled backward. "Well, damn!" With a grunt he got on his belly again. He peeked over the edge, carefully taking aim for her head. The air popped in front of her. He lashed several more times, scooching his body farther out to get a better angle. Pebbles and dirt began to drop beneath him. He quickly wormed back. Even hanging his arm over the side, he could only blindly lash the air. "Shit! I shoulda brought a gun and just shot you. I never thought you'd be this tough to knock off." He threw a rock, bouncing it off her body. He winged a couple more, studying her. She didn't move. Maybe it was better this way. Wasn't the gover'ment always saying, "Leave no trace?" No bullets. No marks. It'd look like the old broad had stumbled over the edge—if she was ever found.

Heaving himself to his feet, he looked at the horse with its ears laid back, ready to kick him again. "Why don't you just run?" Letting the frayed popper-tip drop onto the rocks, he worked a firm grip on the whip's corded handle. With one winging motion, the air snapped. A pink line of flesh split open across Curly Dogs' hind quarter. The horse bucked, then dashed up the trail. Boxer smiled as he coiled his bullwhip. "Rest in hell, Belle Chere. Thanks for the livestock." He kicked dirt and pebbles over the side, and limped up the trail.

30

Got Mules?

BELLE AWAKENED WITH her face in rocks and dirt. She tried to roll over, but found her feet sticking off a ledge. She froze. Slowly she moved her head, discovering a channel of dirt and rocks above her had disintegrated, pouring onto the ledge, pushing her along with it. An inch at a time, she worked her body off of the slide onto the rock ledge. Running her hands over her arms and legs, she checked herself like she would a horse. No broken bones. The back of her hands were bleeding. Her watch had scraped off as she'd fallen.

Gently, her dirty fingertips explored the lump over her right eye. Had the horse gone over with her? She tried to remember. The ledge could only hold half a horse—and he wasn't here. Slowly sitting up and snugging her back to the wall, she leaned slightly sideways to peek below. No Curly Dogs. But he could've busted through the tree canopy and lay down there in pieces. Jiggs was gonna kill her. First his dog, now his horse. She might as well jump and get it over with.

The thought resonated in her. She stared at the edge. A quick roll to the left. An irreversible decision. It would be done. No worrying about who would take care of her in her final years. Whether she'd outlive her money or usefulness. No need to keep proving her toughness. No—

A sharp whistle cut the air.

She scratched at her jacket, trying to open it. Flakes of bloody dirt cracked from her abraded wrists. Her fingers were stiff, but they worked. She pulled her gun from the holster and pointed. If that sack of shit stuck his head over the rim, he'd need a new skull. She waited.

After a minute, she had to hold her wrist, supporting her Smith & Wesson. Breaks in the clouds showed a blue sky. The sun looked like it had only moved an hour to the west. Something moved above her. A face disappeared.

"Hoooo! Mabel, it's me!"

"Who's 'me'? I didn't get a good look at you."

"Who else calls you Mabel?"

"Was that you who whistled?"

"Curly Dogs comes when I blow."

Belle glanced at the trees below. "Good luck with that."

"Is she okay?" Josie's voice floated over the ledge.

"Get back!" Jiggs yelled. "Both of you stay away from the edge. Rig up a rope." His voice grew louder as he called down, "Don't shoot, Mabel." Still lying on his belly, he peeked over the side again. "You okay?"

"Time of my life. What the hell do you think?"

"Where's my horse?"

She thought about telling him, *In God's corral by now*, but instead called out, "That arsonist knocked me off, and I don't know what happened after that." She holstered her gun. "How'd you know I was down here?"

"Scuffed rocks. Broken edge. Looks like a dance party up here." A rope dropped over the side. "Can you reach it."

"No." The end hung six feet above her.

"Can you stand?"

"Leave me. I'm woozy." She rubbed her head. "I don't have anything I need to live for anymore. It's your turn to fight the assholes of this world. I've done my duty."

"Suck it up, Mabel. Get on your feet."

"Push through, Miz Belle! C'mon." Kick's voice drifted over the side.

Slowly, she stood, her fingers running up the dirt wall for support. A rock broke free in her grasp, making her wobble. "I've lost my house. Everything I cared about—"

"Step on that boulder." Jiggs pointed, but Belle just stared. "If you don't put your foot there, I'll come down and push you off. Quit feeling sorry for yourself. Now put your hand up and grab the rope."

Belle stepped on top of the boulder and lifted an arm, pushing on her elbow to get it higher. "That's as far as it goes. I fell out of a tree and hurt it."

"What's an old lady doing up in a tree?"

"Hell, what am I doing on a ledge?" She reached. "And who-in-the-world carries such a short, piece-of-crap rope?"

"It's all I brought. You wanna wait while I go back to camp and get the longer one?"

"Great rescue, Tool."

"What do you care? A minute ago you wanted to die."

"I changed my mind. I wanna go like your dad, on his horse."

"Keep riding Marly. That mule will kill you. Tell me. What'd you think you were gonna do out here?"

"Right a wrong. The fella who burned my house has cattle in a canyon back in here—along with two gals from our group."

"I've been all over this area. I don't know of any hidden canyons."

"Well, there is, Mr. Know-it-All. Your father never doubted anything I told him. He would've said, 'Show me where it is, Belle.' Ox always treated me like I had a brain."

The rope flounced lower, hitting Belle. "Okay," Jiggs said, "you're tied to the mule instead of the tree. If she takes off like a rocket, don't blame me, you trained her."

Belle put her foot in the loop. Gripping it tightly, she gave it a signal-tug. With a jerk, she moved upward, then back down. Up and down, several times, inching toward the top. Belle rolled her eyes and looked to the heavens. "Really, Lord? I decide there may be a slight reason to live, and You send bozos to rescue me?"

When she finally was dragged over the edge, she could see Kick and Josie yanking on the stationary mule as Jiggs pulled the rope.

"I hate this animal." Josie hurried to help Belle stand, her face registering shock.

"Well, Marly knows you don't like her." Belle looked as though she'd been dragged through a gopher tunnel, her front and backside smeared with dirt, her hands coated with a paste of dirt and blood. Her gray hair frizzed around her face with a purple bruise blooming beside a lump over her eye.

"Kick!" Josie called. "Bring your first aid bag." She poured water onto her bandana and laid the cool, wet cloth over the lump on Belle's head.

"I found your cover on the trail." Kick held out a hat. "Let me look at you."

"I'm fine. I checked myself." Belle took her hat and pushed Kick's hands away. "Munk-girl and Tinkerdink are at the end of this trail, along with the jackass who burned my place."

"Just one guy?" Jiggs coiled the rope.

"All I saw. But thievin' usually requires two or more. Says he's Boxer Gedding. I hadn't met him, 'cept for the time I put birdshot in his backside."

"A Gedding kid works at the feed store, but I thought his dad had disappeared long ago."

"He said they were loadin' cattle real soon. They may be gone by now. They're taking Munk-girl with them."

Kick pulled out her phone and turned it on. "I don't care what any of you say, I'm hiking until I pick up a cell signal, and I'm calling the sheriff."

Belle walked up the trail, the lines of her face deep. "Go with Kick," she said as she passed Josie.

"No." Josie's voice came out like a bark. "Melane left, so Samantha went after her as back up. You, Jiggs, and I are their support, and Kick is our last defense. You once pushed me into a tree telling me to take responsibility. We're sending Kick away from danger. You're walking into it. I'm staying with you."

Belle flourished a hand at Kick. "Go. Try to call someone, but use your brain. Don't stray off."

The young woman ran back down the trail. Belle pointed at Josie. "Take Marly ..."

"No. I'm not escorting that vampire mule anywhere. She nips. And she refuses to budge. Tie her up here."

"If she's alone too long, she'll bray, and it'll echo into the canyon. If that worthless sack of flesh, Boxer Gedding, is still there, he'll know someone is around. Right now, surprise is all we've got goin' for us. You're wastin' our time." Belle hurried up the ridgeline path. Jiggs was right behind her, his stride long and fast, the Winchester crooked in his arm.

"Well, I'm going." Josie declared to the mule and took off.

Marly watched them leave, her ears flicking forward and back. She looked around, then clopped up the hill, following Josie.

"Listen to me ... the most important thing in your life is not to kick a rock down that hillside." Belle had stopped the group just before the path made a dogleg and descended into the canyon. "As soon as we make the turn up here, any stone you move will bounce through the trees into their corral. Don't make any noise until we know where they are."

"And if they're there ... *don't* go in blastin', Mabel," Jiggs pulled the rifle from the case. "We need to figure out how many of them there are and where they're holding Mrs. Jarmin and the other gal. I'll climb down and circle to the other side. Wait for my signal."

"That won't be easy. The boulders around the corral are six to seven feet high."

"I'll figure it out. Stay on the north side and keep watch. Don't go killin' anything. A pistol would be easier for me to carry. Trade?" He held out the Winchester.

"Be aware, Boxer has a bullwhip." She pulled off her holster and belt and gave him her K-38. "Listen, Tool, the Smith and Wesson has a hair trigger. Don't shove it in your pants and ... shoot yourself."

"I'll try, Mabel, because I can't wait to get back here and deal with you for stealing my horse." He turned and picked his way downhill.

"Push through," she murmured, watching him disappear from view.

"What should I do?" Josie elbowed Marly's muzzle away from her.

"Stay here with the mule." Belle clicked off the gun's safety and shoved the bolt forward and back, loading a shell into the chamber. "And no matter what you do!" she threatened. "No noise. Got it?"

31

The Day We Fear As Our Last, Is the Birthday of Eternity

~Seneca

"I WASN'T GOING to stay behind," Josie whispered as she stepped behind a fir, scanning the lot below. "Will Marly be quiet? I staked her back there."

"Doesn't anybody follow orders?" Belle peered through the scope, moving the rifle slowly, trying view the corral between the boulders and trees studding the hillside like a slatted fence. "Check on her every fifteen minutes. If she's not alone too long, she'll be quiet."

"Well, the cattle are still here. Geez. It stinks down there."

"Too many cows in too little space. Can you see Boxer?" Belle whispered.

"No. I think I glimpsed Melane and Samantha sitting in the dirt, but just for a moment, then the cattle moved in the way. See the feed bucket? Look over the top of the cows' heads. The bucket is sitting on top of a big post. Our ladies are tied to that post."

"Well, that's dandy." Belle's face clouded. "That snubbin' pole is for breaking broncs, and it sits smack in the middle. We can't get to them very easily."

To the west, a rock rolled down the embankment. Eyes wide, both women listened to it *thump-thump-thump* down the hill. It ricocheted off of several trees, but kept rolling, dropping into the lot with a soft *thwop*.

Belle let out the breath she was holding. "You see anybody? Any movement down there?"

"No. A few cows at that end of the lot shifted. What caused—"

"Boxer may have gotten behind us. Stay here. Keep watch." Belle stepped out of the trees onto the trail, her rifle to her cheek, aiming up the canyon path.

Kick strolled toward her, leading Marly. As soon as she saw Belle aiming a gun at her, she skidded to a stop, sending two more rocks drumming down the hillside. Belle lowered the .30-06 and held up a fist. Kick held still, hands clenched to her sides.

When Belle reached her, the young woman's eyes were round with the whites showing. "Sorry I scared you," Belle whispered. "Thought you were Boxer. What're you doin' here?"

"I climbed up, instead of jogging toward the trailhead. There's cell reception on top. I left a message for the sheriff and hurried back to where I left all of you. And when I saw Marly, I ..."

"Okay, okay." Belle patted her shoulder. "Go about six feet off the trail and tie the mule to a tree."

"What's happening?" Kick nodded toward the gun.

"We're still reconnoitering."

"Someone else has been on top of the ridge, probably making calls. There were brown cigarillo butts all around." She handed Belle a filtered end.

"Gauchos." The old woman made a face and dropped it in her pocket. "Where'd you tell the sheriff to come? Do you know where you are?"

"I gave them the GPS coordinates on my phone." Kick looped the mule's reins around a tree and pulled them into a jerk knot.

"C'mon," Belle whispered and headed back down the trail. She added, "No noise," but figured it really didn't matter. They'd already rung the doorbell with rocks.

"Anybody moving down there?" Belle murmured as she stopped next to Josie.

"Melane and Samantha are staring at something. That's all I can see. The cattle are stirring." Josie squeezed Kick's arm. "I was worried you'd get lost. That didn't take—"

"I see a man." Kick pointed down toward the lot.

Belle jerked the scope to her eye.

"It's a young man," Kick whispered. "I've seen him at the feed store. Don't shoot anybody. Please?"

"Crap. He's gone." Belle moved the gun, searching for a target.

"Have you ever killed anyone, Miz Belle?" Kick leaned close. "My dad said it was a terrible weight to carry. Think of what you're ending for them."

Belle looked away. As a medic, her dad would've understood. He'd have known about the self-doubts and the what-ifs that pick at your mind. If only you'd been faster, smarter, less tired, or less panicked, then the person in your care might've lived. "Yes." Belle's lips barely moved. "I've killed. None of them deserved it, but this one—"

"I see Jiggs," Josie gasped. "He's bent over, sneaking among the cattle."

"Shit! Not yet. I don't know where Boxer is. I can't cover Jiggs from here." Belle turned and hurried down the trail. Before she made it to the log barring the corral's entrance, a woman screamed. Animals shoved and shouldered each other, moving away from the center. Belle stopped at the make-shift entrance. Resting her hand against a tall slab of granite, she steadied her aim, and sighted through the scope, peering over the ears of the cattle.

The short distance made the figures slightly fuzzy, but she could see Boxer Gedding had Melane bar-armed across the neck, holding her in front of him, and a pistol in his other hand. Jiggs stood nearby, pointing the .38 and yelling for Samantha to find a place to hide. Behind him, Samantha was crawling through the muck.

Boxer yanked Melane closer against his body. "Get your gun on him, Gil. He can't shoot both of us."

A young man, holding a .22, rose from his crouched position on top of a boulder.

"Do you remember me, Woolsey?" Gil called out. "You interrupted a fight. Tried to teach us boys to use our fists. Took away my baseball bat."

"I remember." Jiggs kept his eyes on Boxer.

"You shoot me," Boxer yelled, "you gotta go through this little honey." He jerked his arm, gagging Melane. "Then Gil or me will still put a bullet in you. Drop your gun—"

"Jiggs!" Belle yelled across the lot. "I got the young 'un in my sights." The cattle in front of her milled back and forth, trying to get away from the shouting.

Her crosshairs sat on the middle of Gil's chest. He hadn't been aiming at anything until now. He raised his barrel in her direction, seeking her voice. His face had lost color, his eyes round. She knew that look. She'd seen it on plenty of young men.

Jiggs muttered words she couldn't make out, his voice low and threatening. She had just changed the odds: two on two. Jiggs whistled. Curly Dogs trotted through the cattle toward him; Samantha Jarmin's Tennessee Walkers and Winston followed.

Boxer rolled his eyes, shaking his head. "Is that you, Belle Chere? Damn! You're a pain in the ass." Melane dead-weighted, slouching against him, slipping down on his chest. He yanked her up by the throat.

Footsteps pounded toward Belle. She kept her eye to the scope as someone thumped into the fir a few feet from her. "Do *not* kill that boy," Josie ordered. "Do you think you could last, caged in a prison cell for the rest of your life? Is that how you want to live?"

Belle didn't answer. Her daddy had taught her not to talk when the rifle went up to the cheek. With a slight correction, she moved the crosshairs to Boxer. If the boy took her out, then so be it.

"I thought you was dead, Belle," Boxer yelled. "I was peeved, 'cause I didn't finish our earlier conversation before you rudely dropped off a cliff. You must be pretty gimped up, or you'd be down here in the middle of things, firin' off your gun along with your mouth. You even have a gun? Or did they all burn up?"

She didn't answer. Slowly, she let out her breath, listening to the voice in her head. *Pay attention to your premonitions.* She had the feeling the situation was about to go sideways.

"Does she have a gun, Gil?"

"I see her movin' behind a tree, but I can't see any weapon."

Josie gasped and slid down the tree trunk onto the ground, pulling her arms tight to her sides. She glanced at Belle, standing immobile behind the tall boulder. It was quiet except for the cattle crowding each other, trying to avoid getting close to the men.

Belle focused on her breathing, ignoring Josie crawling toward her to take shelter behind her boulder. This was like deer hunting. Wait for the right moment. Only take the perfect shot.

"Hey! You been to your house lately?" Boxer called. "You might be missing a few cattle." He laughed ... a real chuckle as though it were the funniest thing he'd heard in a long time.

No answer.

He twisted to glance where Belle should be. Melane, heavy in his arms sagged low. He throttled her. "Stand up, dammit!"

and added another curse at his bum leg as he tried to hip lever her higher. A three-inch gap appeared between them. A space between her back and his chest. It grew slightly larger as he swiveled more.

Before Belle had taken her position, she had gauged the wind. As she'd put the rifle to her cheek, she'd estimated the distance. Everything she needed to know had been taken into account. Through her nose, she let out a slow breath and aimed. Slowly, she squeezed the trigger ...

Josie grabbed her arm. "Don't."

The gun jerked hard against her shoulder. The *bang* bounced from boulder to boulder across the corral.

"Shit!" Belle stared.

32

All Hours Wound, The Last One Kills
~Latin phrase

SHE'D CALCULATED EVERYTHING—everything!

With Boxer's twisting, Belle had the nagging premonition her bullet would exit through Melane. So she'd centered the scope's crosshairs on Boxer's gun hand. At that range, it was an easy, clean shot.

With Boxer un-armed, Jiggs would be able to free Munkgirl. The boy on the boulder didn't seem likely to fire, but if he tried, Belle had a clear shot at him. She'd gauged everyone's location and their temperament. She'd taken into account everything.

Except being grabbed by the fool behind her.

The lateral compression of the *BANG*! slammed into Josie, making her grip her ears with a shriek, "Ooow!"

Cows in front of them jumped and ran.

The round hit the feed bucket on the top of the snubbing post, knocking it high. The bullet continued upward, blasting into a tree by the boulders, exploding shards and splinters over Gil's head.

The galvanized bucket arced and turned over. Tumbling downward, it flung cattle cube pellets over the herd before banging the head of an Angus steer. The bucket ricocheted between two Herefords before it clattered to the ground among bug-eyed calves—which bawled and ran from it. The corral moved into a rotating frenzy.

Belle yanked the gun bolt back and slammed it forward, ejecting one casing and loading another. Rifle to shoulder again, she searched for Boxer. Both of Melane's hands gripped the bearded man's gun hand, pushing it away as she stomped on his foot.

A cow and calf clipped Jiggs, spinning him sideways. They continued straight ahead, plowing into Melane and Boxer, knocking them apart. Melane bounced off of another passing cow as she tumbled to the ground. Boxer landed on one knee before he was knocked down again.

Curly Dogs moved next to Jiggs, shielding him from the rushing cattle. Samantha's horses clustered behind them. Jiggs worked his way to Melane, grabbing her by her collar, pulling her through manure and dirt toward the big stones at the edge.

Scanning the tops of the boulders, Belle didn't find the boy. The *bang* of a pistol made her jerk her scope back at the lot. Boxer had fired into one of the Tennessee Walkers. It reared and shrieked, then ran, blood pouring from its neck. Dragging one leg, Boxer stumped forward, shooting his way through livestock to get to Jiggs. A passing steer staggered and went down, sliding to a stop in front of him.

Belle peered through the scope as Boxer wobbled and dodged cattle. He pointed his pistol at Winston.

She pulled the trigger.

The man spun sideways and fell on his back, a red hole blooming in his shoulder. A white-face Angus barreled over him, making his legs jerk and his gun flip out of his hand.

Cattle pounded past. Jiggs grabbed Curly Dogs reins. One of Samantha's horses whinnied and reared. Winston kicked at anything that rushed by. The entire lot had become a circling mass of legs and barrel bodies.

At the other end of the corral one of the cows had found the exit into the slot canyon. The first animal made it out, the next four piled up, trying to wedge into an opening two-cows wide. More animals crowded around the mound.

Jiggs was on the back of Curly Dogs, cutting back and forth, attempting to slow the pace of the remaining cattle.

"Where's Melane and Samantha?" Josie yelled.

Rocks clattered down the embankment, rolling into the lot as Kick ran down the trail, calling, "How can I help?"

Belle held up a hand. "Everybody, stop yelling." She punctuated her orders with a glare. In a few minutes Jiggs had herded the cattle to a slow trot. Then they stopped, looking around as though confused about the silence. A groan floated through the air. Boxer lay near the snubbing post.

"Wait here," Belle said, watching him.

"No." Kick stared at the man's leg angled like an "L."

"Nobody your age should have to deal with somethin' like this."

"Miz Belle, I grew up early a long time ago."

Belle studied the young woman's face and finally gave a nod. "All right. Maybe this'll help you decide if you want to go into medicine or become a librarian instead. I wish the lesson hadn't come this way."

In slow, calm steps through the cattle, they walked to the middle of the lot. Kick knelt beside Boxer, her fingers immediately checking for a pulse. A red line trickled from his mouth; his right eye had begun swelling shut. One arm was twisted over his head. A wheezing sound traveled up his throat from his concave chest. Blood ran from the blown-out hole in his right shoulder. "Come to finish our conversation?" He whispered then coughed blood.

"You're a mean sonuvabitch, but not even *I* would've wished this kind of end for you."

"Where ... my son?"

Belle looked around.

Josie was pulling Melane from the gap between two boulders. Samantha was helping Jiggs limp toward her wounded horse. Belle shook her head. "I don't see him. He's gone."

"They both are." Kick said as she closed the man's eyes.

33

The Space We Call Home

TWILIGHT SHADED THE mountain passes. Sagebrush sparrows trilled their five-note evening songs. Hours had passed while Belle and Jiggs had ridden down the slopes. Now she sat in an ambulance at the trailhead, as the EMT moved his finger back and forth in front of her face. "Tool, a deaf alley cat could follow a plan better than you. Whatever happened to 'circling to the other side' and 'wait for my signal'? Nooooo ... you had to jump right in the middle of things."

Jiggs lay on the opposite side of the ambulance, making *ough* and *ufff* sounds as another med tech prodded his foot. "When rocks started rolling down the hillside, I had to do something. Boxer was headed toward the ladies. Either he'd get to them first, or I would."

"All right. Maybe I'll give you that one for thinking fast." Belle batted the EMTs hand from in front of her. "I know the drill. I don't know what day it is because I've been in the woods too long. I don't know who the president is because I've never given a shit, and I don't care what year it is. It keeps changing. I can tell you it's spring and that jack-a-dope over there thinks he's John Wayne."

"Can't you give her something to knock her out?" Jiggs said.

"Ma'am …" The EMT frowned. "We might need to keep you overnight. According to this man, you've been hit in the head by rocks."

Belle let out a squawking laugh. "You're taking the word of a man who got trampled? Worry more about how he got on a horse with a broken foot."

"It's more like Curly Dogs got under me," Jiggs said. "He's the smartest animal in the county."

Belle fought to keep her face from squinching as the EMT bandaged her abrasions. "You *do* know that Boxer had a pistol pointed at your back, Tool? I was gonna let him shoot you as a public service, but Curly Dogs got in front of you, and then Winston stepped in front of *him*. So actually, my mule saved the smartest horse in the county. And if Curly Dogs is really a genius, you should let him do all the ranchin' and rescuin'. I swear, a person has to have a Ph.D. and a crystal ball to know what you're gonna do next."

"Can't you hush her up?" Jiggs pleaded.

"Sure," the tech nodded. "We won't hear a word from her in a few seconds." Both EMTs stepped outside the ambulance.

"They're probably goin' to see if there's any *real injuries* out there." Belle stared at Jiggs. "Say … I never noticed before, but you look like your dad." She pointed. "It's your nose. Get in many fights?"

"Okay. You still sound like you've been clonked in the head."

"Oh, shut up. Get over being peeved about your dad and me. I wanna make it clear, he *never* betrayed your mother. He and I didn't start seeing each other until after she'd passed. He was always in love with her. Everybody was a distant second. He was the only man in this county worth knowin'."

"Sneakin' afternoon delights like two teenagers." Jiggs shook his head. "And running over my dog, high-tailing it from one of your *social calls* to our house."

"Most mutts chase cars, that one actually bit the tires. I'm sorry he didn't free his teeth from my Firestones before the rubber met the road. I think he was showin' off because you were drivin' in."

"Probably. Dad hated him. I think the only animals he ever really liked were his horse and a demented Holstein."

Belle glared at him. "I gave him that Holstein calf. I thought it would make him laugh. He hated getting older. Pissed him off. He couldn't do what he used to do."

"At the end, everything ticked him off or disappointed him—especially me. I even tried to become a big landowner, save the county from urban development. I thought that would shut him up."

Belle rolled her eyes. "How'd that work out?"

"You know there was no pleasing him. When I finally worked to satisfy myself, not Dad—life got better. Now I'm just an ordinary rancher." He looked at her. "And I still have *your* cow. Nuttier than a candy bar. She dances with butterflies."

"The timing never worked out for Ox and me." Belle let out a long sigh. After several moments she lay down, crossing her hands over her chest, grasping her arms like she was cold and stared at the ceiling.

Jiggs rubbed his elevated leg, studying the purple bruises blooming on his swollen foot. They'd cut his boot off. He'd liked those boots. They were a bit run-over at the heels, but still had wear in them. He glanced over at the old woman. She looked small and frizzled, lost in bandages around her head, hands, and arms. "I'm ... late saying this, but ..." He took a breath and blew it out in a long silent whistle. "I'm sorry I kept you and Dad apart. You might've made each other miserable or happy—who knows—if I hadn't thrown such a fit about you taking Mom's place. I was young and angry and ... well ... later I just stayed mad. I'm sorry."

Belle bit her lip and nodded. "It wasn't your fault. And ... I'm sorry about your dog."

Neither spoke. After a while, they could hear Josie's voice outside, asking, "Are they okay?"

"Good grief," Belle whispered, "what do you see in that woman, Tool? She's as goofy as that cow. Isn't one enough for you?"

"Put a plug in it, Mabel."

Josie stuck her head inside the ambulance door. "Hey, you two. The last riders have brought the rest of us out of the mountains. Everyone's okay ... except ..." Her words faded.

"Boxer Gedding." Belle said and let out a long breath. She propped herself up on an elbow. "Any sign of his son?" Josie shook her head.

"And you, missy ..." Belle's eyes narrowed. "You grabbed my arm as I was—"

"I'm sorry. I'm sorry. It was stupid! But I couldn't let you kill him."

"I wasn't, but you might've made me hit someone else."

"I know! I know. I've been thinking about it. I was trying to keep you out of trouble. I've made some stupid decisions, lately. I'm sorry." Josie shook her head. "This sure wasn't the trip I'd planned."

"What trip is?" Belle gave a humorless laugh, staring at nothing. "For that matter ... you could say the same thing about life." She lay back on the gurney. "This sure isn't the life I'd planned. Maybe we each need a good butt kicking every now and then to get our priorities straight."

"Are you saying that's why all this happened?" Josie gave her a skeptical look.

Belle opened her mouth and paused. She blinked. "I don't know why it happened to you, but for me ... I needed a whack on the head. I'd forgotten we're pack animals. We need one another to drag us back from the edge, back into the pack when we're in danger of falling off—or taking a life." She stared, images rolling through her mind as she gently rubbed the bandages on the back of her hands.

Nap broke the moment of silence as he stuck his head into the ambulance. "You okay, Dad?"

Jiggs lifted his leg a few inches, showing off his foot. "One of the horses stepped on me. Broke something. I'll be gimpy for a while. You'll get to do more chores."

"Oh boy." He gave an unenthusiastic glance at the fat, purpling foot. "Some of the cattle were ours. I'll load 'em and call the vet to stitch up Curly Dogs."

"Take the mules, too. And when you finish, would you come to the hospital and get us? Mabel's going to be staying at Ox's house."

Belle looked at him.

Jiggs shrugged. "She needs to watch Harriet the Holstein for a while—maybe make her laugh. If that's okay with you, son."

"Fine!" Nap flashed his lop-sided grin and winked at the old woman. "You can be like the grandma I never had—if you want."

Belle could think of a few quips, but she couldn't get them out. She pressed her lips tight, her eyes shiny and simply nodded.

Sheriff Meyers stopped by for a quick visit and to ask a few questions, then the ambulance emptied of visitors. In the quiet, Belle and Jiggs listened to the noises outside.

"Good thing we're not shot and bleeding like that horse. They're gonna take all day. Probably stop at the Latte-Da for doughnuts on the way." Belle pulled a blanket from a shelf and covered herself.

The hearse from Archer's Funeral Home had arrived. The quiet drone of Morris Archer's voice drifted through the air as he gave instructions and began his solemn duties.

"I guess I got justice." Belle stared at the stainless steel instruments and surfaces around her. "You know ... in the end, I didn't try to kill him. Just stop him from doing more damage. Either way, it doesn't make my house magically resurrect. I don't feel righteous. I feel shell-shocked. None of it makes sense. You'd think I'd have learned by now ... the world doesn't make sense."

Jiggs gave a single headshake. "*That's* a lesson we get to learn over and over."

Belle's voice cracked when she tried to speak again. She cleared her throat and started over. "I wanna thank you, Jiggs. I know you've stood in your father's shadow all your life, but I want you to know ... you're a good man in your own right. A good rancher."

He stared at the black rubber mat on the floor and gave a single nod.

With a breath of relief Belle added, "Now I can teach you the proper way to ride a mule, Tool."

"Just laugh at the cows, Mabel."

A week later Nap sat in Enterprise, Oregon tapping the steering wheel of the Range Rover, staring at the Veteran's Med Center. As soon as he saw Belle leave the building, he hopped out and opened the passenger door. "You get what you needed, ma'am?"

"Sorry about the wait." She got in the SUV and straightened her red skirt and matching embroidered jacket. Her signature coon tail trailed off the back of her Stetson. "Since we were in town, I thought I'd talk to them about some men that have been on my mind. I'm coming back next week to talk again." As Nap began to speak, she held up a hand. "No questions. Maybe someday. Right now, let's go to my mouthpiece, then get outta town."

"No problem. But I have an errand, too. If I'm not back when you've finished, I'll be there soon." Without looking at her, he held up his hand. "No questions."

Belle sat in the pinewood office of Ezra Holtz, J.D. "Hell's bells, you've had these same chairs for the last forty years. Couldn't you invest in some comfortable ones?"

The attorney reached across the desk and tapped a neon-yellow arrow stuck on the papers. "Sign there, too." Belle leaned forward, one bandaged hand anchoring the documents while she scratched her name on various flagged lines. The chair creaked as the attorney stretched backward, crossing his legs at his ankles, and locking his fingers behind his head. "*My* chair is real soft. 'Course this is the fourth one I've bought since I hung my shingle."

"Proof that you sit on your ass too much. And they only had ten laws when you started practicing. Moses hauled them around on stone tablets. When're you gonna retire, Ezra?"

"Never." He gave her a quick smile. "What would I do?"

"You'd let that young 'un in the next office take over." Belle pushed the stack of papers back to him.

The lawyer straightened the sides of the documents with his fingertips until they formed a perfect rectangle. "I believe you have just made Jiggs Woolsey the largest landowner in the county."

"He'll take care of the property. And after that his son will look after it. It's in good hands."

"I agree. I suppose some day we all have to move on."

"Well hold on, I'm not dead yet. And don't you tell him what I've done. News like that tends to swell a fella's hat band." Belle stood. "Send me your over-priced bill. I'm stayin' at the Woolsey place."

"So you said." The attorney walked around his desk. "Do you have time to go to the cafe?"

"I hate to miss a free meal off of you, but it'll have to be another day. I'm meeting a buncha people at the Bar and Grill in Two Pan." She smiled. "I haven't said that in fifty years." She walked out of the office, peering through the lobby window. "I see my chauffeur is here. I feel like the queen of Sheba."

"Give 'em hell, Belle." Ezra opened the door of the old building.

"I always do." She gave him a wink which felt more like having something stuck in her eye. She silently cursed for being so out of practice.

Nap got out and met her before she crossed the sidewalk. "Miz Belle, I haven't been exactly honest. I had a reason I wanted to drive you."

"Yeah?" She put her hands on her hips, squinting up at his six-foot frame. "Is this gonna tick me off? 'Cause I don't wanna be prickly today."

"Well, I had something I needed to pick up , and ... well, get in I'll show you."

She eyeballed him as he opened the door for her. At the rear of the vehicle, he pulled something from the back compartment. A soft *rrrrrrrek, rrrrrrrrek* sounded through the cab. When he got in, he gently placed a raccoon on her lap. Pink crusty scabs covered its left hip and leg. "I just got him from the vet."

"Spanky?" The old woman's stared. She gently stroked the coon's bandit cheeks, examining the shaved fur and wounds.

"On the day of the fire, I saw him run out, but couldn't catch him. I didn't tell you. I didn't want you worrying about him. I've been searching and finally found him wandering around the ruins of your place, covered in mud. He's been living at that little swampy pond south of your house. The vet says the mud is what saved him. The hair's not gonna grow back, and he doesn't have a tail. Do you still want him?"

"Oh … my …" Belle held the animal up and nuzzled her face in his belly fur as he chirred. "I want him." She placed her palm on Nap's cheek. "Thank you," was all she could get out.

Nap nodded and swallowed. "You can pet him while I drive." He handed her a bag of coon treats the vet had given him.

When they pulled into Two Pan, Kick and Josie waited on the bench in front of the Bar and Grill. Jiggs stood next to them, crutches wedged under his arms, his left foot in an over-the-heel cast.

The old woman wiped her cheeks. "Do I look okay? I don't wanna appear like I've been bawlin'."

Nap took the raccoon and smiled. "You are—and always will—look like Miz Belle Chere." She patted his hand, and stepped from the Rover.

Samantha and Melane were hurrying from the empty store where the Two Pan photos were displayed. Melane squealed as she ducked away from Millie Capper spritzing the two women with glass cleaner.

"Ignore her. Come over here." Josie beckoned.

When everyone, including Nap had gathered around, Josie smiled, holding up her hand like a teacher waving for attention. "I have announcements. First of all, because of Kick's inspiring dedication and help on this trip, I want to officially name her as the recipient of the Roggs Student Loan." The women clapped. Kick grinned, her palms together, giving little bows.

"Melane, Samantha …" Josie turned to them. "I'm refunding your money. Instead of a Trek of Self-discovery, it became a march to the seventh circle of hell."

"No. No." Melane fanned her offer away. "You had outlays for food and supplies. Keep the fee. Where else would I have learned a hundred and twenty-two uses for duct tape, how to gut a fish, start a fire, and carve my very own *stoon*?"

Samantha nodded. "I agree. I never dreamed I'd boulder hop up a mountain or find out that crawling through manure won't kill me. And while I learned something from all of you, I'm most happy about meeting two inspiring young women, one of them my step-daughter." Samantha slipped an arm around Melane. "Being tied together, surrounded by thieves and crazy cows, forced us to work out a lot of issues. I'd say the trip worked. We went out looking for ourselves and came back as different people."

There was applause then hugs. "And I've got news." Belle announced. "Everybody. Come see Spanky. Nap here is my hero."

As they moved to the SUV, Samantha placed a hand on Jiggs' arm. "Wait. Can I have a private word with you?"

He nodded. The voices faded as the others moved to the Range Rover. Samantha looked at Jiggs then at the cracked sidewalk. "I want to thank you and apologize."

"For ...?"

"Now that I've been here a while, I realize I haven't always been the best neighbor. There's a culture here. A way of doing things ... and ... I'm sorry Richard and I didn't honor that."

"Eventually, we'll work out our differences, I suppose."

"Uh ... well ..." The corner of her mouth bunched as she squinted. "Maybe not. You know about Melane being Richard's daughter, and he ignored her until he needed to use her?" Jiggs nodded. "Well, she and I are discussing opening a realty firm together in Seattle."

One of Jiggs' eyebrows rose. "And what's Dr. Jarmin say about that?"

"I don't know that he has any say in it. He and I are talking—barely. It's complicated. I don't know what's going to happen, but I have a long way to go to respect him again. I thought you should know ... our ranch—the land you wanted before we came into it—may become available in a property settlement soon."

"I'm sorry to hear of your troubles, ma'am. I don't wish you any grief."

"I'm telling you because I'm truly grateful you risked your life to rescue us. I'd be happy to pick up your medical bills."

Jiggs shook his head. "I'm sorry I couldn't save your horse."

"You tried. And you stopped him from suffering more." Samantha looked around. "People here are ..."

"Connected?" Jiggs offered.

"I was going to say 'stubborn'." Her gaze finally landed with a smile on the ladies. Nap was stowing the coon in its carrier. The women petted Hermes the donkey as he wandered past. "But yes, you're 'connected' in a better way than we are in the city."

"I'm not sure what to say, except I hope it all works out for you."

Samantha gave him a smile and squeezed his shoulder. "Mr. Woolsey, we survivors of the Ladies Trek say ...'Push—'"

"Oh, good grief." Belle interrupted as she walked up. "If you're starting to quote me, then we've dilly-dallied long enough. Let's eat."

"Miz Belle?" the rancher offered his arm.

"Jiggs." She gave him a smile and took his elbow. The group moved down the boardwalk, Jiggs crutching slowly, Belle advising how to do it better. Nap and four women sauntered after them. Hermes the donkey followed, only because he thought one of them would give him a treat.

Behind them, Spooner Hunter taped a photo in the window.

34

For One Brief Moment

A MONTH FROM now, Walter Winn will have his picture taken. He's never been one to jump into the latest hoopla. The only reason he's agreeing to a photo is because Spooner Hunter, the director for Project Two Pan, will promise him a cup of coffee and a hunk of Lottie Lubach's Pecan Carmel Pie if he'll pose.

Walter's photo will make the collection complete. For one brief moment, all 165 residents will have been captured. Their pictures will be taken down, and they'll live in a cardboard box. In ten years, they'll be displayed in the window again—if the box doesn't get lost. Or if someone remembers: "Hey, whatever happened to that artsy project—how long ago was it?" Or if Spooner Hunter is still around. Things change.

Residents here don't much care for change. They feel safe living in a place where they can tell time based on who's in town, or know the seasons by coyote pups' first attempts to join the night choir. If a couple of residents have the same first names, they're at ease with being distinguished as Little Mae and Big Mae or Rooster Joe and Bull Joe—even after one of the duo dies or moves. Sometimes they'll carry a nickname for so long, the original reason for the moniker has been forgotten.

Ten years from now, when the photos are pasted back in the storefront, they'll show change. People won't be able to deny it. Older, thinner, divorced, elastic-waist pants instead of denim. Glasses instead of contacts. A few kids will have kids of their own. Off to the side, there will be pictures of the residents who've moved to their heavenly mansions or their sweatshops in hell. (Or for any closet atheists in town—just to sleep.) People will point and tell stories. The tales of long-gone residents will come alive once more. Bound by kinship, hard times, or living on the same road, folks will continue to choose this space as home for their daily ride around the sun. It's what makes them a little creative, a little eccentric, and sometimes a little sleepless.

Together, they find hope here. Not the waving, jumping, and shouting kind of optimism, but the comfort that comes with clasping a shoulder and assuring one another, "We're gonna make it." And then punctuating it with a nod.

It's the kind of expression you see in the photos. Particularly in the 8X10 colored picture of five women. They hold onto a mule and stand next to a trailhead sign—each wearing a 'Push-through!' smile.

Thanks for visiting Two Pan. If you stay long enough, you'll change.

Jottings

I had no idea there were "cattle cops," until I talked to Roger Huffman, Administrator-Animal Health and Identification Division. Thanks for telling me about your job. And a big shout-out to Donna and Suzanne at the Oregon Department of Agriculture for your brand research.

The Two Pan Project was inspired by the Oxford Project. It's actually an inspiring, brilliant grassroots program, and I hope every small town in America joins them in capturing photographs of its community. You can read about it in *The Oxford Project*, Welcome Books, 2008.

Guns—Ken, thanks for keeping my calibers correct.

Horses—Kristi Beyer, thanks for sharing your beautiful Tennessee Walker, Fancy.

Hoofs, Horses, and Mules—Michael's Farrier Service, thanks for the pedicure tips.

Ranchwoman Extraordinaire—Julie Kooch, I truly appreciate your encouragement and insights.

Military Research—Many thanks to Tracy Thoennes, Curator, Brigadier General James B. Thayer Oregon Military Museum, Camp Withycombe and to the Oregon National Guard, particularly Staff Sergeant Gene Edwards and Staff Sergeant John Mueller

To the *We Honor Veterans* program of Hospice, Thank you for your time and the gracious care you give in dealing with the many warriors and combat stories that have been hidden until end of life ... because as you told me: one out of every four dying Americans is a Veteran.

Information for a general overview of life in Vietnam and in the 12th MedEvac Hospital was inspired by the historical research collection of the Army Medical Department Center of History and Heritage: *Skilled and Resolute*-Sanders Marble, 2013, and the Army Women's Museum.

Thanks to all of the amazing women who **volunteered** to go to Vietnam. You made a difference at such a personal cost. To the men and women who served in Vietnam...and to the families of those who died, please know there aren't enough words to show gratitude for your service and sacrifices. The repercussions of every war ripple through lives long after the guns have stopped firing.

The development, design, and editing of this book would not be possible without: Ken Knorr, Helen Wand, Etta Place, Pat Lichen, and the women of Chrysalis. Thanks for your sharp eyes, and enduring patience.

More humorous stories about change at ...

Before Morning Breaks
www.barbfroman.wordpress.com

Or visit at: barbarakayfroman.com

Other books in the Two Pan Series.
Book 1: Mornings in Two Pan
Book 2: The Lights of Two Pan

To readers across all eras, all geography, and those who love small towns, I so appreciate you joining me on this journey.

Thanks for Reading!